Y0-BQK-309

DONE IN BY INNOCENT THINGS

DONE IN BY INNOCENT THINGS

WILLIAM EISNER

GreyCore Press

Cover Art: René Magritte, *The Tempest,* courtesy of
Wadsworth Atheneum, Hartford, Connecticut.

Cover and text design: Kathleen Massaro

Eisner, William
Done in by innocent things / William Eisner. — 1st ed
p. cm.
LCCN 2001091435
ISBN 0-9671851-6-5

1. Interpersonal relations—Fiction. 2. Man-woman relationships—Fiction. 3. Aging--Fiction. I. Title.

PS3555.I89D66 2002 813'.54
QBI01-700902

for

Elisabeth, Robin and Stephanie

TABLE OF CONTENTS

Heist

ONE

I look up from a cash flow statement and decide that I need a break. I drink coffee, gaze out the window and down three stories to the right, where the Bank of America is located. It's around four in the afternoon. An armored car pulls in front of the bank, the word Protectall across the side. The truck is square and resembles a tank; two lines of rivets along the side add to the sense of solidity. One door with a small window is in the back, no windows are along the side until you reach the passenger door and its window is also small. The back door has a black hole in its center, probably a gun port; there is a similar port in the passenger door.

I keep watching, for some reason interested in the scene, as though I'll be given an exam on it later. The passenger door opens and two guards emerge. Both are in dark blue uniforms, weapons at their sides. One guard enters the bank, the other remains standing by the back door of the truck, gun drawn. A young woman walks by, professional looking, good legs; the guard's head tracks her like a radar dish, gun dangling at his side. In about three minutes the guard who entered the bank emerges holding a single yellow sack by its handle. By the bend of his body I judge that the sack is heavy. While the guard with the drawn gun stands lookout, the guard with the sack takes a key from his pocket, opens the back door, then heaves the sack into the open door where it is grabbed by someone. The guard who heaved the sack slams the door shut, the other replaces the gun in his holster, then they both return to the passenger side and enter the truck. The truck lumbers off.

I watch all this while finishing my coffee. When I return to my desk I have difficulty concentrating. Instead, and without my thinking about it, the scene before the bank replays itself in my head.

I do not think further of this but on the days when I'm in the office, in late afternoon, I take to gazing out the window. The armored car arrives every day around four, the same two guards emerge. I would guess they are both men in their late forties, early fifties, paunchy. The guard exits the bank usually with one but sometimes with two sacks; he slows and his shoulders sag as he walks toward the truck. The second guard always stands with his gun drawn, scanning the street, and never helps the first guard heave the sack toward the person in the interior. Impossible to say from where I view the scene whether the person inside who helps load is the driver or a fourth guard. Fridays, however, one guard opens the back door and before entering the bank pulls a hand-cart from the truck. When he exits the bank the handcart is piled with yellow sacks.

One night, post coital, lying next to Linette, my fiancée of six years, and stroking her thigh (mechanically, I must confess, because she once told me she liked that afterward, though frankly, afterward I'd just as soon read a book or go to sleep), I think of the Protectall armored car. I'm dressed in black, wearing a mask and resembling Batman, and carrying some impossibly lethal weapon. In an imperious voice I order the guards to drop their guns and at gunpoint have them load the yellow sacks into my car (not my Chevy Lumina but a Ferrari or Lamborghini-like vehicle resembling a batmobile), then I speed off. Bystanders stare in amazement, some applaud; even the guards seem pleased at my audacity. I'm still in this idiotic Walter Mitty fantasy when Linette says, "What are you thinking about?"

"Robbing an armored car," I say. "How about you?"

"I'm thinking about getting married."

"Who's the lucky man?"

"Well it sure as hell isn't you, Ronnie."

My knee jerk reaction in this situation—which, as you may have guessed, is not the first of its kind—is to suggest that we just live together. I know this isn't going to work. Linette is from an Irish-Catholic family, has three brothers and two sisters, and there is no way they are going to allow Linette to cohabitate outside of wedlock. Anyway, I'm not their first choice. The brothers are all in manual labor—construction, automobile repair, aircraft maintenance—and look with suspicion at anyone pushing paper as being somehow dishonest. When I see them they're usually lolling around like turnips, drinking beer, watching some sporting event on the tube, witless and happy. They all call me professor, even her old man, a big red-headed, dirty-talking cop with large unreasonable hands. "We could live together," I say despite all of the above.

"We've been through this," Linette says. She waits a minute then sits up, covering her breasts with the sheet. "I think it's time you put up or shut up. My best years are going by. My sisters have five kids between them and I'm on the pill. You think about that, Ronald. Just think about that seriously because I don't plan to stick around much longer."

Actually, what I was thinking about was Protectall but with a new scenario where I hijack the whole truck. But I notice that when I think about this I don't concern myself with the money, what I would do with it or how it would change my life. Only the robbery seems to matter.

You have to understand that I'm not a criminal, though I have at times fantasized about a life of crime. In fact, I have never stolen anything in my life except for a pair of earrings from Woolworth's for a girl I had a crush on when I was fifteen. But maybe I have some affinity with felons, or have recently developed it, because one of my assignments, and the one I enjoy most, is auditing the books of California's state prisons. I've done Lancaster, Norco and Chino. These days I'm assigned to Tehachapi. Once a week I drive from Los Angeles to Tehachapi and check their invoices and ledger entries. The prison assigns an inmate to me as an assistant. Of course, going into one of these places will make you think twice about a life of crime. The odor of unwashed bodies, screamed obscenities, clanging doors—noise echoing off the cement floors and walls—is not something you want to live with. But then nobody inside ever planned to be there.

"One of the salesmen in the office asked me out," Linette says. "I'm going to take him up on it. My dad says I'm nuts to have hung around you this long."

"Let me think about it," I say rather lamely.

"Check it out with your mother," Linette says.

I must admit I *am* close to my mother. But then I'm an only son and my two sisters live on the east coast, so no one else is around. My father died three years ago, his Pontiac with him in it demolished by a runaway big rig outside of Colton, and my mother has no family. She gets social security and Cal State disability money because she's legally blind. But she does have a good-sized stash from the proceeds of my father's life insurance. She manages her little apartment in Santa Monica on her own and does surprisingly well. She belongs to a blind person support group, where I suppose they sit around and discuss the various ways they cope with their affliction. I bought her a special receiver so she can tune into the audio portion of TV programs without bothering to turn on the television. She keeps the little black cube on her night stand. She thinks Linette has a "dishonest voice," is "below my level" and has "poor breeding." All of this may well be true but Linette is fun to be with, is good in bed and is no fool. As you might expect under the circumstances, Linette doesn't much care for my mother either. I have thought about marrying Linette, you know, thought about it more than once. But that's about where it ends. Thinking about it.

When I drive the ninety miles from Los Angeles to Tehachapi, I always experience a sense of freedom when I exit Smogville, leave the San Fernando Valley at Sylmar, drive over the Soledad Pass past Palmdale and Lancaster toward the Tehachapi Mountains and the high desert. The sense of freedom instantly disappears when I pass through the guard gate and the metal detectors.

At Tehachapi, the only window in the room where the financial records are kept faces west and in the morning you can see the peak of Cummings Mountain bright white, snow covered all year round. My assistant at Tehachapi is a black man, Abdullah, who enters data for me into a ledger and into a spreadsheet program on an ancient 486 machine. He doesn't look at the mountains when he prays, which is a couple of times a day; instead he faces east, toward a wall blank except for a large clock.

Abdullah's head is shaved, egg-shaped, burnt almond in color. His eyes are always a little hooded and he doesn't talk much. But Abdullah is trim as a washboard, fingernails clean, well-groomed generally, and his Day-Glo orange prison uniform always neat. I never have to explain anything to him more than once.

Bored and curious, I try to draw Abdullah into conversation. "Why are so many African-Americans in prison?" I ask.

Abdullah's eyes become more hooded yet: I've stepped out of character. He gives me a wary look. "Because they got caught," he says.

"But what drew them to crime in the first place?"

Abdullah turns from the computer screen. "Is that a serious

question?" His speech is unaccented.

"Yes. It's a serious question."

"You're a smart man, Mr. Klein. Why do you think we're locked up?"

"Lack of opportunity," I say. "Drug dealing."

"Too easy," Abdullah says. "You don't know much about the life of a black man, do you, Mr. Klein? The black guys you see locked up all have one thing in common. Can you guess what that is?"

I can see that Abdullah goes in for the Socratic method. I decide against a flip comment. "No I can't," I say.

"You're not alone," Abdullah says. "No white guy can." He stares at me. "Abuse. That's what they have in common. They've all suffered abuse in their lives: physical, mental, drugs, alcohol. But when a black man comes up against the criminal justice system nobody wants to hear about abuse. They don't want to know about it. They just want to put him away. And the longer the better."

Though Abdullah answers in an even voice, his words have become clipped while the sudden tightness of his face gives the impression of an imprisoned genie, rage bottled. When he says "criminal justice system," his tone drips hatred.

"I don't want to give you a bad time, Abdullah," I say, "but it seems to me too easy to blame the system instead of yourself. Life isn't so damn simple for a white man either."

Abdullah contemplates me. "You've never been in a court room, have you? I mean one where a poor son of a bitch black kid is on trial. Where some clown public defender, who's got a hundred other poor son of a bitch black kids to worry about, is his lawyer."

I confess that I haven't.

"Well you should do that." Abdullah's face is rock hard, a

face, I must say, of considerable power. "All white America should do that. If you want to see lies, trickery, deceit and bias in action, you should do that."

"I've always managed to get out of jury duty," I say. "I might just do it next time."

"Do that, Mr. Klein," Abdullah says, "and watch carefully. You'll see the cops lie, witnesses intimidated by the police and every objection overruled by the judge. Anyway, the judge is a biased turd, whether he or she is white or black. The whole trial thing is just a form of Masonic ritual. Everybody knows how it's going to turn out."

I decide there's probably some truth in what Abdullah is saying, but the discussion is hopeless. For one thing I don't have any data. For another, blaming the system must make Abdullah feel better. Then I ask, though I know it's tactless, "Were you unjustly accused, Abdullah?"

"No. I was caught robbing a bank, and that's that. But the ten-to-twenty sentence was crazy. White guys who robbed a hundred times more than me in phony stock deals got five-to-ten or went scot-free on probation."

Then I say, out of nowhere, and the words surprise hell out of me, "What would you think of robbing an armored car, Abdullah?"

He stares at me as though I've mutated into some alien life form then says, "That's one dumb idea."

TWO

Mason regards me through his bottle-bottom glasses, his magnified eyes shifting around. "How do you know it's not fraud?" he asks. Mason is perpetually nervous. He'll give me an assignment then hover around the edges, keep nagging. His problem is that he was an auditor for thirty years then was finally promoted. Becoming a boss made him a worrier.

"I think it's just sloppy bookkeeping," I say in a soothing voice. It's a tone I've adopted with Mason, a placating everything-will-turn-out-fine voice. The other day I noticed it was the same tone I use with my mother, another worrier. "I mean the errors are random. There's no pattern, as you'd expect if there was embezzlement."

Mason's eyes dart about like fish in an aquarium. "*Think* is a bad word in the auditing business," he says. Thirty years of looking for financial chicanery has left Mason permanently leery. "You've got to *know*."

I'm tempted to say that some things are just unknowable but that would not go over well with Mason, for whom all things are knowable. "I'll do more checking," I say. This reply usually works, whether I do more checking or not. Mason appears relieved. "Good," he says, and his eyes drift toward his in-basket.

"Anything new?" I ask Wyomia, my secretary (actually the secretary for five of us auditors).

"The McGregor backup material finally came in," Wyomia says, her long brown fingers, nails bright red, a blur as she wacks away at her word processor. I have had fantasies about Wyomia's agile fingers but she looks at me with the same loving glance she gives her keyboard. McGregor is a cut-and-sew sportswear house that runs a string of sweatshops in L.A. and San Diego counties, manned by illegal Hispanics and Asians. They recently went public, so they're now saddled with quarterly 10-Q reports and annual 10-K and audit certifications. They view this as an evil similar to government safety and health regulations. When I show up I'm treated with the courtesy reserved for a leper.

"Anything else?" I ask Wyomia.

"Mama Bear called," she says without looking up from her word processor.

I sigh. I've asked my mother a hundred times never to call me at the office unless it's an emergency. Unfortunately, we don't agree as to what constitutes an emergency. Still, if you're blind, a lot of things you and I take for granted can be an emergency. She wasn't always blind. It started about ten years ago, something about macula degeneration, rare in people her age, and nobody knew why it was happening or how to stop it. My father sent her everywhere, including the Mayo Clinic. They studied her as if she were a lab rat but could do nothing. Dad could never accept his wife going blind. It soured his life and when he died I suspect Mom was secretly relieved, though she cried for days afterward.

I call my mother. "Thank God!" she says. "The dishwasher overflowed." You'd think there'd been an earthquake the way she says this.

"You might want to call a plumber," I say in my Mason voice.

Dramatic silence.

"*I'll* call a plumber," I finally say.

"Ronnie," she says, voice now plaintive, "I'm sick."

"Sick of what?" I ask.

"*Physically* sick," she says.

"What are the symptoms?" I relax. This may take a while.

"Female stuff. You wouldn't understand."

"Do you want me to make a doctor's appointment?"

"They don't know anything," she says. "Besides, they're bad for your health." She adds "ha! ha!" after that last comment.

"Well, they know more than I do," I say. We've had these sickness conversations before. She has a morbid fear of doctors. Her biggest fear though is of hospitals. She claims that most people who die in hospitals die of illnesses they contracted while in the hospital. The threat of seeing a doctor, who might admit her to a hospital, usually cures her.

"Let's wait," she says. I make sign-off noises, which she ignores, and rattles on about her two ungrateful daughters, my sisters, one of whom has escaped to Boston and the other to Pittsburgh.

I sit at my desk, the door open, Wyomia's willowy legs on display. More fantasy. I make the plumber call then turn to the McGregor material: incomplete, mistakes, sloppy. Mr. Shisgal, the head of McGregor, still thinks of the place as a family business though the stock is traded on the American Exchange. His son-in-law, whose name is Neal but whom I think of as Junior, heads up Finance. The kid treats me like janitorial help but grovels before his father-in-law as if Shisgal were at the very least a Bishop. At our first meeting, with Mason along, Shisgal and Junior took us to lunch. The kid watched the old man salt the bejesus out of a bloody New York sirloin, no doubt imagined Shisgal's arteries beautifully clogging with a thick yellow blubbery substance, and he, the son-in-law, taking over the Holy See, head man at McGregor Sportswear. Why not? But then Shisgal has the build of a Nepalese sherpa, an animal vitality about him, so Junior may be in for a long wait. In the meantime, Shisgal treats the kid the way the kid treats me.

One late afternoon while I drink coffee, I stare out the window at the B of A across the street. I check my watch: the truck is late; it finally shows at 4:21. The guards go through their drill. That evening, on my way to my mother's, I stop at the Santa Monica mall, find their electronics store, and buy a Panasonic video camera. It's not the smallest they have, but the output is a regular video cassette that you just plug into a VCR, no need for an electronic dimwit like me to try to figure out how to hook the damn thing to my TV. It sets me back three-hundred bucks.

"It's important to know who you are," Abdullah says to me one day after prayer. (This he does toward the eastern wall, shutting his eyes. He doesn't mumble or shake or prostrate his body, just shuts his eyes. But there's an intense concentration about the man—you don't have the impression that he's asleep—and I'm respectful of these interludes. When he opens his eyes he always looks refreshed, as though he *had* been asleep.)

"If you think you're just a low good for nothing shit," Abdullah goes on, "then that's what you are."

"Is that what religion does for you, give you self-esteem?" I ask.

"Mr. Klein," Abdullah says, always surprised at how little I know, "I'm not talking about *any* religion. Being Buddhist or Shinto wouldn't do it. Do you know what the dominant religion in Africa is?" Abdullah is back in his Socratic mode.

"I have no idea," I say, "except that the Pope visits every once in a while, so maybe it's Catholic."

"No way," Abdullah says. "The Pope is just trying to drum up converts." He pauses, stares at me to be sure he has my complete attention. "Islam," he says. "Africa is populated by Muslims. That's what *I* am. A Muslim." He straightens as he says this, head higher. "*That's* what gives me cultural identity." He leans back, apparently decides to instruct me further. "The principles of Islam are simple: belief, prayer, charity, pilgrimage, fasting. That's it. That's what's spiritually satisfying. That's what confirms your human identity."

I poke around, on the pretext of deepening my audit procedures, gain access to the inmates' files. I look up Abdullah's history. His real name is Elmore Carter and his record is a yard long, usually armed robbery, booked for six offenses as a juvenile and seven as an adult. Elmore's career started at the age of eight, when he and another boy burned a waterfront warehouse to the ground after the owner refused the children access to a swimming pier.

The next time I show up at Tehachapi, Abdullah is gone and there is a pile of invoices in the in-box. "Where's Abdullah?" I ask the guard.

"Lockdown. The place is in lockdown."

"Meaning?"

"There was a fight, two guys were stabbed and a guard hurt. Everybody is confined to their cells. No visitors, no exercise, no work."

"What about eating?"

"Box lunches in the cells."

"How long does it last?"

"Depends on the warden."

"I guess the warden is a believer in communal punishment."

The guard shrugs. Lockdown makes his job easier. I met the warden my first day at Tehachapi, a middle-aged bald guy with soft predatory eyes. Dressed in a gray business suit, rep tie, he looked like the corporate treasurer at one of our clients, a man nailed for insider trading.

Though it's not my job, I decide to enter the invoice data myself. Once again I'm surprised at the neat careful way Abdullah keeps his ledger. All the entries are hand printed and there are never any errors. I try to imitate Abdullah's precise printing but it takes too long so I switch to script. I notice doodles on the pad next to the computer, no doubt Abdullah's. One is the word motherfucker, carefully written, with arabesques around it, another is the crest of Islam. Some look like Arabic script. I wonder whether Abdullah is teaching himself Arabic so he can read the Koran in the original. There are a couple more motherfuckers in different forms and embellishments, apparently Abdullah's favorite doodle.

Whenever I'm in the office in the afternoon, I videotape the proceedings at the B of A across the street. I zoom in, take a close-up of the guards, the truck, then study the images at home. The two guards are always the same men. Their uniforms are worn, pants shiny. I'd be surprised if they're paid more than ten dollars an hour. (Imagine hauling millions for ten bucks as hour. You wonder if they think about that.) It would appear that Protectall is into cost containment. My prior estimate of their ages is about right, late forties to early fifties, and overweight. Neither strikes me as ready to lay down his life for the good of Protectall, a company no doubt heavily covered by theft insurance. The guard at the truck, gun dangling at his side, continues to be distracted by passing women. He doesn't appear too concentrated on possible danger around him. I can't see the man inside the truck. On Fridays, when the guard goes into the bank with a handcart and emerges with the cart piled with yellow sacks, he hands the sacks through the open back door to the man in the truck while the other guard scans around, gun at the ready. I catch a glimpse of the man in the truck on the video and freeze the frame. He is younger than the other two, in a blue short-sleeved shirt, no jacket. His arms are muscular. That's all I can see.

Now you might ask why am I doing this. I ask myself the same question. I don't have an answer. I chalk it up to fantasy, to trying to keep my life interesting. Maybe it's something deeper. I don't know. I'm not much good at analyzing my own life. Are any of us? Life isn't simple and orderly, you know, like cash flow charts or income statements. Life isn't accounting or physics, neat, circumscribed by laws of logic and reason. Sometimes I have a slippery sensation, no traction anywhere, the world gliding by and me left behind, as insignificant as last year's balance sheet. I suspect that thoughts of a robbery float around the world like wind-blown seeds, searching for a speck of fertile ground and a drop of water to grow. I was innocently standing at my office window when one floated into the room.

My mother's living room has a sofa and two stuffed chairs, all decorated in yellow and pink and blue flowers, covered in transparent plastic. The plastic is slithery, somehow feels greasy, and though it's been on the furniture for years, it still has a plasticy smell; at least I smell it as soon as I enter the apartment. My mother says it's easy to keep clean—just wipe it with a damp cloth. Keeping things clean is important to her. She spends most of her day dusting, tidying, rearranging. She usually eats cold food.

Mom has a cat named Chair. She's into Chinese culture, thinks Asians possess extraordinary wisdom. She probably remembers those old Charlie Chan movies on late night television that she and dad used to watch, where the droopy-mustached oriental and his number one son solved the most diabolical of crimes with pure logic. Chair is short for Chairman Meow. Chair leaps onto the plastic-covered sofa like a leopard, nudges his head under Mom's arm, then nestles in her lap. Mom scratches behind his ears. Chair purrs. Mom claims Chair is very bright, though he looks like any old alley cat to me and Mom never gives me examples of Chair's brilliance. She tends to interpret the cat's comportment in human terms. I worry about her tripping over the animal, but they have been together two years and that's never happened so I guess it's okay.

"You look pale, Ronnie," she says as she scratches Chair. I have no idea how she can tell.

I'm suddenly struck by the misery of her life. In this plastic-covered apartment, yakking with the sightless types in her support group, taking care of a cat. Mom's not old, you know. Middle fifties. Her hair is still dark, complexion okay, body a little heavy but not fat and she does carry herself well. She deserves better. "Why don't we go out for dinner," I say.

Her hands flutter. "That would be nice, Ronnie," she says. "I'd like that." She's suddenly girlish. Makes you want to cry.

We go to an Italian restaurant on Wilshire Boulevard. Mom orders a soup and spaghetti with meat sauce. No need to cut anything on her plate that way. She treats herself to a glass of red wine, then reaches across the table, takes my hand. "You're a good son," she says. She studies me with her sightless eyes. "Are you happy, Ronnie?" she asks.

"No," I say.

"I thought so. Linette doesn't make you happy?"

"Sometimes yes. It's something deeper, Mom. I don't know what it is. Maybe nobody is really happy. Maybe everybody wants more than they have but they can't say what."

"Some people are happy. When you're healthy and have a job you like and a good wife and children..." Then she looks down and I notice she's crying. This bit of life counseling has saddened her. It sure as hell has saddened me.

"Jesus, Mom, don't cry."

"I'm not crying. It's allergy."

We eat. Mom drinks her wine. Her mood lightens. "A man is interested in me," she says. "The brother of one of the women in the support group. A widower. He took me dancing."

I'm amazed. My mother dancing.

"A sweet man. Sells jewelry. His name is Murray."

I wipe a spot of sauce from my mother's chin with my napkin. "I'd like you to meet him," Mom says.

"Sure, anytime."

"He's a sweet man," she repeats. "Starved for love."

"Most people are," I say, not too sensitively I have to admit.

"What makes you so cynical, Ronnie? At your age you should be full of optimism. Your whole life ahead of you. Why are you so bitter?"

There's no way to answer this. I can't tell her about Mason or Junior or old man Shisgal or Linette or Tehachapi or Abdullah or about anything really. "I hope things work out with you and Murray," I say.

"Mason wants to see you," Wyomia says. She's standing in front of my desk, hands on her flat hips. "He doesn't look too happy." Her small, aggressively pointed breasts stare straight ahead. Wyomia doesn't seem saddened by Mason's unhappiness.

"What's he upset about?"

"He doesn't usually confide in me," Wyomia says. She treats me to a smile, her teeth even and bright white against the milk chocolate of her skin. "He says right now." Wyomia emphasizes this with a little stamp of her foot, then leaves. Wyomia has the high extraordinarily rounded and protruding ass that some black women have. I have fantasized much over that ass.

"Neal complained that you never showed up," Mason says. "You had an appointment and never cancelled. What happened?"

Mason is indeed unhappy, unhappy and worried. His lips look thinner, grape-colored, and his magnified eyes glisten like little damp gray stones and they do not wander.

"I was held up at Tehachapi," I say. "The inmate who does the books is in lockdown, so I made the entries."

"What's lockdown?"

I explain.

"You're a ledger checker not a data enterer," Mason tells me; he sounds indignant, as if he's been personally insulted.

I decide to switch to Junior. "I *did* call Neal," I say, "and left a message with his secretary. Maybe she never gave him the message." This is likely since the secretary is Shisgal's niece whose most important task seems to be the care of her fingernails.

"McGregor is a new customer," Mason says. "This is the time to show them we're on top of things, not canceling appointments because you're helping some felon who's in solitary confinement." Mason has a talent for explaining the obvious. I'm tempted to point out that Abdullah is in lockdown through no fault of his own, but decide against it. "I understand," I say to his neatly arranged desk. Humility always works with Mason. His gaze drifts toward his papers. You have to wonder whether Mason has ever felt anything, either pleasure or pain.

That afternoon I wander across the street to the bank. There is no guard inside. That night I watch the videos with a stopwatch. From the time the guard emerges from the bank with the handcart of sacks until all the sacks are loaded into the armored car, the cart hauled in and the door slammed shut, forty-two seconds elapse.

THREE

Lockdown lasts a month. When I see Abdullah he grumbles that my ledger entries are sloppy. He's sullen, regards me with hostility as though I'm at least partially responsible for the lockdown. "He's not very fair, is he?" I say.

"Who?"

"The warden."

Abdullah shrugs, answers impatiently. "It's not the warden. He's just part of the system... Imagine yourself locked up, nothing to read, no TV, no radio, no daylight. Locked up with some kid nailed for the fourth time for car theft, who's going crazy because he's a heroin addict and can't get a fix. All this because of a fight you had nothing to do with. If it weren't for Islam I'd go nuts myself."

"It's a lousy deal," I say. It's all I can manage.

"Nobody on the outside knows how lousy a deal it is," Abdullah says. "They're happy to see blacks locked up. Makes them feel safer. All you see on local TV are robberies, murders, freeway chases. The guys they catch are always black. You don't develop much compassion for the poor son of a bitch, do you? You couldn't care less what formed the guy. Lock him up. That's all you want. Society doesn't take any blame even though it created this so-called criminal."

I have never heard Abdullah make so long a speech. In solitary for a month with a deprived addict. Make anybody talkative. He speaks quickly, the skin across his face drawn tight. He looks thinner; probably not too well fed in lockdown.

"Do you understand population control, Mr. Klein?" Abdullah asks.

"What do you mean?"

"Prisons are a form of population control. Fewer black men on the outside means fewer black babies."

This strikes me as too much. "Come on, Abdullah. People are put away for a crime. Not indiscriminately." I sense this argument won't wash with Abdullah and in fact it doesn't.

Abdullah again shrugs impatiently. "Blacks have been imprisoned for no good reason since the Civil War. If you don't buy population control, how about cheap labor? That's what chain gangs are all about, an extension of slavery."

Here, I have to admit, he has a point. All the chain gang pictures I ever saw were of black men.

When I agree with him, Abdullah leans back, away from his

computer, and goes into his tutorial mode. "All those white history books want you to believe that the blacks in the south were just cotton and tobacco pickers." A note of pride creeps into his voice. "That's bull. A lot of them were brick masons, carpenters, weavers, craftsmen. Those African slaves built most of the south."

Though it might have some truth, this strikes me as revisionist history, Abdullah style. There's no point in arguing. I don't have any data and I suspect Abdullah doesn't either.

Abdullah cracks a smile. "You don't believe me, do you Mr. Klein?"

"I'm skeptical," I say.

"Well, that's better than most people." Then Abdullah looks at me in a wary inquiring way. "I'm coming up for parole review next month," he says.

"I hope it works for you," I say.

"You can help."

"How is that?"

"They're going to want a reference. Whether I'm doing good work for you. Cooperative. All that bull."

I can see that asking is costing Abdullah a lot of effort. "Not to worry. If they call me, I'll say the right words."

Abdullah does not appear completely convinced. "Thanks, Mr. Klein," he says, then glances at the clock on the east wall. "Time for prayer," he adds.

"Hi professor," says Kevin, Linette's oldest brother. "What's happening?" His hair is deep red, almost burgundy, like his father's, his head heavy, oblong, punctuated by two blue marbles for eyes. He's sporting a couple of days' growth of beard, a lighter red than his hair.

"Not much," I say. "Same old grind."

"What *is* the old grind?" Kevin asks. "You've already told me but I can't keep it straight." Kevin was a muffler man at Midas but was recently promoted to brake pad replacement. This has made him cocky. His face breaks into a smirk after he asks the question.

"Not much to it," I say, resolved to answer Kevin seriously while keeping it simple. "Companies write down their transactions in books. Sometimes they screw up, sometimes they cheat. I check what they do. Keep them honest."

"What's to check in a prison?" Kevin asks.

"Well, they buy things—food, uniforms, maintenance stuff—and they pay people. So they keep books, like a company. Somebody has to check."

Kevin takes a swig of Coors. I can see his attention has wandered.

Linette shows up. Her hair, a lighter red than her brother's, is her best feature; she wears it long, below her shoulders, and coupled with the dark green of her eyes, it gives her so much color that she doesn't need makeup. She's smart enough to know that. Unfortunately, her legs are heavy and she's a little knock-kneed. She's smart enough to know that too and favors long skirts or slacks. Now she's wearing a silky dark olive blouse and khaki pants, colors that nicely set off the red of her hair.

"Ronnie was telling me about his job," Kevin says.

"What did he tell you?" Linette says as she surveys herself in the hall mirror.

"That he's into books."

Linette regards Kevin critically. "Dad wants you to slow down on the beer," she says. "He's worried about you becoming an Irish drunk." She pats his gut. "You're also getting fat." I notice that Linette too has put on a little weight, around the hips.

"Fuck you, Linette," Kevin says amiably.

"Don't wait up," she says as we cruise through the door.

We drive to an Italian restaurant, Tre Cugini, in Santa Monica. Italian food strikes me as neutral ground in my relations with Linette, part way between her Ireland and the Russia of my ancestors.

Linette is a receptionist, typist, secretary and general helper in a real estate office and has been in the same job for years. One thing you can say about Linette, she's stable. Most of the sales agents are women; Linette doesn't hold any of them in high regard. Linette frowns at the menu, grumbles that there's not much in the way of low-cal food in an Italian restaurant, then settles for a salad with lemon juice as dressing and broiled sea bass with steamed vegetables. Linette, I see, is also smart enough to have noticed that she's putting on weight. Reluctantly, she agrees to a glass of white wine.

"The real estate market is heating up," Linette says. "I'm taking a course for the broker's exam. I want to get a license. If those dumb housewives can sell real estate, I sure can. Maybe one day I can open my own office. It's not all that tough, you know. Old man Kleeber rakes in a fortune and barely raises a finger." Her eyes glitter. Inexplicably, ambition seems to have taken possession of Linette.

"You look skeptical," she says.

"No, no," I hasten to say. "That's great. Sure, do it. You'll never know unless you try."

"Do you really think I can sell real estate?"

"Sure. You're smart, organized. Why not?"

"Anyway, I'm tired of working for other people, tired of being told what to do. The woman who teaches the real estate course encourages us to get out on our own. She said something pretty good: better to be first in the village than second in Rome." Linette's gaze is steady and unblinking as she adds, "I think she's right."

"That's great, Linette," I say. "Just do it."

She touches my hand. "Thanks, Ronnie."

I figure I've put a little gratitude in the bank so after dinner, instead of a movie, I say, "Why don't we go over to my place, have another glass of wine, relax."

Linette regards me with the expression that I have learned precedes something serious. "No," she says, "we're not going to do that anymore."

This catches me totally off guard. "Why not?"

"Because you've had a free ride for years, that's why not. If you want to have sex with me, Ronnie, you'll first have to put a marriage ring on my finger. Then you can fuck me anytime you want, morning, noon or night. But not before. That's the new rule."

"That's one hell of a rule, especially these days."

"There are no rules in this business. You make them up as you go along. Though if it makes you feel any better, think of me as having gone old-fashioned."

I have learned that when Linette makes up her mind she can be stubborn as rock. I don't even try to persuade her. But then I see that she isn't through. "I'm also not available this Friday... I'm going out with someone else."

Despite myself, I say, "Do the same rules apply to someone else?"

"That's no business of yours, Ronnie."

I feel sudden pangs of jealousy, rejection, etc. Linette's strategy, I have to admit, is effective. Still, I'm not ready just yet to march to the altar, though I can see Linette is depending on time and jealousy to work their magic.

A woman with a professional voice calls to inquire about Elmore Carter. She's impatient. At first I don't know what she's taking about. Then I catch on that this is the Abdullah reference call.

I say all the okay words I can think of: diligent, responsible, trustworthy, reliable, conscientious, etc., etc. The woman's tone never changes. She might as well be announcing the marine weather forecast. I refer to Abdullah as Mr. Carter. Forget that Muslim alias business: I doubt if Ms. Professional Voice would understand. She signs off with a Thank you, Mr. Klein in the same tone as the rest. I think if she were telling me a meteor was about to strike L.A. she would use the same voice.

When next I see Abdullah I tell him of the phone call. He thanks me but does not appear heartened. The parole board is all white, he tells me, except for one black guy who might as well be white. This despite half the prison population being black. "You never know how those sons of bitches are going to react," he says. "They might be trying to lighten the prison load because of budget cuts one day, or keep every black guy locked inside forever because the governor has just made a law and order speech. I'm just another black monkey in the system. They don't give two shits about justice. It's all today's politics and how they got out of bed in the morning and whether the old lady put out last night."

Abdullah does not say any of this in a resigned way. His lips tighten and his eyes glint. There's raw hatred in his face.

"What'll you do when you get out?" I ask, trying to get Abdullah to focus on a future of freedom.

"I haven't thought about it," he says. "It's dangerous to think about those things until you're out."

I can see his point.

Before meeting with Junior, I walk through the McGregor shop to get a feel for the place. The factory is not air conditioned and smells of lint, dust and sweat, the air filled with the staccato ripping sounds of sewing machines. The women on the production line are crammed side by side like oarsmen in a Roman galley.

Everyone is on piecework, an intense desperate quality about the workers.

Junior and I meet in his office, on the second floor, the room small, a single window facing the parking lot, desk and chairs chipped. Papers are scattered over Junior's desk and on a filing cabinet; you wonder whether his mind is equally cluttered. I patiently point out the errors in his financial statements. Junior has no feel for double entry bookkeeping. He'll peer at the numbers as if they're specimens under a microscope, but by his questions I can see that he really doesn't understand any of it. When I explain his face is dazzlingly blank.

What Junior wants, and is working up the courage to approach old man Shisgal for, are a couple of supercomputers instead of the ancient Pentiums his finance staff uses. He thinks of computers as super beings that miraculously will make the entries, keep the books and cause his father-in-law to love him. I give Junior a brief lecture on garbage in, garbage out, but he's not listening. Then he tries to convince me of the need for the miracle machines. What he's really doing is honing his pitch to the old man. I don't think Junior stands a chance. When it comes to spending money Shisgal is hard as flint. I tune out. Then, as if by magic, the Friday scene at the Bank of America as it appears on my video replays itself in my mind. I see it all in slow motion as if it were happening under water: the Protectall truck, the guard entering the bank with his handcart, the other beside the truck, gun dangling at his side, big gut, shiny pants, watching the women strolling by, the guard emerging from the bank, the yellow sacks loaded on the handcart, then the same guard hoisting the sacks into the truck, the unseen guard inside grabbing the sacks. How many guards are there in the truck? One or two? Is the driver now in the back helping load the truck? Or is the driver on his rear end behind the wheel thinking of nothing at all while a helper loads the sacks?

"What do you think?" Junior asks, yanking me back to reality.

"It's ambitious," I say.

"I want you to put in a word with Mr. Shisgal for the computer," Junior says.

"You'll need more people," I point out. "For example, a programmer, data entry clerks. But it's bigger than that. You'll have to automate inventory control, receivables, payroll... Everything that passes through here."

Junior squints at me. I'm becoming an enemy. I decide to be positive: losing the account would not sit well with Mason. "But you could start slow," I say. "Take it a step at a time."

Junior is still squinting. "I'll mention it to Mr. Shisgal," I say.

"I hope you'll be more enthusiastic with him than you are with me," Junior finishes.

"Sure," I say, but my thoughts are elsewhere. I've decided it's the driver who helps load the sacks. All signs tell me that Protectall, like old man Shisgal, is into cost containment. I'm certain there are no more than three guards, but to be sure I'll check it out.

I've been assigned a new man at Tehachapi, an older white guy with a narrow string of a mouth who calls me Sir with no hint of irony. I ask him what happened to Abdullah. Paroled.

FOUR

"Ron, this is Murray," my mother says, introducing me to her boyfriend. She grins a big satisfied grin. Murray is lumpy, wears a knit suit the color of horseshit, combs wispy hair across a shiny skull. He has an odd pallor, like those asparagus the French grow underground. He smiles a cap-toothed smile, teeth too white. "So this is the young man I've heard so much about," Murray says and shoves a paw that looks like a raw chicken breast at me. Murray is a wholesale gem salesman and sports a fancy ring on each hand to prove it. "You're the genius accountant," he goes on. I turn toward Mom, who's staring God knows where with her blind eyes. "Just accountant is fine," I say, disengaging my hand from the chicken breast. "I like a modest man," says the gem salesman.

We stare at each other, neither quite sure who has the next move. "Sit down, sit down," Mom says. "I'll make some tea." She feels her way to the kitchen. "Need some help?" Murray calls. "No, no," Mom calls back. "You two boys get acquainted."

"As a guy close to the action," Murray says, "have you figured out how to make a million?"

I decide to take the question at face value. "You can own all or part of a company," I say, "or you can rob a bank. But you can't get there working for someone else."

"What route are you taking?" Murray asks, capped teeth on display.

"The bank route," I say. "It's quicker and probably easier than starting a company and making it succeed."

Murray laughs. "I like a man with a sense of humor," he says.

When the tea kettle whistles Murray jumps up. "I think I'll help your mother." In the kitchen I notice he puts his arm around her waist. Mom giggles girlishly. I wonder whether she's sleeping with this guy. I mean, she's not really old, then she doesn't have to look at him. And he does seem attentive. I sigh: why not?

All of this gets me thinking of Linette who, true to her word, has ceased putting out.

Murray has also gotten me thinking of those yellow sacks. I could forget Linette. And Mom is well fixed financially, what with her social security disability payments and dad's life insurance. I could go to the South Seas, wherever that is, and screw myself stupid. Or maybe go to Paris. Fuck every whore in the city, of which I understand there is a vast number. Then my thoughts shift away from sexual fantasies. The scene of the handcart piled with yellow sacks appears. I point some incredibly potent weapon, like a grenade launcher, at the guards, who cower in fear, then I suavely take possession of the sacks and drive off into the sunset as onlookers applaud. I sigh: more Walter Mitty nonsense; if only it were that easy. But the following day when I see the Protectall truck pull up, I hustle out to the street and walk past the front of the truck. Sure enough, there's no one in the driver's compartment, but a door leads into the storage area. When the guard hoists the yellow sack into the now open back door of the truck, I peek in as I recross the street. Only one guard inside.

"We lost the prison contract," Mason says.

"What happened?"

"The job is rebid every year and some shlock house underbid us." He glares at me as if it were my fault. I'm suddenly apprehensive: am I going to disappear with the lost contract?

"I'm reassigning you to the Sunshine account," Mason says. Sunshine is a chain of retirement homes from San Diego to Santa Barbara. To tell the truth, I'd rather work prisons. "Jaime will fill you in. He's the lead auditor." Jaime is an ambitious Hispanic who once told me something I couldn't believe. He's an only child. I observed that he's probably the only Hispanic only child in California if not on the whole North American continent. Jaime gave me a friendly slap on the back and said that I'm a Jewish racist but that was okay because everybody one way or another is racist.

So Jaime and I set out for Van Nuys, where Sunshine is headquartered, in his Mercedes C-Class AMG Sport Version. He's going to introduce me to the Sunshine executives. They turn out to be a bunch of young hustlers who took over the operation in a leveraged buyout and are now intent on squeezing every penny of cost out of poor Sunshine. We arrive at lunch time. The inmates, mostly jabbering old ladies, line up cafeteria style with aluminum army trays. The place smells a little like Tehachapi; an odor of decay and ruin floats in the air. The meal is white: white mashed potatoes, no doubt from dehydrated flakes, some strange meat, possibly chicken, that looks as if it had died in the Carter administration, a white sauce, white bread and, to break the monotony, soft drinks, coffee or tea. "We have a dietician prescribe our menu," says an exec. I'm tempted to say that they eat better at Tehachapi.

Which gets me thinking of Abdullah. I've got to make two more trips to the prison to pass the baton to the "schlock house" that low bid us. I could find Abdullah's address from the prison records. Then a scene enters my mind, a scene that I conclude is never far below the surface: the handcart and the yellow sacks and the overweight guards and their shiny pants. Yes, I'll find Abdullah's address.

Jaime and I and the Sunshine V.P. Finance, who resembles a Nazi youth leader, take a fast pass through their records. They have a monster IBM mainframe machine, everything ship shape. The Finance Department looks like mission control in Houston. The executives take us out to lunch: no way, I'm sure, would any of them eat that white shit they feed the inmates at Sunshine.

The prison records give Abdullah's address but no phone number. So one Saturday morning I drive around South Central L.A., very carefully, searching for the address. Streets are littered with trash, fly-blown paper, the cars big old Ford Crown Victorias, ancient Cadillacs and Pontiac Bonnevilles. The address is a three-story apartment building, no names listed, not even on the mailboxes. The front door is open; I knock at the first apartment, clutching my video cassette. "Yeah?" calls a female voice. "I'm looking for Abdullah," I call back. "Who?" "Abdullah." "Never heard of him." "Elmore Carter?" "Never heard of him either." I go through this drill with the other apartments, some answer, some don't, but "never heard of him" is always the response. Finally, on the top floor, there is a door with a small hand-written sign, Sons of Islam. I knock, ask. "He's in the mosque." "Where's that?" "Down the street." "Which direction?"

I'm having second thoughts about this whole endeavor but look for the mosque. It's a store front, the windows painted black, the words Sons of Islam and the crescent moon with a star inside painted in white on the black of the window. I peek in. "What?" asks a voice. "Abdullah?" "Who wants him?" "Ron Klein."

Abdullah comes to the door. He wears a dark blue dashiki and is a far more commanding presence than he was in orange prison garb leaning over a ledger in Tehachapi. "Mr. Klein!" he says and seems truly surprised, an apparition from a previous life. "What brings you here?" I'm not sure how to go about this. Anyway, the whole idea now seems wacky. "Can I come in?" "Sure, but take off your shoes." The interior is dim, the front room about the size of a Mom and Pop grocery store, bare floor, podium in front. Several men sit at a table in a corner, also in dashikis. They look me over, poker faced. I'm obviously the wrong color and can only mean trouble.

Abdullah pulls a couple of chairs to a corner, motions me to sit, then waits. "Do you have a television with a VCR?" I ask. "A what?" "A television with a VCR. I'd like to show you a video." "Are you selling something?" "Sort of." "What?" I hesitate: impossible to explain. "I think it's best if I just show you the video." "There are TVs around but I don't have any VCR... What's the matter with you, Mr. Klein? You look shaky. Why are you looking for me?"

"I'll tell you what," I finally blurt out, "my car is down the street. We can drive to my apartment and I'll show you the video there." Abdullah's eyes narrow. "I'm busy right now," he says. "Give me your phone number and I'll call." I'm uneasy about giving Abdullah the number but decide what the hell, it's okay.

Days go by. No message on my machine, no call in the evening. Maybe Abdullah, a parolee after all, is wary of entrapment. Finally, after I've lost hope that Abdullah will ever call, the phone rings, early, before I go to work. Abdullah makes no apology for having taken so long to get back to me. A friend of his has a TV plus VCR. If I'm still interested, we can meet this evening, seven o'clock, at the friend's apartment. He gives me the address. Second floor.

The apartment is in the same neighborhood as the mosque. A young black woman carrying a baby answers my knock. "Abdullah is out but he'll be right back. Come in. Sit down." She leads me to the living room. "Can I get you something? A beer?" "I'll have a coke, thanks." The interior has an odd odor that I can't place; a crack in the plaster traverses the ceiling like a lightening bolt. A sagging couch and two worn stuffed chairs furnish the room. A threadbare oriental rug defines the central space. The TV is in a corner, a VCR on top. I sink into the couch. The woman brings my coke then sits opposite me, opens her blouse and breast feeds the baby. A gold bracelet gleams against her wrist. "I hope this doesn't bother you," she says. "No, no, not at all. It's perfectly natural." She gives me a friendly smile. "I'm just more comfortable here," she adds, then relaxes in the chair, expression remote, a black madonna and child.

Abdullah shows up, in street clothes, dark slacks and a sport shirt. He kisses the woman on the cheek. She rises heavily from the chair, disappears into the interior. "Well, Mr. Klein," Abdullah says without preamble, "there's the TV and the VCR. You're on."

We both watch the Protectall armored car, guard waiting, gun at his side, eyeing the passing women. "Why are you showing me this?" Abdullah asks. "Hold on," I answer, "until you've seen the whole thing, then I'll tell you." "I'm a busy man, Mr. Klein. What is it you want?" "Please be patient another minute." The guard pushing the handcart piled with yellow sacks appears at the bank door then loads the sacks while the guard beside the truck stands vigil. "So?" asks Abdullah. I decide that being blunt is the best strategy. "I'm thinking of robbing those sacks," I say. Abdullah breaks into a laugh, then throws back his head and laughs and laughs. The woman's head appears in the doorway; she smiles then disappears. "You're a funny guy, Mr. Klein," Abdullah finally manages.

"I'm serious," I answer.

Abdullah gives me a huge smile. "What would my parole officer say if he even saw me watching your video? And how would I explain it? I think you'd better take your pictures and leave."

"I'm not into entrapment, Abdullah," I say. "I just wanted your advice."

"Mr. Klein, you could no more pull that off than fly to Mars. Do you understand the planning, the pressure of a job like that?" He smiles again, a you-poor-misguided-idiot smile, and says, "Have you ever fired a gun? Do you even *own* a gun?" I meekly shake my head. "Between wanting and doing there's an ocean," Abdullah says, not unkindly. "Even if you could convince some madman to do this with you, you'd be dead weight. Just a burden, that's all. He contemplates me, sighs. "I suppose everybody has some larceny in him. Everybody wants a quick hit." He nods. "Go back to your books, Mr. Klein. That's what you were cut out to do. Don't mess with fate. You'll just get screwed up."

I go about my life, not messing with fate. Sunshine is depressing; Linette won't put out; Mom and Murray go dancing. I watch Protectall pull in front of the bank afternoons, rather wistfully now I have to admit. It's a bit like seeing a girl you once loved who picked someone else. When you see her she seems more beautiful than ever and you sigh and fantasize over what might have been.

Linette is going out with someone else. When I ask who, she answers haughtily. "None of your business." When I want to see her she's now often busy. I mope around, trying to sort out my life. Weeks go by and I haven't sorted anything out.

Then one evening at home, I'm watching the news and feeling sorry for myself, when the phone rings. It's Abdullah. He wants to meet. "And bring those tapes," he commands.

We meet in the apartment of the TV and the VCR. Abdullah is dressed in jeans, black denim shirt. "Three of my brothers, Muslims, fine people, have been locked up," he tells me. Abdullah is different. His face is tight and he looks dangerous as hell. "The cops say they conspired to violate narcotics and prostitution laws. *Conspired.* That's what they said. Those guys didn't *do* anything. They *conspired.*"

Abdullah paces the threadbare oriental rug, head down. "Conspired!" He turns to me. "Can you believe that shit?" My mouth opens and shuts. Some soothing words are in order but I have no idea what they might be.

"Sure there's a conspiracy," Abdullah says. "But it's the *government* that's doing the conspiring. They see us and Islam as a threat, that's what they see. We're a menace. That's how they see us. A fucking menace. They're going to lock up every one of us because we're a fucking menace."

"How can I help?" I ask, a born straight man.

But Abdullah pays no attention to this. I'm not sure he even heard. He keeps pacing around. "Destroy," he says, "that's what they want to do. Destroy us all." Then he stops and stares at me, his eyes narrowed to the look of a predator. I have the impression that before me is not Abdullah but Elmore Carter, wronged by the law from childhood to Tehachapi. A man who wants to get even.

"There's only one way to fight the government," Abdullah says. His eyes are black hard agates, bloodshot. "You got to fight them with their own weapons. Courts, procedures, red tape. Tie those low shits into knots, show the world how pitifully incompetent they are. That's what O.J. did. But it takes money. Bushels of it... Okay," he says with the finality of a general taking command of the field of battle, "Let's take a good look at your tapes."

FIVE

Abdullah leans forward as he watches the video. "I would guess there's two-hundred to three-hundred thousand dollars in each of those sacks," he says. He continues to watch. "The problem is the guy in the truck, or maybe two guys inside—" "There's only one guard inside," I interrupt. "I checked it out." "Good," Abdullah says, "good," then goes on. "See the porthole in the back of the truck, in the door? He can fire through it but he can't aim too good. He might worry about hitting people on the street... But they would scatter at the first sign of trouble." He now seems to be musing to himself.

"We need equipment," Abdullah says. "Good weapons, bullet-proof vests, masks. And another man." "Another man?" "That's right," Abdullah says. "You can be there to drive and hold a gun so you look intimidating, but I couldn't depend on you for firepower. The odds are you'd fall apart under pressure." He says this clinically. “Gogan,” he goes on, “Gogan is the man. That’s if he’s interested.”

“Who’s Gogan?”

“A smart guy I knew at Tehachapi. He’s now tending bar in Westwood. The man is quick and can analyze things. And he knows weapons and can get the equipment.” Abdullah stares at me. ”We’re going to need money to pull this thing off.” That obvious thought had never occurred to me. “How much are we talking about?” I ask, suddenly wary. The word money has brought all this out of its abstract world. “I’d be guessing,” Abdullah says, “but Gogan would know.” Abdullah comes to his feet, hoists his pants in a virile gesture. “Take your video,” he says. “I have your phone number. I’ll be in touch.” My real role is now clear: I’m the angel expected to bankroll the job.

In my last visit to Tehachapi, I check Gogan in the prison files. Luckily, there’s only one, a certain Patrick Gogan. He has a record a yard long, starting with petty stealing as a child and graduating to breaking and entering, auto theft, illegal weapons possession and narcotics trafficking. Despite his intelligence, it would appear that Gogan has a propensity for getting caught. He has spent about a third of his thirty-three years in various penal institutions, from reformatories to Tehachapi.

Gogan, it turns out, is not sure whether he’s interested or not but he’s willing to listen. “Why don’t we meet at your place?” Abdullah says to me. His friend, the renter of the apartment where we met, is leery. He’s worried that his place may be under surveillance. I’m leery as well: two parolees converging on my apartment. I suggest a MacDonald’s, or meeting in Griffith Park, but Abdullah says that Gogan has to see the videos. Well, I rationalize, we haven’t *done* anything, so what’s the harm in meeting at my place? There’s lots of time to back out.

Gogan has a white chunky face, disfigured by a nose scarred

and brutally indented half way down, his eyes a faded blue like much washed denim. I offer soft drinks but Gogan wants whiskey. I poke around, find a bottle of Old Grand-Dad, which Gogan mixes with 7-up. We watch the video. "Stop!" Gogan says, raising a finger. "I want to look at the guy's gun." He peers at the screen. "That's a long-barrel .38 caliber revolver. An old cop gun. Accurate, but not a big deal weapon."

"It'll kill you all the same," Abdullah says.

"That's for sure," Gogan says. He takes a swig of his whiskey then lights up. By the sweet smell of the smoke I gather it's marijuana. He offers the joint around; both Abdullah and I pass.

"We've got to intimidate those guys and fast," Abdullah says. "Scary masks, like Halloween masks. That's the ticket. Sounds dumb but it works. And heavy-duty automatic weapons to make it clear we're serious. Show firepower. That'll get their attention. They're old guys. They didn't get that way by being reckless."

"What about the guy inside?" I ask.

"He's a problem," Gogan answers and takes a hit on his joint. "He might try to fire through the porthole. But to do that he's got to see. Look at the window on the back door of the truck. It's small. They sell spray paint cans, not those puny shits for the home, but high-output professional numbers. You could black spray that little window in a second or two, before he knew what was going on." Gogan's voice is hard, gravel-like, the voice of a much older man. "If the guy does come out of the truck he's faced with all that firepower," Gogan says, echoing Abdullah.

"Let's get one thing straight," Abdullah says. "We don't want to kill anybody, just make sure they know real fast that they're outgunned." He looks first at Gogan then at me, a born leader with the reflexes of a man of action, not troubled by irresolution, a man who would have made his mark in any profession. "As Shaka would tell you, more battles are won in the mind of the enemy than on the battlefield."

"Who's Shaka?" I ask.

"A great Zulu general," Abdullah says. "The guy lived a couple of hundred years ago. Beat shit out of the British."

Gogan's joint is out. He reaches in his pocket, fishes out a book of matches and a rosary comes along with it. He dumps the rosary back in his pocket, lights up, again offers us a hit. We both shake our heads.

Abdullah turns to Gogan. "How much?" he asks.

"Well, you'll need guns, protection, cars... I'd say ten grand minimum."

"Why don't we split it three ways," I say, trying to avoid the obvious.

"Whoa!" Gogan says. "Whoa! First off I didn't say I was in this thing. Second, I'm just a poor parolee with a wife, two kids and a dog. And my wife works so we can stay afloat."

Abdullah makes a broad gesture toward me as if conferring some honor. "You're the banker, Mr. Klein," he says. "It takes money to make money."

"You can't do this on the cheap," Gogan chimes in. "You can't pull off a million dollar job with nickels and dimes."

I hadn't visualized my money disappearing. My role is doubly clear, the only reason these two are talking to me at all is for me to bankroll the project. Then as I look at these two ex-convicts, the ridiculousness, the improbableness, of the whole affair strikes me. Then I have another thought. I work up the courage to say, "By the way, how do I know you guys won't just disappear with my ten grand?"

Abdullah stares at me like a tombstone. I feel myself wilting, then finally he says, "You don't. That's a chance you'll have to take."

"I'll have to think about it," I say.

"I have to think about it too," Gogan says.

Abdullah, who now looks disgusted, says, "We'll all think about it, but not too long. A week seems long enough to me. I'll call you guys in a week. It's yes or no."

Like a good accountant trying to bound the problem, I ask, "How do I know ten thousand is enough?" The amount seems like a fortune to me and is most of my savings, though I don't even know why I'm asking because I suddenly don't give a damn.

Gogan's answer is the same as Abdullah's. "You don't," he says. "It should do it, but then I don't know how much high-quality guns cost these days. Or how much other things cost. I've been out of action for a while. But I'm not going to ask around until we've made up our minds. Just asking can get you into big trouble."

"I'll call you guys in a week," Abdullah says.

All the high tech razzle dazzle finance machinery at Sunshine notwithstanding, their accounting practices are at the ragged edge, actually over it. They depreciate old dilapidated facilities over forty years when they'd be lucky if the buildings were still standing in ten. They take to revenue receivables way past due and that will probably never be paid, and their bad debt reserve is minuscule. I point all this out to Jaime and he makes excuses for Sunshine. They plan to upgrade the buildings every five years, the receivables are from old and reliable customers, and so on. It's clear that he likes the account, likes the storm troopers that run the place. It occurs to me that some bread may well be passing from the gestapo types to hustling young Jaime. "It's a go-go world," Jaime tells me, "*everybody* is at the edge. If they're not actually breaking the law, leave them alone."

"How are things going at Sunshine?" Mason the Worrier asks me. I don't want to undermine Jaime but I don't want to lie either, so I tell him what I've found but tone it down. "What does Jaime say?" he asks. I give him Jaime's whitewash logic. He nods, in sort-of, kind-of agreement with Jaime then, brow wrinkled, he stares out the window as if something important were happening there. You can almost see in Mason's head the size of the Sunshine account whirring into place like the numbers in a slot machine. "When I get a chance," Mason finally says, "I'll check it out myself." Since no one can remember Mason ever leaving the office since his appointment as top honcho of the audit department, I view this as firing for effect. What I really wanted to tell him was that Sunshine's dietician had got a deal on a truckload of some oddball Scandinavian cheese and now the breath of all the inmates smells like sperm. But I don't think that would have interested Mason.

I leave Mason's office to find Wyomia holding an imaginary telephone to her ear and pointing to me. "Mama Bear," she says.

"He's disappeared," Mom says. "Just disappeared and hasn't called." Her voice is quavery.

"Who?"

"Murray," she says. "Who else would I be talking about?" She could have been talking about the cat, but I let this pass.

"How many days has he been gone?"

"Three."

"Is that all? He's probably on the road."

"He used to call me every day, even when traveling."

"Maybe he's closing some big deal. He's a busy man. Don't panic, Mom. He'll show up." I wonder whether Murray is shacked up with someone—though this doesn't strike me as likely—or maybe he just got tired of his blind girlfriend.

"Do me a favor, Ronnie," Mom says.

"What?"

"Find him. Call him for me. Tell him I'm worried about him,

worried about his health, that maybe he had an accident."

"That's a mistake," I say. "He'll feel henpecked, tracked. I mean you're not his wife. And besides, it's only been three days."

"Call anyway," she says. "I'll give you his office number. Make believe you're a client."

I'm tempted to say, why don't *you* call, but can't bring myself to do it. "What's the number?"

I call Linette. "I can't," she says. "I'm busy."

"What do you mean, *busy*?"

"Do I have to spell it out for you? I've got a date. The sun is shining and I'm making hay."

"Who's the lucky guy?" I inquire, though heaven know's why.

"I don't see where I have to inform you, Mr. House Detective, of my comings and goings. I'm not available. That's the bottom line. In your business you should have a real appreciation for the bottom line."

I'm about to ask about next week but then decide screw it. I'd sound like Mom chasing Murray. "I'll check in some other time," I say.

"Yeah, do that," Linette says. But I sense an edge of disappointment, as if she expected me to ask about another time.

"Take care of yourself, Linette," I say and mean it. You can't be close to someone for six years and not care for that person.

"I will," she says. "Thanks Ron." Her voice has softened. We both hang up and I feel alone as hell.

In the meantime the McGregor Sportswear account is screwed up. Old man Shisgal hires the cheapest labor he can find and that includes the help in the Finance Department, and accuracy is beyond Junior, so their books are fouled up. Erroneous entries, debits and credits that don't match, inventories wrong, receivables aging not updated, cash flow statements in error, etc., etc. It didn't matter much in the old days but now the company is publicly held and is stuck with quarterly 10-Qs and a yearly 10-K and annual report. All this goes to the SEC and we auditors have to certify that it's true and correct. I patiently point this out to Junior, the subtext being that unless it's right we can't sign off and he's in deep shit with his father-in-law. Junior's attention wanders. All this bookkeeping stuff might as well be higher mathematics. He's a big picture man, likes to be on the road, shaking hands, buying dinners, ordering wine. "Why don't you hire a professional?" I say. "A Controller, V.P. Finance, whatever you want to call him."

Junior nods, evidently recognizing the wisdom of this. I can see the wheels turning: how to sell this happy idea to old man Shisgal. He leans back, studies me, then says, "Do you want the job?" I can see he's serious. No way in this world would I work for Junior and godzilla Shisgal. I give Junior a humble smile, tell him I'm flattered that he would consider me, then gently say that I'm happy where I am. "Do you know somebody qualified?" Junior persists. I can see he's smitten with the idea. "I'll look around," I say, "but I'd suggest you get a headhunter to work the problem." Junior nods: the big hurdle, convincing the old man without implying his own incompetence, must look a thousand feet high. "Anyway, for now," I say, "this is what I suggest you do to get your books shaped up." Junior sighs, leans forward as I scratch action items on a pad. Oddly, I experience a moment of affection for poor Junior who must have thought he'd hit real pay dirt when he married Shisgal's daughter.

I'm debating whether to try to track down the disappeared Murray when Abdullah calls. "Are you in or out?" he asks, voice abrupt. "Do we do this or not? I can't wait around anymore."

"How about Gogan?" I ask.

"He's in."

"He is?" I say despite myself.

"Yeah," Abdullah says. "He checked the Bible and the Bible said it was okay."

"How's that?" I ask. "I thought the Bible said Thou shalt not steal."

"Well," Abdullah says, "the Bible isn't like the Koran. It's not the most consistent book in the world. In Proverbs there's something about men do not despise a thief if he steals to satisfy his hunger. Gogan, his wife and kids and dog, are all hungry. So...in or out, Mr. Klein. Do we have a deal or not?"

I'm not sure whether I'm in or out. "Let's meet," I say, "the three of us." We decide on my place the following evening. What am I doing? I have the feeling that I've boarded a plane and it's about to take off and in a short while there will be no way to get out. I'm apprehensive but also elated, as if something bright and alert has leaped up at me. Maybe it's the danger, but I sense that something deeper is going on. For the first time I'm doing something positive. I, Ronald Klein, CPA and auditor, am taking control of my destiny. Or at least seriously thinking about it. Then I can tell them all to go screw themselves: Mason and Jaime, Junior and Shisgal, the storm troopers at Sunshine, yes the whole lot of them. I elaborate this theme, see them all, small timers and small thinkers, at the end of their miserable lives, in retirement communities, dying of a heart attack or stroke while on the golf course. Or maybe they'll end their days in a concentration camp like Sunshine, eating white shit and being ordered around by a crew of gestapo nurses. And by God maybe I'll also say sayonara to Linette and damn it, maybe even to my mother. Yes sir, I'll do it. But as I think all this I sense the foundation of my world rocking and fear and confusion rising within me. I sleep badly, agonize, but in the end make up my mind.

SIX

So I hand over ten-thousand dollars in one-hundred dollar bills to Abdullah. I notice I'm perspiring as I do this. It is, after all, a good chunk of my life savings. Abdullah takes the packet of cash and looks at me not unsympathetically. "Do you want a receipt?" he asks and treats me to a big smile. I shake my head. Abdullah hands the cash to Gogan.

Gogan, it turns out, has surveyed the site. "Ron's right," he says. "There's no guard in the bank." Gogan then pulls out a local street map that he has annotated. "We'll switch cars twice before the final get away," he says. "We'll unload the first car at a Vons supermarket, right here." He points to a location on the map. "They've got a giant parking lot. After we transfer the sacks to the second car, we drive two miles to a Sav-on drugstore and another good-sized parking lot." He points again. "Those are wide streets with lots of traffic, so our cars will be lost in the crowd. At the drugstore we pick up Ron's car, drive to his house, split the take and everyone goes his own way."

"Why my car and my place?" I say, raising the first question that comes to me.

"That's one less illegitimate car we have to worry about," Gogan replies. "Then we want to go someplace totally unsuspicious where we can transfer the cash to our own suitcases."

I still don't like the idea but I hold off further argument. "Where do we get the other two cars?" I ask.

"There are a couple of possibilities," Gogan says. "One way is just to rent them." He now speaks directly to me. "I'll get you two phony drivers' licenses with a couple of phony credit cards that match the drivers' licenses. You can use those to rent the cars."

"That doesn't sound too good to me," I say. "First off it leaves a paper trail. Second, somebody will remember me as the renter.

Then what about the picture on the driver's license? There's just too much risk."

"Well goddamn!" bursts out Abdullah. "Damn right there's risk. We're not stealing jelly beans. If you want no risk then just keep doing what you're doing and we'll forget this thing right now."

I'm amazed at Abdullah's outburst. He glares at me as if I'm an enemy.

"Wait a minute," I say. "I just handed over ten grand to you guys. That's an act of faith. And also risk. All I'm asking is whether there're other ways to get the cars without exposing myself so much."

"Well," says Gogan, ignoring Abdullah, "I could steal the cars a couple of days before, or even the day before, switch plates with other cars so at least the plates won't be suspicious and use those."

"I like that a lot better," I say.

"I bet you do," Gogan says, "because now *I'm* taking all the risk."

"Let's knock off the bullshit," Abdullah says. "We'll go with you getting the cars," he says to Gogan. He turns to me. "You'll drive all the cars."

"Why me?"

"Because you're the only one with a driver's license."

After Abdullah and Gogan are gone with my ten-thousand dollars, I wonder—admittedly a little late in the day—whether these men can be trusted. Then I switch to developing a plan to insure my own safety. I think about this for quite a while but all the thoughts melt into mush. I give up. No such plan exists. I finally conclude that I have no alternative but to trust Abdullah and Gogan. It's either that or bail out of the deal and kiss my ten grand goodbye.

Gogan and I are sitting around my place waiting for

Abdullah. He's casually smoking a joint and invites me to take a hit. I politely decline. "My dog won a frisbee catching contest," he tells me.

"Where was this?" I ask, making light conversation.

"At our church picnic. It was a pot luck. My wife made potato salad. She makes a super potato salad." His voice carries the pleasant memory of the potato salad. He reflectively inhales, French style. "My kids threw the frisbee and the dog caught it. Jumped a mile high and caught it." "What kind of dog is it?" "German Shepherd. Name's Blarney." He gives me a benign smile; apparently cannabis makes Gogan gentle. "His full name is Blarney Stone, but we just call him Blarney."

"Is he mean?" I ask, not caring one way or the other but you've got to talk about something. "No way!" exclaims Gogan. "He's not a guard dog and not trained to be one. Blarney is just a family dog and great with the kids. He's real smart, though. Responds to something like thirty commands. Can you believe that?"

"That does sound remarkable," I say. "He's a buddy," Gogan goes on. "Always glad to see me, never gives me shit."

Gogan sucks up a draft of smoke, gives me a conspiratorial smile. "If you're going to embark on a life of crime," he says, assuming an instructional tone, "you should learn a little about arrest etiquette." I had never considered the possibility of getting caught. I stare at Gogan's friendly face, a man who has gotten caught many times. "Two rules to keep in mind," he continues. "Cooperate physically. And keep your mouth shut. The first rule will preserve your skull, kidneys and bones. The second will shorten the time you're locked up. Just remember four words: I want a lawyer. You get *no* benefit by saying things to cops and prosecutors for free. You only talk in exchange for something." He takes on a far away look as he finishes. I have the impression that much hard-earned wisdom has been distilled into those few words.

"Where did you learn about guns?" I ask. Gogan, it turns out, has been fascinated by weapons since he was a kid. He has an encyclopedia on guns at home, subscribes to *Guns & Ammo, Shooter's Bible*, and assorted other weapons magazines. "Of course, as a parolee," he says sadly, "I can't own a gun."

I ask Gogan about his family: did any other family members operate outside the law? Probably loosened by the marijuana, Gogan tells me about his brothers. One was killed in Pomona as he fell face first through the ceiling of a bicycle shop he was burglarizing. Death was caused when the long flashlight he had placed in his mouth to keep his hands free rammed into the base of his skull as he hit the floor. Gogan doesn't appear particularly saddened as he recounts the demise of his brother. "Aubrey wasn't too bright," he observes philosophically. Another brother was badly wounded when he stabbed himself trying to prove that an ice pick could not penetrate the flak vest he was wearing. "But he's okay now," Gogan reassures me. "Graeme runs a gas station in Anaheim." I begin to have doubts about the Gogans. They seem badly accident prone.

Abdullah shows up wearing black denim jeans and a black denim shirt. He's allowed his hair to grow in and it's now braided in dreadlocks. I have to admit, he's a menacing-looking figure.

"Guns are harder to buy now than they used to be," Gogan complains.

"What guns are we talking about?" Abdullah asks.

"For Ron here I thought I'd get a Smith and Wesson Model 10 revolver. Cops use it. It's easy to shoot. Good for a newcomer."

"We don't care if it's easy to shoot," Abdullah says. "We don't want to shoot anybody. We've been through this. We want guns that *look* like they mean business." He stares at Gogan. "Remember Shaka, the Zulu general? You win a war in the mind of the enemy? We want those guards to take one peek at our guns and know they don't stand a chance. We want to look like Rambo going in there. If we have to fire the damn things we've failed."

"Okay," Gogan says. "We could use an Uzi or a Tec-9 or an AK-47 or the MP5." Gogan is now visibly brightening as he warms to his favorite subject. "They're all automatics but I like the MP5. It has the highest rate of fire and it's the most reliable. U.S. Special Forces use it, so does the INS and so does NATO. I'd vote for the Heckler and Koch MP5. It's the meanest looking of the lot. That sucker looks like it could wipe out an army. In fact it probably could."

"Now you're talking," Abdullah says. "When can we get them?"

"A couple of weeks."

Abdullah does not look happy. "Try a couple of days," he says. "Now let's talk about the cars. I like Pat's three-car idea, the second in the supermarket and the third at the drugstore. But where do we park the first car? Then exactly where does each of us stand while we're waiting for the truck? We have to go look."

I'm concerned about being recognized by someone from the office coming out of my building. "Why don't we go on a Sunday morning?" I suggest.

Abdullah shakes his head. "No good. The scene will be totally different. No people, no cars. We have to go on Friday afternoon, about the time the truck arrives."

"Parking next to the bank is going to be a problem," I say. "The street is full of cars."

"It's metered parking," Gogan says. "I'll get a couple of No Parking, Violators Towed canvas bags the city uses for parades and stuff. I'll hang the bags over two of the meters. We'll park then pull the bags after we've parked."

"How about vests?" Abdullah asks.

"I thought I'd get the ones that are like T-shirts," Gogan says. "You wear them under a regular shirt. You can't see them so we look like everybody else. They wrap around and adjust with velcro straps so one size pretty much fits all. They do bulk you up a little but that's okay."

"Are they any good?" Abdullah asks.

"Yeah," Gogan says. "They're kevlar, same as the outside ones, and they have a shockplate. They'll stop anything except armor-piercing bullets."

As the planning continues I become aware that what had been a fantasy is now becoming reality. Suddenly my hands are cold, mouth dry.

"We'll do a run through this Friday," Abdullah says, "say at a quarter to four. Check out parking, where's our best positions, watch the truck pull up, see up close how they handle things. Then we'll check out traffic to the supermarket, how crowded the lot is, drive to the drugstore, check that out. We'll need your car to do that, Ron." I notice that "Mr. Klein" has disappeared. We're all equals now. "Then we'll do another dry run the next week," Abdullah finishes.

I'm thinking of my car and the three of us driving around in it. "Why two dry runs?" I ask.

Gogan answers. "It's the unknowns that kill you. You have to prepare for them."

"How do you prepare for them if they're unknown?" I ask.

"By being flexible," Gogan says. "By thinking through all possible what ifs."

I think of a couple of what ifs that I find frightening. "What if the guards refuse to comply and fire at us?" I ask.

"Then you have to kill them," Abdullah says. But his reply is not dispassionate, analytic, as his other words have been. Instead there is a sudden glint of hatred that I find disturbing.

"What if the guard in the truck fires through the porthole?" I ask.

"I'll spray his window in the first seconds," Gogan says. "He'd never fire blind."

These men, I must admit, seem to know what they are about. But then it occurs to me that both of them have been caught many times and spent a good part of their adult life locked up. Presumably they've learned from their mistakes, at least I hope they have. They no doubt learned the need for all those what ifs the hard way.

"What if a passerby intervenes?" I ask further.

Gogan gives a mirthless laugh. "Small chance staring into all that firepower," he says.

"What if he decides to be a kamikaze?" I persist.

"Goddamn!" Abdullah exclaims suddenly losing patience and startling me. "Then you kill him too." He stares at me. His eyes are hard, black. "You kill anyone who's an immediate threat."

That Friday we meet at the corner down the street from the bank. I had never really considered the bank building before: it's brutally modern in glass and steel, formidable as a prison. I had not noticed the large number of pedestrians before either. Gogan arrived an hour earlier and placed two No Parking bags over the two parking meters adjacent to the bank. God knows where he got the bags. "We want to test compliance," he says to me. And sure enough there is compliance: both spots are empty. "When you park there on D-day," Gogan says to me, "be sure you have some quarters for the meter."

Abdullah arrives dressed, I'm relieved to see, in blue jeans and a denim shirt and resembles an ordinary citizen. He decides where we stand so the guards will feel themselves surrounded, and

Gogan will have an immediate shot at spraying the windows.

The Protectall truck shows up. The usual guards are on the job and seem as lackadaisical as ever. One guard takes the handcart into the bank, returns with the cart piled with yellow sacks. The other guard waits with his gun drawn. The back door to the truck is opened and the sacks hauled in by the guard inside. The handcart is handed in next. One guard slams the door shut, then they both jump in the passenger entrance and the truck drives off.

We reconvene while I look around apprehensively to see if anyone I know is exiting my building or is on the street. "We move as soon as the sacks are in front of the truck," Abdullah says. "That's about five seconds after the guard leaves the bank. We have to move fast so position is important." He readjusts our locations relative to the truck. Gogan removes the signs from the parking meters, I get my car from the underground garage in my building and we drive to the supermarket. The lot is jammed with Friday afternoon shoppers but there are open parking slots. Abdullah decides to place the car as far out in the parking lot and away from the store as possible and, since I'll be doing the driving, indicates some candidate spaces to me. We then go through the same drill at the Sav-on parking lot.

We meet the following day at the home of Abdullah's friend with the VCR. Abdullah has asked me to bring the tapes. "Let's review this one more time," he says. "Look where the portholes are. Forget the one in the passenger door. The one that matters is in the back door." He turns to Gogan. "You've only got seconds to spray that little window." Abdullah stops and peers at Gogan. "Hey, are you listening?" He raises his voice as though Gogan were on the other side of the room. "Sure," Gogan says and smiles something of an idiot smile.

"Well goddamn!" Abdullah exclaims in total disgust, "this dumb son of a bitch is drunk. ARE YOU DRUNK?" Abdullah screams this last sentence at Gogan. He has taken on a primitive barbaric look that I at least would find thoroughly sobering.

"I'm not drunk," Gogan says indignantly. "Who says I'm drunk? What makes you think I'm drunk?"

Abdullah grabs Gogan's shirt, twists it and pulls Gogan's face close to his. "Listen you motherfucker," he hisses, "and listen real good. My ass depends on you. So do the asses of my brothers in the lockup. We're going to meet here again tomorrow, at ten in the morning. You be here and you be sober. If you come here drunk again this deal is off, but I'm going to kick shit out of you for all that wasted time." I notice Abdullah has not mentioned *my* ass or my ten grand.

"I got to go to mass," Gogan says.

"Mass?"

"Yeah. We go to Sunday ten o'clock mass."

Abdullah sighs. Mass is evidently a force majeure. "All right. Let's make it at three tomorrow afternoon."

Murray, to my mother's relief—and mine as well because I never did call to inquire as to his whereabouts—has resurfaced. "He was in Russia closing an important deal," my mother tells me. I doubt this but Mom is enthused about her big time boy friend and there's no point puncturing her balloon. Then, for all I know, maybe he *was* in Russia.

Mom invites me to dinner. I could use a square meal so I accept. Murray is there though she never mentioned him when she invited me. He's looking a little worn around the edges, eyes pink-rimmed and watery, clothes a trifle shabby, cuffs frayed, spots on his pants. He doesn't look like a man who just closed an important deal. Over the pot roast he gives me a capped-tooth smile and says, "Ron, I've got a proposition for you. We, you and me, can revolutionize the diamond business." He pauses, presumably for dramatic effect. "The deBeers guys in South Africa put out over eighty percent of the world's diamonds. They got a monopoly so their prices are sky high. What that spells is opportunity. They've put a big umbrella over diamond prices." Mom nods. Murray suddenly looks around as if concerned there is a stranger in the room or a bug hidden in the pot roast. He lowers his voice as though he's handing over some precious secret. "I can get diamonds at way below the deBeers wholesale price and sell them at a sizable profit." Now Murray nods. He has a triumphant look, as if he's elucidated some complicated theorem in mathematics.

"So go do it," I say.

"This is a big time operation," Murray says. "And requires big time thinking." Chair the cat looks at Murray doubtfully. My mother nods some more.

I get the picture. "So you're looking for investors."

"That's right," Murray says. He turns to my mother, teeth on display. "Your boy is a quick study." She beams. "I've always been proud of him," she says.

Now there's no way in this world I would entrust Murray with a dime of mine but by my mother's nodding I sense something more disturbing in the air. "How much do you need?" I ask.

"A hundred grand," Murray says.

"There's no hundred-thousand dollars around here," I say, while knowing that Mom's stash from Dad's life insurance is well over that. Then I ask the same question I had posed to Abdullah and Gogan. "Tell me," I say, "if somebody did lend you the money how would he know that you wouldn't just take it and disappear?"

"Ronnie!" cries my mother.

Murray appears shocked, eyes round muddy puddles as he stares at me. "Business deals are based on trust," he says piously.

"They're also based on credibility," I say. Murray looks offended. As far as I'm concerned, Abdullah and Gogan are a lot more credible than Murray. "Where do you get these el cheapo diamonds?" I ask.

"They're artificial diamond," Murray says. "Made in Russia."

"And they're the same quality as natural diamonds?"

"Not quite, but so close you can't tell them apart."

"Can't an expert tell them apart?"

Murray sighs. "I see you don't know much about diamonds," he says.

"I may not know much about diamonds," I say, "but I know a lot about baloney."

"Ron!" my mother cries.

Murray, who no doubt has faced much resistance in his life, is not terribly fazed. After a meditative silence he says, "A real expert can tell them apart, but it's not easy."

I suspect that anyone who knows anything at all about diamonds can tell them apart, but by my mother's scowl I decide to drop the subject. "I'll think about it," I say.

I call my mother the following morning. "You weren't thinking of putting money into Murray's phony diamond venture, were you?"

"I was thinking about it," she says. "And it might not be phony."

"Well stop thinking about it. I'm an auditor, Mom. My job is to find four-flushers. This guy is a con man. Don't you dare give him a penny."

"He's a nice man, Ron."

"All con men are nice men. After he's disappeared with your money, you'll always remember him as a nice man."

Maybe I'll call Murray and give him an ultimatum. If he touches a cent of Mom's cash, I'll sic the FBI on him. It's a thought anyway, to see how the asshole reacts.

I notice that I've grown impatient, more aggressive. I treat

Junior at McGregor's as if he's not worth my attention. He's getting sulky so I had best be careful. I'm also impatient in reviewing the books of my clients. Auditing is a meticulous business. Little things matter. There's no room for impatience. I try to concentrate but my thoughts return to the what ifs. I make mental notes of the things that bother me. Then another phenomenon is occurring: events around me, my own actions, seem cloaked in unreality. It's as if my true existence is now in another world, that of Abdullah and Gogan and the yellow sacks, and I'm only mouthing a script in the world of Mason and Junior and the others.

At our Sunday afternoon meeting, Gogan sober, I bring up my concerns. "How do we hide the weapons while we're waiting for the truck?" I ask.

"Duffle bags," Gogan says. "Ordinary looking things, like the bags you use to carry around athletic equipment. I'll get them."

Gogan turns to Abdullah. "Masks," he says.

"Like we said," Abdullah says. "We want masks that intimidate, like the guns. Halloween masks. Sinister-looking shit. Remember how they painted shark's teeth on those fighter airplanes? That's what we want to do. Scare those mothers... I'll get the masks."

"You know," Gogan says, "I've been thinking. Instead of just going for those yellow bags, what if we went for the whole truck? They've been picking up all day so the truck must be loaded. If we got hold of the truck, I know a warehouse where we could drive it—"

"I'm against that," I interrupt. "There are enough unknowns just getting the sacks. To take over the truck we'd have to deal with the guard inside. The bank or a passerby will call the cops in any case. Helicopters would spot and track that truck before it ever got to your warehouse."

Abdullah gives Gogan a viper-like stare. "That's a dumb

idea," he finally says.

"Some of your ideas are pretty dumb too," says a suddenly aggressive Gogan. "So don't give me shit, Elmore."

"Abdullah is the name," Abdullah says very slowly, menace emanating from him like a dangerous light.

"All right you guys," I say, seeing the need for peacemaking, "let's get on with this."

"About the money," says Abdullah.

"What about the money?" says a sullen Gogan.

"For at least a year afterward you can't spend the money freely."

"It's none of your fucking business when and how I spend the money," Gogan says.

"It fucking-A is," says Abdullah. "If one of us gets caught, it won't be long before the rest are too."

"What about your friends in prison?" I ask Abdullah. "I thought you were going to use the money for their legal defense."

"Our lawyers don't ask questions when they get paid," Abdullah says, then he stares at Gogan. "No big deal spending spree afterward or the whole deal is off."

"I'll be careful," Gogan says, back into his sullen mode.

"What about the guns?" Abdullah asks.

"I'll get three MP5s," Gogan says, "with full loads of ammo."

"Good," says Abdullah.

"Are you all right?" Linette asks me. "You seem sort of absent, or nervous about something."

I'm tempted to tell her about the nightmares I've been having—being buried alive, chased by prehistoric animals, being in a room that's on fire and no way out—but instead and to my amazement I say, "I'm planning to rob a bank and I'm a little nervous." I try to recover by giving her a big grin.

Linette laughs. "Ron, you *are* a funny guy... Maybe I could help. We could do a Bonnie and Clyde number."

"That's not a bad idea," I say, "but I've got a better idea."

"What's that?"

I stare at her with my new macho look. "Let's fuck."

She takes on a look that I recognize and that I haven't seen in months. We hustle into the car and, my hand gripping her thigh, tear over to my apartment. She strips off her clothes quick as a rabbit. Then, as we get into the action, I make a horrible discovery: things aren't working. Linette tries to help. No dice. "Let's just relax for a while," I say, perspiring.

"Sure," Linette says. She cuddles up close. "It's okay, Ron. These things happen."

It must be the robbery, I tell myself. It's frightened me somewhere inside. Holding a loaded gun... I've never held anything more deadly than a bread knife. What am I doing and why? Some internal map of where I've been and where I'm going has grown blurry. I now think of the whole improbable event as a form of madness that possessed me for a while and is now gone. I can still back out I suppose. The heist is on for this Friday. I have a passport now and a ticket on Air France (economy), non-stop Los Angeles to Paris, leaving at 9:30 the night of the robbery. I'll head for LAX as soon as the money is split. Take a cab. I don't know about carrying all that money on board. I've agonized over that. I'm worried about somebody examining my carry-on case and finding all that cash. I know there's some risk but decide to pack the money in the checked luggage. Linette huddles against me and I hold onto her, tightly. I'm tempted to ask her to come along with me to Paris but decide that's crazy. I hold on, my mouth dry; the air seems glutinous, hard to breathe. I suppose I can still back out.

"Are you sick, Ron?" Linette asks. "You're shaking."

We meet again at my place. "Here are the guns," Gogan says, and removes them from the duffle bags. "Careful, they're loaded." I hold the weapon. It's black, heavy, beautiful in a way. "Here's the safety catch," Gogan says. "Press down and rotate the lever and you can fire. It's an automatic weapon. As long as you keep the trigger down it'll fire, 800 rounds a second in fact."

Abdullah examines the gun in an experienced way, appears satisfied. "There are thirty rounds in the clip," Gogan says, "but here's an extra clip anyway. Just in case." Gogan hands each of us a spare magazine. He shows me how to unhook the old clip and jam in a loaded one. He's very professional in doing this. Then he removes a shell from a clip. "In case you're interested," he says, "this is what the gun fires. It's a Federal 9mm FMJ American Eagle, metal jacketed. Powerful shit." The yellow cartridge, plump and round, sits in his palm. It seems both deadly and innocent, beyond praise or blame, and I suppose it is.

"Here are your flak vests," Gogan says and hands each of us a heavy looking T-shirt. "They adjust to fit."

"What about the masks?" I ask.

"I've got them," Abdullah says and pulls three folded objects from his pocket. "Try these on. I've got a couple of spares in case these don't work."

Abdullah hands me a mask, a vampire's face in reds and blacks, of a rubbery material like those latex gloves my mother uses to clean the bathroom. I try it on: it's skin tight and difficult to get the eyeholes, nose and mouth to line up. When I have it set I look at myself in a mirror. It is, I have to admit, a frightening sight. Abdullah laughs. "You look real mean, Ron," he says.

Abdullah's mask is a death's head, all black and white, and Gogan's a devil. We're an imposing lot. "You'd better practice getting that thing on and off fast," Abdullah says. "We don't want any fuck ups on the job."

"The duffle bags," Gogan says, "are the smallest that'll hide the guns and the extra clip. They're old and kicked around. You can't trace them to anybody."

"The meter bags?" Abdullah asks.

"I've got those," Gogan says. "I'll put those on the meters around two o'clock."

"The paint spray?" Abdullah asks.

"I've got two high pressure cans," Gogan says. "They fit in my pocket."

There's now a sober professionalism about these two men as they go through their checklist of actions that gives the auditor in me a sense of comfort and confidence. It occurs to me that these men in their field are far more competent than Mason or Jaime or Junior or the Sunshine Nazi youth leader, or any of the other arrogant shits I deal with. But the consequence of failure in Gogan and Abdullah's world are far more severe than simply losing your job.

I feel myself again on an airliner, borne toward some unknown destination, impossible now to get off. The heist is on for tomorrow. I imagine Gogan in church tonight, kneeling before a saint, fingering his rosary, praying for the success of our venture.

SEVEN

I'm all set now: passport, one-way ticket to Paris, and the bag that'll hold the money. It's a good-sized heavy-duty suitcase, one of those that in the TV ads they drop off speeding trucks and have gorillas stomp on. Oddly, when I now think of Paris, I'm not at all sure why I'm going. My original fantasy has dissipated. Now it's just a foreign city where you're alone and have trouble ordering a meal because you don't understand the menu. Still, getting away after the heist is surely the prudent thing to do.

Gogan has "procured" the two cars, one we park at the supermarket and the other, a black Chevy Impala, I drive to the front of the bank. Gogan's Tow Away bags over the parking meters worked. I park in an open spot, take off the Tow Away bags and slip quarters in the meter. No one seems to notice. It's 3:45 p.m. The truck should be here in fifteen minutes.

Abdullah looks me over, cracks a friendly smile. "How are you doing, Ron?"

"Okay," I say.

"Everything will work out fine," Abdullah says. Gogan nods agreement. Suddenly I love both these men, my partners in this unlikely venture. Then I notice that Gogan's gestures are staccato, tic-like; he looks like he badly needs a joint. Even Abdullah, despite his words of encouragement, seems in an abstract mood, his movements stiff, robotic. It occurs to me that both these men have put in much time in prison and the possibility of returning for a long stretch, or for that matter for the rest of their lives, is surely frightening.

We all carry our duffel bags and are all dressed casually, Abdullah and Gogan in denim and me in conservative slacks and sport shirt. The bank building, now sinister looking, reflects back the mushroom gray of the sky. Though the day is cool I'm perspiring in my kevlar flack vest that substitutes for a T-shirt. Also, the fabric of the damn thing is rough so I'm itching as well.

I take my appointed position, on the opposite side of the street from the bank and about twenty paces to the left of the bank face. Gogan is directly opposite the bank and Abdullah next to the bank. I look around: the world—people, cars, avenue and buildings—now appear somehow transformed, foreign. I touch the mask in my pocket, feel its slithery surface, like alien skin, and my legs grow watery. A breeze comes and goes in a rhythmic way as though the city is breathing. Suddenly a voice next to me says, "Hey Ron, what are you doing here?" and my heart gives a mighty beat. It's Wyomia. "I thought you were on vacation," she says.

"I'm waiting for someone," I say and smile at her, sort of a Mona Lisa smile, the most I can manage.

"Are you okay?" she says. "You look...I don't know...sort of pale."

"I think I've got the flu," I say.

"Well, take care of yourself," Wyomia says and rushes off.

I feel perspiration on my forehead, in my armpits, and hear the beating of my heart. Now I'm concerned that someone else who knows me will exit the building. I keep my head down, try to shrink into myself, make myself invisible. I become aware of the duffle bag in my hand, the weight of the MP5 inside. What in the name of heaven am I doing, an accountant, carrying a gun? How did I get into this mess? I have an urge to flee, run for my life, forget the whole crazy enterprise.

The armored car should arrive any minute now. I scan the passersby, the cars. They all hurry along, innocently going about their lives, ignorant of the drama about to be played out before them. I feel myself at the rim of time, all things, the world itself, about to change, savagely and irreversibly.

The armored car arrives on schedule. It now seems enormous, tank-like, rivets along the sides, small windows, no doubt bulletproof, porthole in the back. The two guards emerge. These are the same men I have seen many times before: from my window, on video and in our dry runs. But now, heavy weapons at their sides, they seem far more substantial, dangerous. The back door opens, the handcart is grabbed by a guard, the door slams shut. The guard with the handcart goes into the bank, the other draws his gun and takes up his position by the truck. My legs are trembling.

Absurdly, I find myself thinking of my mother, her blind eyes, her voice, whiny and upset, "Ron, what are you doing? Have you gone insane?" Once again I'm seized by an urge to flee that's almost overpowering. Abdullah and Gogan are now exactly on station. People on the street seem to slow as if moving through air that has thickened.

I wait. What is taking so long? The waiting guard, gun casually at his side, tracks a passing woman. His pants are shiny. I touch the keys in my pocket; my pocket is filled with keys: for the two get away cars, my car. Again I scan the passersby. From a distance an older woman is approaching, a dog, a German Shepherd, on a leash.

The guard emerges from the bank, the hand cart piled with yellow sacks. Gogan crosses himself. Abdullah, Gogan and I slide on our masks; my hands are trembling and I have difficulty aligning the eyeholes of my Dracula disguise. When I have the mask adjusted I notice that the German Shepherd has disappeared behind the black Impala. Abdullah's mask is a death's head, Gogan's a devil, both seem to have emerged from some hellish other world. We pull our weapons from the duffle bags. But I cannot bring myself to touch the safety lever. Intimidate, I tell myself. Intimidate. That's all I'm here to do.

"Drop the gun!" Abdullah shouts to the guards, his weapon in clear view. "Down on the ground!"

"Down! Both of you!" yells Gogan. Weapon in one hand, spray can in the other, he sprints toward the truck. At that moment the Shepherd starts to bark furiously.

"Down!" I yell as well, but my voice is drowned by the barking dog.

The Shepherd tears the leash from the hands of the woman and races toward Gogan. Gogan seems paralyzed as his devil's mask stares at the oncoming dog. The Shepherd leaps toward the frozen Gogan. There is a volley of gunfire, shattering in its intensity, a great yelp, and the dog is writhing on the pavement, shot by Abdullah.

In the diversion the guard on the street, who has not dropped his gun, fires at Gogan. The MP5 and spray can drop from Gogan's hands and he falls to the ground clutching his head. Abdullah screams something that sounds like "motherfucker" then guns down the guard that fired at Gogan. The second guard has now drawn his weapon and Abdullah shrieks something else and blasts the second guard. Abdullah's screams seem demonic, Abdullah killing not only these guards but *all* guards, in prison and out, that have tormented him his entire life.

The guard in the truck, no doubt alerted by the gunfire, gets off a round through the porthole. Abdullah staggers then goes down, grasping his thigh. Abdullah is now apparently out of the line of fire of the guard in the truck, who does not emerge or fire again.

I stare in disarray at the scene before me: Gogan, in his devil's mask, is sprawled on the pavement along with the two bleeding and unconscious guards and a dead dog. Abdullah, with his death's head mask, is on the ground still clutching his thigh, his pants turning red. People are ducked in doorways, crouched behind cars. And in the midst of this mayhem sits the aluminum handcart piled with the yellow sacks. A great silence is over everything as if a glass dome has descended over the scene, shutting out all sound. All of life seems to hang suspended.

I haul Abdullah to his feet, grab one sack by its handle, am astonished at its weight, and dragging Abdullah and the sack, make it to the Impala, staying out of the line of fire of the porthole. I shove Abdullah into the back of the vehicle, heave the sack after him, tear off my vampire mask and speed away.

In my rear view mirror I see the guard from inside the truck, outside now, gun drawn, but he does not fire, probably for fear of hitting a bystander. I drive to the Vons supermarket, hear sirens sounding in the distance, find the second car, park beside it and haul Abdullah and the sack into the back seat. I drive carefully, don't want to be stopped for a traffic violation. I hear the whir of helicopters overhead. My face is now covered with perspiration. I think of Gogan: no way I could have dragged him into the Impala. Perversely, I pray that he is dead. I remember that I dropped my weapon and duffel bag when I ran to pick up Abdullah. The words "fingerprints" and "DNA" cross my mind. No help for it now. In the back, Abdullah, mask removed, has fashioned a tourniquet with his belt to slow the bleeding. "You saved my life, Ron," he says. "But you've got to get me to a doctor. In South Central... Where's Gogan?" "On the ground. I think he was shot in the head." "Pray that he's dead," Abdullah says, echoing my thought. I check my rear view mirror: Abdullah is now slouched in a distorted position, apparently passed out.

I reach my Chevy Lumina; sitting quietly in the Sav-on parking lot, it seems an old and reliable friend waiting for me. Again I transfer Abdullah and the sack. I loosen the tourniquet and bright red blood saturates Abdullah's pants. The bullet probably severed an artery. His face is pasty, head slumped to the side.

I drive toward South Central L.A. A new thought now enters my mind. I could dump Abdullah, disappear with the contents of that single sack and onto that Air France flight. But while I may think this, the car continues to head toward South Central.

When we reach the black neighborhood I find that I've lost my bearings and have no idea where to go. I'm thinking of the apartment with the VCR, but now I have even forgotten the street name. I gather the courage to pull slowly alongside a black man walking along the street. I open the window. "Do you know where I can find a doctor?" I ask, accepting the risk of that question. "My friend is badly hurt."

The man looks in the back of the car, at the unconscious Abdullah, at blood everywhere, and without a word hurries off.

Now what? In the name of God, now what? I suppress a wave of panic. I stop the car and am considering just dumping Abdullah on the street when a black woman approaches, maybe Linette's age. In an inspired instant I ask, "Can you please tell me where the Muslim mosque is?"

She looks in back, looks at me, then—and I have no idea what she makes of this improbable scene of a white man driving a badly bleeding black man to a mosque—she gives me directions.

At last I find the store front church marked Sons of Islam where I had first encountered the freed Abdullah. I run inside. I'm suddenly grabbed by the arm, by a huge black man with a vise-like hand. "Hey!" he says. "Where do you think you're going? This is prayer time."

"One of your brothers, Abdullah, is outside in my car. He's bleeding to death and he needs help."

"Wait a minute," the man says.

"We don't have a lot of minutes," I say. "The guy is dying."

"You just wait!" he commands and disappears into the dim interior.

A few minutes later he's joined by a black man in a blue and gold dashiki, of smaller dimensions than the first man but not by much. "Now what's this all about?" he asks in a reasonable voice.

"Listen," I say. "I can't keep explaining. Just come with me out to my car and see for yourself. I'm parked right in front."

"First tell me what's in the car," he says. His voice is patient, unhurried, a man who has just finished prayer.

"Look," I say, *my* patience now gone, "you come and take Abdullah out of the car or I'll dump him on the sidewalk."

The second man regards me appraisingly then motions to the

first man and we go out to the car. Abdullah is passed out in the back, the tourniquet open, his pants and the upholstery of the car saturated with blood. The two men haul Abdullah out of the vehicle and into the mosque. "I think he's dead or close to it," one of the men says. But I'm not listening. I stare in disbelief. The yellow sack is gone. In my hurry to tend to Abdullah, I had not locked the car.

I drive around disoriented then finally find my way home. I clean up, dump the clothes I wore into the trash, then turn on the evening news. The attempted B of A robbery is the first item on their agenda. Gogan is dead. The single shot penetrated an eye and shattered his skull. One guard is dead and the other critically wounded. The woman whose dog was killed is interviewed. The animal was a guard dog, trained to go after weapons. Gogan had been right about the power of the unknowns. After all that meticulous planning, done in by a dog! I stare at my Air France ticket, now worthless.

Using detergent, I scrub hell out of my car interior, trying to remove the blood stains. This, it turns out, is not easy. Some shadow remains.

I go to work, see Mason, Wyomia, Jaime. They appear new to me, as if I have been through some herculean trial—returned from a war, or recovered from some killer disease—and yet I'm pleased to see them. They now seem blessedly ordinary, normal.

I meet Junior at McGregor, review his books, do the same at Sunshine where the Nazi youth leader V.P. Finance gives me a big hello. Through all this, as I peruse balance sheets and cash flow statements, the scene before the bank replays itself in my head. Actually, the scene, reconstructed via television interviews, is played before most of America. The *L.A. Times* carries interviews with bystanders, what they say wildly at variance with one another and with what actually happened. The woman with the dog has become a celebrity. A spokesman for Protectall praises the guards and says that a special award of $10,000 each has been made to the families of the guard killed in action and the guard critically wounded. He commends their dedication and says they represent all the devoted men and women that daily risk their lives for Protectall and its precious cargo. He makes no mention of the disappeared yellow sack.

On TV there is an interview with the widow Gogan who, dressed in black, face tear-streaked, characterizes her husband as a loving family man and father, church going and God fearing. A naive man who had been led astray by unscrupulous associates taking advantage of his innocence. The guards' families are also interviewed, both wives through tears praise their spouses as hard working, responsible men; their children, teens to twenties, appear stunned. Seeing these people stuns me as well: the guards for me had been as detached as tree stumps, with no existence beyond the Protectall truck. Though it wouldn't have changed anything, it never entered my mind that they might have families.

The two getaway cars, parked at Vons and Sav-on, have been found and identified as stolen. The L.A. District Attorney has appeared on television and says that forensic experts from the FBI and the LAPD are combing the vehicles for clues as to the other two felons. They are considered armed and dangerous and no doubt with a long record of crime. The three weapons left at the scene and the duffle bags are also at the crime labs. One of the escapees, based on the quantity of blood in the two vehicles, is clearly badly wounded and DNA analysis is being done on the blood. The District Attorney is confident that the noose is tightening and the other two perpetrators will soon be apprehended.

When I think back—the scene and the action now growing surreal—I ask myself what went wrong. It occurs to me in a vague sort of way that we were done in by our finer instincts. Gogan who loved his dog and so could not bring himself to fire on the Shepherd. Me staying with Abdullah when I could have dumped him while I disappeared on that Air France flight with the money. Abdullah avenging all the wrongs done Elmore Carter. And the guards acting out of a sense of duty toward Protectall, at ten dollars an hour. Protectall was a rift that revealed the soul of each of us. All useless thoughts, all gone now. Though I do ask myself how I got involved in the first place. All the reasons I come up with are really foolish, but then people often do serious things for foolish reasons.

In the ensuing days the failed robbery fades from the news. Nothing is said of Abdullah so he may have been treated clandestinely, though I would bet that he's dead.

My mother calls. "I'm going to marry Murray," she announces.

"It's a mistake Mom," I say soberly. "He's a con man. After your money."

"I'll take my chances," she says. "Nobody is perfect."

"Do you love him?" I ask.

She giggles. "Ronnie, you're a romantic. You don't have to be in love to get married... How about you? You're going to marry Linette, aren't you? I can tell. You're getting antsy, ready to mate... She's no good for you, you know."

"Maybe I'll marry her anyway," I say. "Nobody is perfect."

"We could make it a double wedding," Mom says.

After that conversation, my thoughts drift to the yellow sacks. They appear disembodied as in those strange paintings where unlikely objects float over a familiar landscape. You know, I think there is a certain moment that marks a before and after in your life. Mine occurred the moment I started to seriously observe the

Protectall truck and the guards and the yellow sacks. From that moment forward, all Walter Mitty fantasies aside, whether those observations resulted in action or not, I changed. I had come to be possessed by a secret that would never leave me. That the world offers far greater possibilities than I had previously imagined. That I could do more and go further than I had dreamed.

The disaster in front of the Bank of America is never completely out of my mind though I try to ignore it. I pray that no clue will lead the police to me. And I grieve for Abdullah and Gogan, even for the guards with their shiny pants. Abdullah, a Muslim, would say that the outcome was fated, preordained and unchangeable. Just as he told me that my fate was to audit financial statements forever. But I now know that I will not spend my life doing that. I will strike out on my own, not work for Mason or Jaime or Shisgal or anybody else. Linette will help. Her real estate instructor was right: better to be first in the village than second in Rome. We'll do it together. If nothing else, I owe it to Abdullah and Gogan, two entrepreneurs after all, to make the most of myself. I even owe it to the guards.

I dial the Kleeber real estate office and Linette answers. "I've got a proposal for you," I say. "I couldn't wait to ask so I thought I'd call. How would you like to get married and honeymoon in Paris?"

Arthur

Julie always looked younger than her years. But now her face is deeply lined and the green of her eyes appears faded. Her hair is gray and she has chosen not to dye it. "This is what I am," she says, voice resigned. "There's no point pretending to be another." This aging occurred over the last few years. Her doctor suggests estrogen replacement therapy. Julie shakes her head. "We don't want to fool with nature," she says. And she never did fool with nature. When she was young she wore no makeup, yet because of the rich auburn of her hair, green eyes, the glow of her skin, she seemed extravagantly made up.

Through our life together I have always admired her stubbornness as she fought for her rights, allowed no slight to pass without comment, always stated her opinion, often contrary to mine. Now in our seventies, we have achieved a certain weary peace. She has grown gentle, leans upon me. In the end I suppose I have won though I have no sense of victory.

There is a disquieting development. She struggles to find words where she was once smoothly articulate. She will search for a word or a name and her face will take on a fixed expression, the silence lengthening. She does not try for a work around, or say it doesn't matter and go on, but just stands there frozen, as if rummaging through some inner closet now hopelessly scrambled. I try to help, suggest words, but she keeps staring, determined to do this on her own. It's heartbreaking.

"Why don't you balance the checkbook," she says one day, handing me the latest bank statement.

This comes as a surprise because she has always enjoyed these administrative duties. I find mistake after mistake in the arithmetic but say nothing.

I search for things to interest her. Television and films are so abysmal that we amuse ourselves by reading aloud to each other. She loves Henry James though she laments that his late novels had become so subtle, so artistic, as to be incomprehensible. I try reading aloud James's *Portrait of a Lady*, her favorite, Isabel Archer her favorite heroine. But her attention wanders and I ask whether she would like to do the reading. She hesitates but finally agrees, stumbles over words, then puts down her glasses and says her eyes are tired.

A couple, friends and former neighbors, will be visiting Philadelphia and I suggest to Julie that we invite them to stay at our house. They put us up when we were in Paris and we should reciprocate; heaven knows, we have the room. "The house is not clean," she says. "These are people who notice every spot on the rug, every speck of dust on the furniture." She seems in a panic. "No, no, we can't have them here. Put them in a hotel. We can pay. Not here." But I bring her around, hire a maintenance service to clean the house.

Michel Trenet has remained trim, hair now gray curving around his ears and down the back of his neck, too long for America; his wife Colette has the chic cared-for appearance of French women, head small and neat like a cat. "When did we last see each other?" asks Colette when they arrive. Julie stares at her without recognition. "It's been ages," Julie finally manages. "Too long," she adds graciously.

We take the Trenets to dinner, order cocktails, a bottle of wine, but it's Julie who drinks much of the wine. I know she does this when she is ill at ease. I have never found a way to get her to stop. Trenet says that with the Internet all information travels the world in a day, including jokes. His full mouth breaks into a smile. "For instance, I received an e-mail the other day with this foolish story." He then recounts a tale where a young Jewish woman returns from a Peace Corps tour of duty in Uganda and introduces her new Ugandan husband to her mother. He is black, wears an elaborate headdress, a feathered loincloth, and a necklace of animal teeth. "Fool! Idiot!" cries the mother. "I said marry a *rich* doctor!" Trenet laughs discreetly, his eyes, wide and narrow, search for audience reaction. He obviously enjoys the story and doesn't think it foolish.

Julie stares uncomprehending at Michel. "Arthur," she says, "you were never much of a storyteller." Trenet and Colette, brows wrinkled, possibly thinking they've misheard, gaze quizzically at Julie.

At home we say goodnight and Julie adds, "How nice, Arthur, to at last have you in my own house," and turns and leaves.

The Trenets watch her go. "She's tired," I say, and leave myself.

"Who's Arthur?" I ask Julie. She stares at me. "You called Michel Trenet Arthur. Twice in fact."

"Did I?" she says and seems astonished. "How strange."

"But who did Trenet remind you of?" I don't know why I'm persisting but I've grown curious. For all I know Arthur is the mailman or the grocer or nobody at all. But I'd like to know.

"Did I really call that silly man Arthur?" Julie says. "How unkind."

"Unkind?"

"To Arthur, of course."

"But who the hell is Arthur?"

"Don't raise your voice," Julie says. "You sound like a jealous husband. It doesn't become you." She smiles sweetly. "He's someone I knew many years ago who wrote me letters." Her look grows distant. "Did I really call that man Arthur? How odd."

I do not persist. She is evidently tired and I no longer care.

But for some reason I *do* care. Perhaps when you have lived with someone for fifty years and think you know all there is to know of the other person, when something comes along to shake that assumption, it's troubling.

The following day and for the remainder of the Trenets' stay Arthur does not surface again. But when they are gone I casually remark, "Well, Arthur has left at last."

"Who?" Julie asks.

"Why Arthur of course," I say assuming a joking tone.

Julie squints at me. "I don't know what you're talking about," she says.

We have three children, spread all over America: New York, Chicago, Los Angeles. They're busy, successful, rarely come to Norristown, the Philadelphia suburb where we live and where they grew up. Sensing that bad things may be ahead, I urge them to visit with us over Christmas. Reluctantly, they agree. Instead of making her happy, this puts Julie in a panic: "Where will they all sleep? And what about the grandchildren? Five little kids." I correct her. "Eight," I say. "We have *eight* grandchildren." "And what about presents?" she goes on, ignoring the correction. "And a tree?" She wrings her hands, looks about, paces the kitchen. It all seems insurmountable to her.

To minimize the strain on grandma, our younger daughter and her husband, who have but one child, are the only ones to stay at our house. The other two children, with their multitude of offspring, stay at a nearby hotel. Our two daughters and daughter-in-law volunteer to do the Christmas dinner with Julie supervising. Our son, who is a surgeon, might as well not be there because much of the time he's on the phone. When we are all together Julie turns to our older daughter and son and asks,

"Where are you staying?" When they tell her she flies into a rage. "We could have fit you into the house," she cries, then stares accusingly at me.

The children are all in their forties now, each touched by life in his own way. The older girl is on her third husband; my son might as well be single for all the time he spends with his family; only the younger girl seems at peace though her husband cannot hold a job for more than a year and they live on her income. I say grace over dinner then Julie insists on making a speech. "I thank you all for taking the time to visit with your doddering old parents," she says. "I remember you as children..." She then goes on to recollect the youngsters they once were, confusing one child with another. There seems no end to this. The adults look to me for guidance, the grandchildren fidget. I decide to let her go on. Julie pauses a moment and our oldest seizes the opportunity. "Shall we eat, Mom?"

Julie glares at her. "You were always a rebel," she says to Margaret, mouth turned down. "You have been trouble since you were a child."

"I only suggested that we eat," Margaret says soothingly. "The children are hungry. We can reminisce over dessert."

Julie suddenly bursts into tears. "Only Arthur knows how much I have suffered."

"Who's Arthur?" our youngest asks.

"Why your father, of course." She stares at her daughter, face strained. "Surely you're not so busy as to forget your own father."

The reunion has only gone well for the grandchildren. They tear open their presents, have a snowball fight in the yard, cousins discovering each other. The children catch up on one another's lives, are awkward together. "Do you have any idea who Arthur might be?" I ask. They shrug, shake their heads: no one has a clue. "But I doubt if he's our father," my son says, "because we all look like you." They all hasten to leave.

"Mom's not going to get any better," my son the doctor says clinically when at the door. "Later, you might want to hire a caretaker for her." He looks me in the eye. "Otherwise, she'll pull you down with her." Diagnosis delivered, he and his family are gone.

I work at remembering the names of all our past neighbors, friends, husbands of Julie's friends, etc. No Arthur. I try again with Julie. "You said Arthur was the father of our children... What in the world did you mean?"

She stares at me. "Did I say that?" She collapses in confusion. "I have no idea what I was talking about."

My son was right: things begin to fall apart. Julie can't find the iron. I help her look for it: the iron finally turns up in the freezer. She wanders out of the house in her bathrobe, gets lost on our own street, prepares a meal then forgets she ever made it. Always neat, but now like a molting bird she leaves items of clothing, bits of herself, lying about, disorder everywhere. She interrogates me when I leave the house—where have I been?—even though suspicion was always alien to her. When problems arise in personal care—bathing, brushing her teeth, dressing—I give up. I have grown short-tempered with her, intolerant of her forgetfulness, her suspicion, fears, fits of crying. I am, as my son said, being pulled down. This is another Julie, one I do not know, one who can quickly turn your heart to stone.

I consider putting Julie in a nursing home, visit several, am appalled by what I see. Mostly women, white-haired, bent, shabby, some staring blank-eyed at a television, some babbling incessantly, a gulag for the aged and dying. I decide on the home care option. I visit employment agencies, search for a caretaker. I try to make Julie part of the interviewing process, telling her we're hiring a maid-of-all-work. Julie doesn't understand why we need one; she stares suspiciously at all the applicants during the interviews and doesn't say a word. But she momentarily smiles at a large black woman named Earline and that's the one I hire.

Earline doesn't mess around. She has grab bars installed in the bathtub to prevent falls, places nonslip adhesives on the bathtub surface, and tests the water temperature before allowing Julie to get in. She has Julie brush her teeth by the numbers: hold toothbrush, put paste on brush, brush top teeth, and so on. Julie takes to following Earline around like a duckling as the woman goes about her chores; this doesn't seem to bother Earline at all. Earline hums, whistles, says to Julie, "Why don't we do a greens omelette for lunch?" and Julie nods enthusiastically. Julie prattles on about something and Earline says, "No foolin'" or "Well I'll be..." and laughs. When Julie refers to me she calls me Arthur more and more frequently. Earline smiles, nods and pays no attention to this.

I am steadily building Julie out of my life. She is happy with Earline: they eat together, dust together, make the beds, etc. I sit alone and try to sort out how I, a man on the lee side of his seventies, will spend the little that's left of my life.

I have always had an interest in history. Many years ago, it seems in another geological epoch, I had considered writing a history of the lesser presidents—Polk, Fillmore, Buchanan, Harrison—and had taken copious notes on the subject. I set about looking for those notes. I search all the boxes accumulated in the attic, the garage, the basement, locate old Christmas tree decorations, an ancient turntable, the elastic collar I wore when I injured a nerve in my neck, and assorted other castoffs. But no notes on the presidents. In desperation, I ask Julie, hoping for a moment of lucidity. "Why Arthur," she says, "they're probably with your letters." "And where are those?" I ask. "In my love chest," she says. "Where is that?" She takes on a confused look, then shuffles off to the kitchen and Earline.

I don't recall any love chest. But I do remember a steamer trunk that we had years ago, a huge wooden affair where Julie stored odds and ends. But that had been disposed of years ago. Or had it? You couldn't hide something that big. If it existed at all, it had to be in plain view. I again search the garage, basement. Nothing. Then another possibility comes to me. There is a crawl space under part of the house, to get at the water and sewer lines. Years ago we had stashed bulky items there—discarded drapery fixtures, a dilapidated awning—things we no longer needed but that for some reason we could not bring ourselves to throw away.

I unscrew the wood frame that is the entrance to the crawl space. The inside is cold, musty, smells of damp. I scan a flashlight beam across the space: the awning is still there, mildewed, and old Venetian blinds that I had forgotten existed. In a corner is the steamer trunk. It takes me half an hour to move it at all: it seems to have rooted itself to the ground. I finally drag it through the entry and into the snow in the yard. The sides and top are rotted, probably by termites, and the clasps rusted shut. I knock off the clasps with a hammer and chisel and pull the top open. The top falls away as the hinges have rusted clear through. I feel as though I'm opening a long-sealed tomb, expect an odor of mortar and plaster. But the smell is like that of the crawl space, musty and damp.

There are items of clothing: children's scarves and gloves, baby items, old dresses, saved bits of time, all mildewed. I scavenge down to the bottom of the pile. There is a looseleaf notebook, indeed my presidents notes, still legible. But that's not really what I'm searching for. At the very bottom is a shoebox. I lift it gingerly, the cardboard coming apart in my hands, and inside are the letters. Everything smells of damp, of far away time, of things long dead. I find another shoebox in the house, transfer the letters to it, and take it to my study. Snow is falling in big cottony flakes as I wrestle the steamer trunk back into the crawl space, close up the entrance. I feel somehow guilty, as if I had desecrated a cemetery.

The letters are arranged chronologically, the paper fragile, of different sizes, yellowed, the ink faded but still legible. There is never a return address. They are all written on hotel stationery, sent to a post office box in Norristown and postmarked from cities all over the U.S. Clearly, Arthur got around. The closing ranges from "Affectionately, Arthur," in the early letters to "With deepest love, your Arthur" in the later ones. I have an impulse to throw them out, pitch them into the trash without reading any of them, for what do they matter now? They are dated some thirty years ago, when Julie was about the same age as our children are now. Astonishingly, they extend over a period of five years. Hesitantly at first, then more quickly, obeying a force greater than myself, setting aside all logic and reason, I read the letters. Arthur wrote in a neat confident hand, without crossouts. I have the impression that each letter had gone through several drafts before the final version was written. He called her Juliana, her real name, rather than Julie like everyone else.

Arthur liked to quote poetry, most of which I do not recognize, phrases like, "If thou must love me, let it be for naught/ Except for love's sake only," or "All in green went my love riding/ on a great horse of gold/ into the silver dawn."

From a shred here, a fragment there, I piece together Arthur's life. He was an antique dealer with a show room in Manhattan who traveled to auctions, tried to sort out the antiques from the merely old, buying pieces and shipping them off to N.Y. He was married with two grown children and by the terms of endearment he used ("my sweet newly blossomed rose," "but thee, thou still hast the dew of thy youth") much older than Julie. They had met at the Philadelphia Museum of Art during an exhibit of 18th and 19th century silver. She was "a rare and exotic flower improbably hidden in an ordinary bouquet." So I gather she was with friends. He made some knowledgeable comments about the coffeepots, trays, punch bowls, candelabra, then, no doubt with charm and modesty, said he was in the business and handed her his card. And Julie's call "caused my heart to leap with pleasure, as if a door had opened and the future walked in." After five years the letters abruptly cease. There is no cooling of ardor toward the end. The letters just stop—or were the later ones destroyed? Impossible to know. But I conjecture that Arthur had a heart attack or a stroke or just plain died, found in his gallery slumped in a Chippendale chair.

He describes Julie's body—alabaster is his favorite word—at length, in detail, and often (I imagine horny Arthur in a lonely hotel room in the bowels of some strange city fantasizing over Julie): "you came to me in shy nakedness, through a silvery haze of light. It made me worshipful, a miraculous vision in the desert of my life, but it also aroused in me a pagan lust." Their trysts are afternoons at an anonymous Marriott or Sheraton or Hilton around Philadelphia. Though once he mentions the Barclay and the charm of their French Provincial room and the high four-poster bed and the Louis XIV bergere on which they had made love. "You, my sweet and lovely darling, and that room are inseparable." He is amused that Julie complains his beard tickles, is pleased that she appreciates how lean he has kept his body, admires his wide-set eyes and how dark they become when he is sexually aroused. She thinks he resembles Cardinal Richelieu. Sometimes Arthur grows philosophical and reflects on "the riddle of life," or "our mother the sea." He reminisces over their lunches at La Ciboulette or Girasole or Isola Bella, mentions a walk along the river where they chanced on a collegiate rowing event and Julie said it reminded her of an Eakins painting. He recalls the time they took in a performance of *Swan Lake* at the Academy of

Music and afterward, his "hot house flower" sang the Swan theme and she was so fetching that he had to have her immediately. And every year, at the anniversary of their meeting, he takes her to dinner at Le Bec Fin, where, in its old world elegance, he feels at home. At times he thanks her, immensely grateful that she "has turned on the lights in the theater of my life, appeared miraculously, like a pearl in an oyster."

Later letters take on a cozy old-friends quality: he muses over a decision whether to buy a Louis XVI fauteuil or a Roman gilded wood poltrona. Sometimes he speaks of his family: his son, "an Adonis," is a bit actor in off-off-Broadway theater and in constant need of money, his daughter helps run the gallery, drinks too much, and is luckless in love. He characterizes his wife as "morose," "unappreciative," "jealous." Once, he refers to her as "a gloomy owl-like creature who flees daylight." But there is never any talk of divorce, of he and Julie running off together. Arthur's life, it would appear, isn't much different from that of a lot of other people.

The spacing of the letters is uneven. Sometimes Arthur will write twice a week, other times a month will go by between letters. There are maybe two hundred letters in all, some only a paragraph long, others several pages. Did Julie ever write to him? Probably not, because he never refers to any letter of hers.

I was always mechanically inclined—souped up an old Ford as a teenager—and after receiving a mechanical engineering degree from Temple worked for a while as a tool and die designer in Reading, Pennsylvania, then saved, begged and borrowed enough money to open my own tool and die shop in Norristown, in a cramped former grocery store. I made precision parts for the textile machinery manufacturers in Reading and York, the manufacturers of food processing machinery in Allentown, the makers of packaging equipment and paper processing machines in Pittsburgh and everyone else who made machines in Pennsylvania and the northeast. I review the years of Julie's affair with Arthur. Our children were in their middle teens then. My memories of the time are a haze of struggle with the business, traveling to drum up sales, scrounging to find competent help, pay the bills. I remember Julie as occupied with the children, in no way unhappy, sex available on request, she responsive. At least I think that's how it was. We quarreled, yes, but we had always done that. I don't recall our arguments in that period being more acrimonious than usual. I marvel that she was able to find the time and invent the subterfuge needed to get away and meet with Arthur.

Our older daughter, who lives in New York, will be visiting Philadelphia on business and I arrange to have dinner with her. She's an attorney, street-smart, and the shrewdest of the bunch. I ask her again, as I did at Christmas, if she knew of Arthur and she says no. "Well, he's the guy your mother was sleeping with while you were in high school."

Margaret stares at me. "How do you know?" she asks.

I tell her about the letters.

She laughs. "Well, good for her!" She touches my arm. "No offense, Dad, but every woman deserves one good fling outside of marriage."

I decide to ignore this observation. "Was she unhappy then? Do you remember?"

"I can't say. I was too involved with my own problems. Anyway, a woman doesn't have to be unhappy to have an affair... I mean, were *you* unhappy? From what I can tell you had your share of one-night stands and adventures over the years... Am I wrong?"

"They don't count," I say rather lamely. "They were just a

form of entertainment. Not a five-year relationship."

Margaret shrugs. "That was a long time ago. Why does it matter?"

"She calls me Arthur now."

Margaret shrugs again, sighs. "I can see where that would bother you." She pauses a moment as if debating whether to go on then proceeds. "You know, Dad, you and Mom did not have what I would call a happy marriage. You guys disagreed on most things, and didn't communicate too well either. All you worried about was your business. That's where all your time and energy went. Mom worried about us, sulked sometimes, found buddies outside the house... I wouldn't even call you two friends... I can see where she might be tempted into an affair... Then this guy *was* attentive. Look at all those letters. That must have meant a lot to her. Otherwise why now, with all those synapses blinking out, would she hang on to that one shred?"

Julie now calls me Arthur all the time. I go along, answer to the name, do not correct her. Margaret was right: what difference does it make? Sometimes Julie refers to our walks along the Schuykill, behind the art museum, men fishing off the embankment, in April bursts of azaleas and rhododendrons. Or our lunches in some out-of-the-way restaurant, or the silver bracelet I gave her with the name Juliana engraved on it. (I wonder where the bracelet is now but I'm not going to bother looking for it.) I go along with it all. To please her, I refer to incidents I pick out of the letters—a matinee where we saw Shaw's *Major Barbara,* a visit to the Barnes exhibit and her delight at Matisse's mural *The Dancers,* spring in Fairmount Park, dogwood and cherry trees in bloom on both sides of the Schuykill, a visit to the zoo, how I think the Philadelphia City Hall is itself an antique, one that resembles an overiced wedding cake—and she is delighted that I remember. I grow a spade of a beard, call her Juliana and she accepts all this as perfectly natural. "Hold me, Arthur," she says, "the way you always did." And so I hold her tightly and she sighs in contentment.

Our fifty years of life together have disappeared, wiped away like an erased tape. All that remains for us are her five years with Arthur, and me becoming more and more the man I never was.

The Baby Rocker

I study the three baby rockers that have been on life test for four and a half months. They're standard units taken off the production line. I've been observing with increasing anxiety the wire that leads across the frame to the motor and cam that impart the rocking motion. On one of the rockers the wire is caught between two metal bars and is gradually chaffing. On the other two rockers the wires are intact but slowly migrating, because of the rocking motion, to where they can be trapped. Once the wire is chaffed down to the bare copper, the full line voltage will be across two of the metal bars. An infant in the rocker would then be in danger of electrocution.

I issued an order to reroute the wire as soon as I saw the chaffing, but by then some two-hundred-and-fifty-thousand units had gone out. The rocker, called Rock-A-Bye, has been a great marketing success. Just shove in your infant, plug in the rocker, hit the start switch and the kid is rocked to sleep. In a new version there's even a cheap tape recorder and speaker attached. You can play the Brahms Lullaby or record your own crooning to help lull the kid to sleep without feeling guilty that you're abandoning the child.

Every day I check the wire, stupidly praying for a miracle. I have the impression the wire itself is begging for help. I'm the chief engineer of Omega, Inc., a privately held company that specializes in children's products: cribs, strollers, high chairs, and the like. The president, CEO, owner and founder is a man named Arthur Creal—Dr. Arthur Creal—in his late sixties now, who a year ago married his fourth wife, a beauty named Melissa, thirty years younger. This has made him more short-tempered and irascible than he had been in the past. In the last year he has grown a beard, which has come in salt and pepper and which he keeps carefully trimmed; it adds gravity to his face while hiding his jowls. He gave the company the name Omega some forty years ago when he founded the enterprise and thought it would be the last word in baby products.

I have hauled the director of Quality Control down to the life test lab and pointed out the frayed wire. He stared at it with the look the righteous reserve for pornography. "You're not proposing a recall, are you Bob?" the QC man said. "Do you have a better idea?" I asked. "We haven't heard of a field failure," he countered. "It's only a matter of time," I said. "Besides, it only takes one." He continued to stare at the rocker, the frayed wire, apparently much going through his mind not directly related to the problem at hand. "I'll think about it," he said.

I'm trying to decide how best to broach the frayed wire problem to Creal when he appears in my office. "Robert," he says, his bald head reflecting the light from my window as does the Phi Beta Kappa key that dangles across his vest, "let's you and I see what the manufacturing types are up to." Creal likes to do this periodically: appear unannounced at the assembly lines. He always drags a staff member along. Apparently, it's my turn. Creal is about five five with extraordinarily broad shoulders, a tree stump of a man who holds his head very erect and moves with the speed of someone who has only minutes to make a plane connection. Hopefully, I'll have an opportunity to discuss the chaffed wire with him after the tour.

We pass through the shop, low-ceilinged, where the rhythmic hammering of punch presses and the sock of injection molding machines always cause me to squint as though struck by a bright light. We enter a space the size of a supermarket, brightly lit by sodium vapor lamps that cast an amber light. Lines of women perched on high stools are bent over conveyor belts, putting together the sub-assemblies that ultimately converge into the final product. The illumination bleaches all color from their faces other than a yellowish residue, making them all appear to be suffering from some obscure liver disease. Sub-assemblies, since they depend on marketing needs, change often. I've found there's always a certain confusion in the sub-assembly department, though that might be the fault of the supervisor whom I would not characterize as the brightest bulb on the tree.

Whenever Creal shows up in the production area, the V.P. Manufacturing, the Quality Control director and the section supervisors appear as if by magic and trail behind him like the tail of a comet. Creal asks a question of the QC director; the man answers head turned away, as if he wanted the words to reach Creal by a circuitous route. Creal stops to watch a woman take a completed baby carriage wheel assembly, walk twelve feet to a table against a wall and place the assembly in a holding fixture. He watches her do this three times. *"Why is that table against the wall?"* he asks. Now you didn't need a poet's sensitivity to detect the ominous note in Creal's voice. The V.P. Manufacturing, a clever man, turns to the sub-assembly supervisor. The supervisor, who sports a walrus mustache that looks like a disguise, a platoon of pencils, pens and small tools in a plastic holder in his breast pocket, is apparently oblivious to the gathering storm. In fact, he seems to expand in the bracing air of Creal's attention. "That's an inspection station," he says brightly, which of course doesn't answer the question at all.

Creal stares at the supervisor and in a voice that continuously rises in volume, says, "That table is at least twelve feet from the end of the conveyor. The girl has to walk twenty-four feet every time an assembly comes off the line." Creal's voice now reaches a full-throated roar. "If that table were in New Jersey and the girl had to take an airplane to get there every time a piece was produced, it might occur to you that the table is too far away!"

The supervisor's expression has switched to pleading, as if seeking permission to relive the moment of his answer. The women on the line furtively glance at Creal, at the distant table, then bend back over their sub-assemblies. Creal stands rigid facing the supervisor, arms at his sides, fingers extended. His face and bald head are the color of cork under the chemical light. A droplet of spittle hangs in his beard. "That table is where the moving men put it when they brought it into the room!" he yells. "Nobody has even *thought* about product flow in this place!" He then strides from station to station, gesticulates, rants at the stupidity of its location. A purse lies on a table; Creal stares at it in disgust, as if it were a dead mouse, then with a great swipe launches the purse like a cannon shot across the room and into a wall: a tube of lipstick, a circular mirror, a blue comb, coins and pins scatter from the purse and across the floor. "This is a place of business, not a checkroom!" he bellows in a voice loud enough to command a regiment. He then continues his circuit and shouted comments. All the women bend over the conveyor belts, bent further than they normally are, no longer even peeking at Creal. All seem huddled within themselves as if in the midst of some calamitous natural phenomenon, a tornado descending upon them, they rooted in place, powerless to move, praying that it will pass them by.

Creal turns to the V.P. Manufacturing and in a nail-driving voice says, "I want you to spend all your time fixing this layout. You have nothing more important to do." He waves a hand, seems to encompass not only the sub-assembly area but the world. "Wasted motion! That's what this place is. All wasted motion!"

Now everyone has seen angry bosses, but I would wager that you have never seen one like this. In that explosion of rage Creal took on mythological proportions, like some ancient god gone berserk. Creal gives the place one last withering glance then storms out. It does not strike me as the right moment to bring up the frayed wire.

But I agonize over that wire, day after day. I check with the director of Quality Control. He's still thinking. I decide that I can delay no longer. My best bet in approaching Creal, I conclude, is to invoke the plugged drain principle. Simply put, the principle states that one man heading for a drain will be washed away, but two or more will plug the drain and neither will go down. "I think both of us should meet with Creal," I say to the QC man. "What about Manufacturing?" he asks. "I've already talked to them," I say. "They caused the problem. They'd have to be hauled in chains before Creal. They're not going voluntarily." The QC man goes into his Hamlet mode. I decide that hardball is in order. "We can both walk in," I say, "or I can ask Creal to call you into the meeting when I'm with him. You pick."

Creal's office, given its size and elegance, always strikes me as a place more appropriate to conferring sainthood than conducting business. You have to walk fifty feet from the door to get to his desk, which is flanked by an American flag and a globe of the world. As you traverse those fifty feet you have much time to consider whether what you have to say to the president, CEO, owner and founder is worth saying. "Dr. Creal, we'd like to show you a worrisome development in the life testing of the rocker," I say. Creal, the light reflecting off his bald head as if it were marble, says, "What's the problem?"

"It would be easier if we just showed you," I say. "If you would come with us to the life test lab..."

Creal does not budge. His eyes, small, yellow-brown, motionless as a pair of spiders, are difficult to look at. "Just tell me the problem, Mr. Morrow. Then I'll decide whether it's worth going to see." Creal always uses your last name when he senses trouble.

The QC man and I take seats side by side in two of the four straight-backed chairs that sit meekly before Creal's desk. I explain the problem but hasten to add that it's fixed in new production. It's those quarter of a million previously shipped units that have me worried. I'm debating whether to tell Creal that the original routing of the wire was proper, well out of the way. The production people changed the path to shorten the route and save a couple of pennies per unit on the cost of wire. But before I can mention any of this Creal says, "What are you proposing?"

Creal, of course, knows damn well what I'm proposing—it's as obvious as the stripe down a highway—but he wants me to say it. I decide that a simple direct statement is my best bet. "I recommend that we recall those units before an infant gets electrocuted."

Creal leaves his chair and starts to pace the room. The QC man changes his seat, as if lightning is about to strike and he wants to get as far away as possible from its likely target. "Let me get this straight," Creal says. "You've had three units under test for a total of something like ten-thousand hours and so far you haven't had a single failure. You *think* that one of these days you might, just might, have a failure." Creal is now facing me, feet apart, arms rigid at his sides, his expression that of a wrestler at the start of a match. "Is that right?"

"That's right," I say, though his slant on the problem isn't exactly what I had in mind, "but the result of a single failure can be catastrophic."

Creal's voice now rises a fair number of decibels. "Do you have any idea what recalling a quarter of a million units would cost? It would put us out of business, that's what it would do. And all that on the probability of a failure occurring that hasn't even happened. What kind of madness is that?" I'm trying to frame a response, though this isn't easy, while Creal paces the room. He turns again. "You're like the crazy captain of a ship ordering everybody into the lifeboats because maybe, just maybe, there might be a leak." His voice can now be heard half way across Los Angeles. "This is a form of self-flagellation! You want the company to pay because you feel guilty!" He stops, narrows his gaze at the QC man, his head shifting slowly from side to side like a cobra. "Do you concur in this recommendation?"

"No sir," the QC man says.

Now I should make you aware of two things. First off, though my title is chief engineer, I'm not an engineer, that is I do not have an engineering degree. I came up through the ranks, starting as a draftsman and technician. But then you don't need a detailed knowledge of thermodynamics or fluid flow or structures to design a baby carriage or a crib. Second, Creal isn't a doctor, that is he never earned a doctorate. He endowed a chair in the humanities at Cabot College in L.A. and they awarded him an honorary doctorate in gratitude. But Creal apparently has a weakness for titles because he insists on everybody calling him Doctor. He does have a bachelor's in psychology, a long way from crib making.

My options are clear: (1) I can quit; (2) I can find some cheap fix short of a recall and pray that Creal buys it; or (3) I can forget the whole thing.

I think about the second option, discuss it with my staff, and conclude there is no fix we could ask consumers to make. Even if we sent them a longer wire there is no way they could install it since they would have to open the motor housing. And asking them to put electrical tape or some insulating device around the wire is just not reliable. Besides, even proposing this to a consumer would scare the life out of him, or more likely her. Realistically, there are only options (1) and (3).

I stare out the window of my office. I'm thinking of all this when a Mercedes SL 500 sports car, top down, pulls in front of the building. Creal's long-legged beauty steps out, pops the trunk and leans in for some reason. She has an absolutely remarkable bottom. She slams the trunk, looks around and I make a stunning observation. The old man still has lead in his pencil: Melissa is pregnant!

Creal shows up, holds the passenger door for his wife and jumps in the driver's seat. She puts her arm around Creal's shoulder. Even from a distance I can see the sparkle of the rock on her finger. Melissa must be expensive as hell. Creal dons a cap with the Greek letter omega above the bill and buzzes off.

A problem, and by no means a small one, is do you follow orders even when you know they are wrong. In what I think of as another life, I was a second lieutenant in Vietnam in command of a platoon. There was a dug-in concentration of Viet Cong that kept sniping and laying land mines along a route the South Vietnamese were using as a supply line. Aerial bombardment hadn't budged them. My orders were to wipe out the VC concentration. But in reconnoitering I discovered there was no need to attack the VC position and risk high casualties. There was an alternate route, somewhat longer but one that would circumvent the VC. It had been hidden by the jungle canopy and so was not visible through aerial reconnaissance. But I couldn't be absolutely certain that the alternate route was viable. So there was my quandary: do I follow orders and attack the VC position and almost surely see some of my men die, not to mention risking my own life? Or do I fall back, do nothing and risk court martial for disobeying orders? And what about the risk to others if that alternate route doesn't pan out? So I followed orders. We wiped out the VC position; half of my men were killed or wounded, and I took a bullet that shattered the tibia of my left leg. Now one leg is shorter than the other; I have to wear special shoes and have a permanent limp. And in the end the South Vietnamese changed the route anyway and all that bloodshed and dying was useless.

So you might conclude that I learned to think for myself and not blindly follow orders. But it's been a long while since Vietnam and I'm not a hero. One thing about Creal: he pays well. Without a degree, an oddball specialty—designing baby contrivances—I doubt if I could do half as well elsewhere. I have two kids in college, both in engineering school if you can believe, and another going in next year. All reasons not to be heroic.

I drop the subject of the chaffing wire, which in the life test ultimately does wear down to the bare copper, though it takes three more months for it to happen. In the meantime a second unit under test is chaffing. But I've given up on persuading Creal.

Creal throws a big party when his baby is born and my wife and I are invited. Creal's house is like Xanadu in *Citizen Kane*. The living room is the size of a basketball court and the cathedral ceiling is high enough to where the room *could* be used as a basketball court. A suit of armor stands like a sentinel guarding the entrance. The furnishings, in blue and gold and mahogany, the vast oriental rug, all have an air of superiority, as do the brocade drapes. Creal has flags, British heraldic things, hanging on masts along the side walls. On the front wall, illuminated by a recessed light, is an oil portrait of Creal in the academic robes of Cabot College. Then there are display cabinets featuring Samurai swords, headsman's axes, daggers, crossbows, spears and other military paraphernalia of the middle ages. Arthur Creal may well think of himself as King Arthur and the lovely Melissa as the new Guinevere.

There are plates of hors d'oeuvres with enough food to feed an army; two bartenders serve the liquor needs of the participants.

Three musicians in a corner play elevator type music. Creal, carefully dressed like an exhibit, a perky carnation in his lapel, moves through the crowd accepting congratulations. He puts an arm on my shoulder while juggling a martini and tells my wife that I'm the finest chief engineer Omega has ever had.

At one point Melissa disappears then returns carrying the newborn swaddled in a blue blanket and passes through the crowd. Much oohing and aahing as though she were displaying the infant Jesus. I get a peek at the kid: the poor little guy bears a disconcerting resemblance to the old man. After a while a nurse's uniform appears and whisks away young Arthur Creal Jr.

The idea occurs to me as I take a sip of my third gin and tonic, a suggestion from some remote corner of my mind. I discard it at first but it keeps returning, nipping at me like a terrier, more insistent as I drink more gin and tonic. I work my way through the crowd toward Melissa. I hover around, waiting for a break in the group that surrounds her. The evening wears on. Melissa, her sheath dress slit down the side to mid-thigh and clinging to her like a second skin, is never alone. The crowd is starting to thin. "Let's go, Bob," my wife says. "I think we've discharged our obligation to your boss." "I've got one small chore to do," I say, "then we'll leave."

The crowd is thinner yet but still no break in the group around Melissa. "What are you trying to do?" my wife asks. "You look worried. And you keep hovering around Mrs. Creal. What's going on?" I beg her to be patient.

At last, when the musicians are packing up and I have almost given up hope, Melissa is alone at the bar. "Mrs. Creal," I say, "my name is Robert Morrow and I'm Omega's chief engineer." Melissa gazes at me through impenetrable lashes then gives me a professional smile and a "How nice to meet you."

I hesitate an instant, intimidated by her beauty, then take a deep breath and say, "You might be interested in one of our products. It'll make your life a lot easier and your baby happy." And I proceed to tell her about the rocker. "You might want to surprise Dr. Creal and just buy it. I'm sure he would be very pleased. The name is Rock-A-Bye. Most department stores carry it."

I wait. Will Melissa buy the rocker, and if she does will she tell the old man that I recommended it? And will she get one of the old production models with the compromising wire or the new model where the problem was eliminated? No way to know.

Three weeks later I come in to work to find a rocker, old style, on top of my desk and a note scotchtaped to it. MORROW, YOU ARE FIRED. CLEAR OUT RIGHT NOW. Signed Arthur Creal, President. I feel short changed: the old man didn't have the guts to tell me to my face. I examine the rocker: the wire has a faint shadow, a slight darkening of the white surface, where chaffing has started.

I find our Polaroid camera in the lab, take a photograph of the rocker and the note, then hustle down to the life test room and photograph the units under test including close ups of the chaffed wires. I then find some boxes, dump in my belongings, and haul the boxes to my car. I say goodbye to the staff, none of whom looks happy about my leaving, if for no other reason than that there is now one less lightning rod around and they are further exposed.

That afternoon I call the *Los Angeles Times* and KCLA television. I'm interviewed, my credentials checked and rechecked. Then, convinced that I'm not a flake, the storm breaks like a hurricane, photos and all. QUARTER OF A MILLION BABIES RISK ELECTROCUTION is the *Times* headline. A spokesman, not Creal but an attorney, appears on television, says the danger has been blown way out of proportion, that no failure has ever occurred, but concedes that Omega has ordered a recall to reassure consumers.

In six months Omega is out of business. The fright caused by the baby rocker cast a cloud over all of Omega's products. Then there was the cost of the recall.

Now you might ask what did I gain by all this? Four-hundred people lost their jobs and that includes me. But I sleep better these nights and I *have* found another job. It doesn't pay as well as Omega but we get by. And all the others will no doubt find new jobs as well. And no kid will be electrocuted by that rocker. Then, for some reason, I also feel better about Vietnam. A great serenity, like a blessing, has fallen on me, and everything appears bright and new as if the whole world has been cleansed. When I think back to Omega, I realize that in my heart I have always despised Arthur Creal.

The Philosopher

You are an avid hiker and mountain climber. You and a group of hiker friends have journeyed to the Himalayas to scale one of the minor peaks. The group has reached 15,000 feet and established a base camp. You go on alone to reconnoiter. You're perhaps five miles ahead of the base camp when you notice the sky darkening. Storms in the Himalayas, you know, arrive suddenly and can be of ferocious intensity. Your best bet is to hustle back to the base camp and quickly. You are about to do this when you notice an elderly man seated on a rock. He lets you understand that he wished to make the peak because he is certain that he will experience a religious revelation there. But he is now terribly fatigued and can't go on. He can barely walk and solicits your help to return. The wind increases in intensity and snow is now whipping at you horizontally. Helping this man may mean that you will both be trapped in the storm and neither of you will return alive. But if you do not help the man he will surely die. You are alone. You and only you will know of your decision. Do you help the man or not?

I used to be one of the Philosopher's students but now I'm his secretary, admin assistant, general gopher. He asks me to invent moral dilemmas for him that he can pass on to his classes. He says I have a special knack for creating these things. I don't. All I really want is the Philosopher's approval. He has a terrific smile: his eyes are a vivid periwinkle blue, skin fair, surprisingly unlined despite his age, the face of one untouched by sun, wind, even by life itself, and it all opens in a dazzle when he smiles. He is appalled at how his students react to these moral dilemmas. To the one above most of them said to hell with the old man. Why should I risk my life to save the guy from his own folly? I must confess, I feel the same way.

I have concluded that the Philosopher really believes the stuff he teaches. Aristotle is his favorite. When he quotes the mighty philosopher as saying, "I do without being commanded what others do only from fear of the law," he sounds as if he's talking about himself. A couple of his other goodies: "The least deviation from the truth is multiplied later a thousand fold," and "man is the origin of his actions." He intones these little aphorisms as though they were the words of God. They often strike his students as quaint, but to him, I've decided, they are signposts for living and he tries to demonstrate to his students their worth through illustration from the lives of great men. Once, groping for examples, he quoted Schopenhauer: "There is no more mistaken path to happiness than revelry and high life." Most everyone in the room thought that was off the wall. His heroes are what he calls reasonable men and it's their writings that he assigns. His favorites are Marcus Aurelius, John Stuart Mill, Ernest Renan, Henry Sidgwick. Heavy shit.

The Philosopher is not a religious man and he handles religion academically, just another milestone in man's search for guidance and truth. But he doesn't appear to espouse or to be especially reverent toward any one religion. He's respectful toward all of them, though when it comes to religious thinkers he believes Spinoza and Saint Augustine were the brightest of the bunch.

The Philosopher's routine is unvarying. He shows up at eight-thirty, gives me a "Good morning, Emma," then sips the coffee (cream, no sugar) that I bring him as he stares out at the campus and the hurrying students and mentally prepares for his nine o'clock class. I make appointments for the students who want to meet with him. He dislikes these encounters—usually complaints over an exam grade or a plea for a B instead of a C or D, otherwise the poor clod won't graduate—and asks me to limit them to ten minutes. He speaks almost not at all in these meetings nor does he nod; he simply fixes the students with a penetrating ice blue stare as though he's reading their genetic code then pointedly glances at his watch after ten minutes. Few students ever return for a second shot at the Philosopher.

He has a wife but no children. Her name is Camilla. She's extraordinarily skinny—legs so thin you'd think they'd splinter walking down a flight of stairs, arms like aluminum rods, and no ass at all—but she has an extraordinary pair of tits. It's as though all her sexuality got concentrated in those boobs. Sometimes she shows up in the late afternoon to pick up her husband. Good evening, Emma, she says and sits in the single guest chair in my cubbyhole office, her knobby knees staring at me. I type up a storm: the quick brown fox jumps over the lazy dog. She watches me, a remote expression on her pale bird-like face. I once suggested she'd be more comfortable waiting for the boss in his office. She gave me an aloof side-to-side head shake as if I'd suggested a wire tap. For some reason I believe she has gynecological problems.

One afternoon as Camilla is sitting there a moral dilemma occurs to me. I type it right then:

A friend, a successful man in his middle forties, comes to you for advice. One of his clients is a woman. He finds her extraordinarily intelligent and, to an ever greater degree, physically appealing. Moreover, he discovers that their interests—in literature, music, theater, art—coincide. He is in love with her. He broaches his feelings to the woman and finds they are reciprocated. On the other hand, while his wife is neither as intelligent nor as attractive as the other woman, he does care for her. They've been married for twenty years and she's made a comfortable home for him and their two children. (I throw in the children as an afterthought.) *The other woman asks that he leave his wife and they live together. She is not interested in an affair with a married man. So he is tugged in opposite directions, toward this splendid woman he's had the good fortune to meet, and toward the stability and solidity of a comfortable family and home. What advice would you give him?*

The following day the Philosopher shows up after nine and dismisses his class early, things he's never done before. At his desk he barely looks at the moral dilemma I've cooked up for him and seems agitated, something else I've never seen in him. When he leaves I investigate his desk for clues as to what's bothering him. On a yellow pad he's written, "Hope is a waking dream." Hmmm...

The next day he says to me when I bring him his coffee, "I'd like you to do some research for me." I think maybe he wants the work of some obscure Greek or a medieval philosopher-saint, but he says, "I'd like you to get information on breast cancer. Therapy, prognosis, survival rates—that sort of thing. I want to double check the doctors." There's a practical side to the Philosopher.

I figure it's Camilla. I think of those splendid tits, now tainted, malignant. I take my best shot at sincerity. "I'm sorry," I say and when I say it, surprisingly, I *do* feel sorry. The Philosopher pays no attention to this. I think about the assignment and beyond. "How far along is it?" I ask, then, drawing on my meager knowledge, "Are the lymph nodes affected?"

He sits there, staring through the walls, unmoving as concrete. I repeat the question. "We don't know yet," he says to the air. "Just look at the whole picture."

So I investigate breast cancer, the various stages, the drugs—anti-estrogens, protease inhibitors, anthracyclines, with names like Tamoxifen, Letrozole, Taxotere—the surgery, radiation, chemotherapy... It's a bummer disease, I'll say that. Treatment starts when a guy wearing a mask and flashing a knife comes at you. He can cut out the lump or lop off the whole boob, but there's no real difference in survival rate. Half the time, though, women opt for the lop off. The latest deal is breast-conserving therapy, though that didn't change survival rate one way or the other. But the literature says large breast size is a contraindication to breast-conserving treatment. That rules out poor Camilla. Of course, if the cancer has metastasized then Camilla is in deep yogurt: chemotherapy gives a big deal ten to twenty percent remission rate.

I type all this in neat term paper fashion and place it in the middle of the Philosopher's desk. My bottom line: take the whole boob then belt the chest wall with radiation. This, the big-time doctors say, is supposed to decrease local recurrence as well as systemic disease. Having read all that, I'm not sure the big-timers really know what they're talking about. My paper doesn't say this, though. I present all the technobabble as if it were gospel.

The Philosopher gives me a distracted Thank you, Emma. But he's not looking well. There are violet quarter moons like bruises under his eyes. He doesn't look as if he's sleeping. Sometimes I can smell his breath: it's rancid, as if he's been drinking too much coffee. "Disease is a crack through which the soul becomes visible," I find written on his yellow pad. Camilla shows up. She doesn't appear ill or agitated, but there's something haunted about her. She must visualize what it will be like to be lopsided, a big boob on one side and nothing but ribs on the other, wearing a stuffed bra so she doesn't look weird. Then in bed... When they leave, the Philosopher takes her arm as if guiding her across a mine field, something I don't recall him doing before.

The Philosopher's routine has become erratic. He's often late, has a TA handle a class for him. For a philosopher he isn't taking any of this philosophically. I try to provide some solace. "I'm sure everything will turn out fine," I say when I bring him his coffee. He looks through me. "Thank you for your concern, Emma," he says. Once he says, looking very wise as he says it, "Life isn't fair, you know." This observation, which even dim people have sorted out by the age of eight, isn't exactly up there with Aristotle. The

Philosopher's beautiful face seems confused: this business has him addled. "Yes, you're right," I say, nodding sagely at so much wisdom. "Please let me know if I can help." He focuses on me for the first time but says nothing.

I poke around the papers on the Philosopher's desk. It seems that Camilla has made a decision. Contrary to my recommendation, she's going for a lumpectomy followed by radiation and chemotherapy.

"You look like you've lost weight," I say to the Philosopher late one morning. (This is questionable, but he *does* appear a bit undernourished.) "There's a decent Italian restaurant two blocks from campus. Why don't you let me buy you lunch?"

He squints at me, seems to be giving this simple suggestion much thought, as if I'd proposed something momentous, like running off to Rio. Then he finally says, "That's very kind of you, Emma. I will accept your offer, but you must allow me to pay for our repast."

The Philosopher doesn't know his way around an Italian restaurant menu so I guide him toward something nutritious. He opts for meat and after much chatter we settle on veal scallopine. "How are you getting on?" he asks. I tell him, but his eyes are focused somewhere beyond Uranus and I can see he isn't much interested in how I'm getting on. I'm about to ask him the same question but instead ask, "How is your wife faring?" and take on a concerned look. He answers, his gaze still focused beyond the outer planets, "As well as could be expected, I suppose. It's an awful thing, you know, and terribly unjust." I have a feeling he's not talking to me but to the gods. "We try to see patterns, to judge the events in our lives as reward or punishment, parse things into good and evil. But there is a randomness to life that is beyond analysis..." He trails off, seems adrift in ultimate questions. I have the impression that for the first time in his life the Philosopher is really coming to grips with philosophy.

"Have you made a decision on treatment?" I ask, yanking the Philosopher back to reality. "Yes," he says and explains. "These things are best done quickly. The operation is tomorrow morning."

In the following weeks the Philosopher seems almost his former self, but not quite. He's grown erratic, is late for appointments or even misses them, and there are complaints that he's dreamy in class and questions have to be repeated. Camilla shows up. Her complexion is sort of gray, face shrunk closer to the bone, and she's wearing a hat, a cloche, something she never did before. I imagine the slow poison they call chemotherapy destroying her insides, then her lacerated boob getting belted with x-rays. There's an odorless odor about her, of decay and decomposition. It's tough to imagine a sex life under those conditions. I occasionally invite the Philosopher to lunch. Sometimes he accepts. I decide not to talk about Camilla, instead ask him about himself, how he got interested in philosophy, his goals, what he thinks about the school administration. To my surprise, the Philosopher is ambitious. He thinks the administration sucks and he could do a much better job running the place. I gaze into his periwinkle eyes, touch his hand and agree with him. He grows expansive, decides on a glass of wine, reorganizes the college right there before my eyes using some Greek school as a model.

I find myself fantasizing about sex with the Philosopher. His body is trim though he's about as muscular looking as a seal. He has attractive hands, masculine and sprouted with golden hairs. I imagine being caressed by those hands. I have grown curious as to whether he's circumcised. I would prefer if he were not. I imagine myself toying with his pecker and watching its head emerge magisterially from the foreskin. I might even give it a kiss in appreciation.

When he comes into his office and I'm at my desk, I make sure there's plenty of thigh showing. I buy skirts loaded with spandex so they cling to my ass, dress in lollipop colors, dab on perfume, expensive subtle shit like Joy, until one day the Philosopher comments, "Do you have a boyfriend, Emma?" He gives me a smile: it's dazzling and I melt. "You seem ready for mating."

I decide to be brazen. "I don't have a boyfriend but I am ready for mating," I say and look at him in a way that any male past puberty would understand.

He blinks a couple of times. "I see," he says and hurries off, but from then on he always pauses when he comes into the office and when he leaves he exchanges a few words with me and his eyes move appraisingly over my body.

Camilla shows up. She moves carefully, as if guarding against a fall, and looks awful. It occurs to me that all that chemo and radiation may have made her bones brittle. If she fell she could shatter like a dropped plate. I type like a whirlwind. The Philosopher departs with her, holding her arm, and on the way out impersonally says Goodnight, Emma.

Now you might ask why am I interested in the Philosopher. I am not an unattractive woman, so why am I not hustling a man my own age and single? I don't have a good answer except that the blue-eyed rascal appeals to me. I can't help fantasizing about him. Sure he's older than I am, by about twenty years, but that doesn't bother me. Or maybe I view the old guy as a challenge. Or maybe all secretaries at some point get curious about their boss, want to get laid by the big man to see how he performs in bed. I can't say for sure.

You're an art expert. A wealthy friend of yours is a great admirer of the American artist Thomas Eakins. Your friend is about to spend a great deal of money to buy a painting by Eakins. He loves the painting and plans to give it an honored place in his home. You study the painting and are convinced it's a fake. Do you tell this to your friend and deny him the pleasure of enjoying the painting in the years ahead? Or do you remain silent and let him believe in the painting's authenticity and enjoy it?

"That's a rather interesting dilemma you posed," the Philosopher says to me over his fettucine alfredo. "Whether in some circumstances a lie is superior to truth... You do realize that you are posing a moral dilemma for me."

"How so?" I ask, doing a born yesterday number.

"You are suggesting an affair with me and the question is do I accept or not?"

"And the answer?" I ask.

"How would you feel if you were married and your husband had the same dilemma? How would you want him to resolve it?" I'm disappointed: I thought the Philosopher would be more subtle than throwing the golden rule at me.

"If I truly loved him I would want him to do whatever makes him happy," I lie.

The Philosopher blinks. "Maybe in the abstract you feel that way, but faced with the actual circumstance I cannot help but wonder. And particularly if your husband were ill and you were cheating at a time when he needed you most." His tone at the end of this speech becomes didactic, as if he were addressing a class. "That would be a moral betrayal of the most reprehensible kind."

All this theory is tiring, and right now I've stopped caring. "You do what you think is right," I say.

Camilla surfaces in the office while the Philosopher is teaching class. She looks more awful yet but is quite calm. "I understand you have proposed an affair with my husband," she says.

I'm flustered for a moment—I can't believe the idiot told his wife—then decide to be indignant. "I have proposed no such thing. Maybe that's wishful thinking on your husband's part. He's old enough to be my father. To be blunt, I have no interest in an affair with an old man."

Camilla gives me a shrewd stare. "I want to believe you, Emma, but I notice you've been wearing suggestive clothing of late and—"

"What I wear has nothing to do with your husband," I interrupt.

"Anyway, he laughed when he told me this," Camilla finishes. "He found it amusing that little Emma would be interested in him."

"I find it amusing that he would think little Emma would be even remotely interested in him... Would you like some coffee?"

Camilla shakes her head no and I get busy, hammer away at the typewriter: the quick brown fox... That "little Emma" hurt. I pray that Camilla's other boob gets infected.

I wonder why the Philosopher told her. I decide it's because in that way it would be impossible for him to have an affair with me. A form of self-protection. Or maybe the son of a bitch *was* amused by it all.

Months go by. Camilla has finished her radiation, chemotherapy and whatever other horrors they inflict on women with breast cancer. I gather she's in remission because the Philosopher's routine is back to normal. I continue to wear suggestive clothing but adopt a cool remote manner. Actually, I'm messing around with a fellow named Breeze who's my age and script writes for a television soap opera. He's mildly successful but always in a state of anxiety over the next episode. I chip in plot ideas. He says his most creative thoughts come to him during sex. That's what helps him last—he's concentrating on plot ideas. I have to admit, he does quite well. My interest in the Philosopher has waned though I continue to cook up moral dilemmas for him to present to his catatonic classes.

You are a medical researcher and have stumbled on a drug that can prolong human life. But the drug does not extend vigor or mental acuity. One will continue to decline, only take longer, much longer, to die. You are deeply troubled. Is living longer even in an ever deteriorating condition worthwhile or not? Do you go public with this drug, or simply discard it?

The Philosopher comments with an indulgent smile that my dilemmas have grown rather gloomy. I point out, philosophically, that lots of life's dilemmas are gloomy. He vaguely acknowledges this to be true. I no longer suggest lunch or anything else. Camilla shows up. She looks marginally better; her hair is cut short and she's now wearing makeup. I check out her boobs. They seem smaller, but symmetric. I imagine the Philosopher being cautious about fondling them. In the back of his mind there's got to be some primitive sense of contagion. But then not only her boobs—the whole sex thing has likely taken on an aura of vague menace. She probably watches to see how he functions, or how often, or whatever other signs of sexual interest there are between them. But who knows? Maybe adversity has brought them closer. Or maybe the Philosopher is turned on by damaged goods. "How have you been, Emma?" Camilla asks. "We haven't seen each other in a while."

I'm startled. Camilla asks how I've been about as often as she asks the lampshade. "I'm fine," I say, bubbling with creativity. "You're looking well," I lie. "Thank you," she says, accepting my compliment at face value. We stare at each other. She seems at a loss. I decide to fill the gap. "It must have been a difficult ordeal."

The Philosopher appears and saves Camilla the ordeal of answering. She rises to greet him, is wearing a pants suit, more assless than ever, and except for her boobs is as sexy as a fence post. He takes her arm. At the door the Philosopher turns to me,

"Hold down the fort," he says and smiles as though he's said something terribly clever. What did I see in that idiot?

Breeze says I have the kind of imagination that's ideal for television. I take this as a compliment, sort of. He pumps me for ideas for those weekly episodes. He thinks of them as monsters for whom a new food supply has to be created every week. I try a couple of the Philosopher's moral dilemmas on him. He thinks about this. Too cerebral, he concludes, but they can be dumbed down. Breeze then says he can get me a job at the studio, sort of an idea person. I consider this and am not enthused. Being creative on a tight schedule, dealing with a crowd of egocentrics, feeding that insatiable beast, generating pap... I don't know. I'm not really ambitious. I like to moon around, gin up moral dilemmas for the Philosopher, wander around campus, study the poor harassed students that come to see my boss on some pretext or other but are only after a better grade. Still, I must confess, I'm getting bored. I conjure up another moral dilemma for the big man.

You are a doctor. A well-off elderly woman whom you have know for years has bone cancer and you judge her case to be hopeless. She, however, has heard of a clinic in Mexico—in fact, has visited the clinic—and they assure her they can cure her cancer with drugs that only they possess. She asks for your advice, but it is clear that she wants to go to the clinic. Do you advise against going and extinguish what hope of living she has? Or do you let her go, even though you believe the clinic will milk her for her last penny and therefore, on her death, she will leave nothing to her deserving family?

"How do you know this?" the Philosopher asks in an agitated way. "Has my wife spoken to you?"

I'm amazed, look closely at the Philosopher. His eyes are red; either he's been up late or been crying or both. Jesus! I've stumbled into his real honest-to-God dilemma. "I'm sorry," I say and really mean it because at that moment I *am* sorry—for poor Camilla, for the Philosopher, for all those who suffer. I'm crying. Can you believe that? I'm actually crying. I look up: the Philosopher's eyes are blurred. As if by some secret signal we both rise to our feet and he comes out from behind his desk and we hold each other. "I'm so sorry," I repeat.

I dab my eyes, the crying jag subsided, and we sit side by side. "It has attacked her spine," he says to the empty chair behind his desk. I imagine the cancer wrapped like a python around her spinal column, crushing all those cables inside. "She's in terrible pain," he says in an uncomprehending way. He sounds like one of his students who has been given a failing grade and has no idea why. "The doctors say it's hopeless but she wants to go to this clinic in Guadalajara anyway."

My heart goes out to poor Camilla, my sister. For didn't we both love the same man, sort of at least? "Take her there," I say. "Give her that last hope."

"It's not covered by insurance," he says.

I push my chair away, turn toward him, stare with disbelief into his reddened periwinkle eyes. "Your wife, your life's companion, is dying. She's grasping at a last straw of hope and you talk about *insurance*?"

"There's a practical side to life, Emma," the Philosopher says, "that you're too young to understand."

I'm upset, really upset. "Don't hide behind that practical-side-of-life bullshit," I say. "You didn't want to cheat on your wife because you said that was a moral betrayal and reprehensible. Those were your words. I'd say it's a hell of a lot more morally reprehensible to deny her that last crumb of hope because it's not covered by insurance. In fact, that's more than reprehensible. It's sick."

I decide that looking into the studio job Breeze mentioned isn't a bad idea after all. The Philosopher seems relieved when I give notice. Maybe he's come to view me as his conscience, something he'd rather do without. I learn later that Camilla died, the Philosopher was appointed chairman of the department, then quick as a rabbit married one of his ex-students. Had I hung around I might have stood a chance, but then who would want a creep like that for a husband?

An Encounter With Venus

Edward Ashley III gazed out of his hotel window across the Arno. The July sun had set and the sky to the west was dull yellow; the river, black and sluggish in the center, was green at the edges where the water reflected the shrubs along the shore. Ashley raised his glance to the Tuscan hills, now dark gray-green masses, the lines of cypresses black silhouettes against the sky. A slender black bird swooped toward the river then wheeled skyward in a series of erratic loops and turns. Ashley watched the bird continue its uneven flight and had the impression that its path was a complex symbol, a hieroglyphic of destruction and ruin. As Ashley continued to gaze at the foreign landscape all things seemed filled with significance, to carry the same ominous message as the bird. For Edward Ashley III had fallen on bad times.

Disaster had struck Ashley's life in a series of thunderclaps. Four months ago his wife had run off with a golf pro; six months earlier his mother had died of lung cancer though she had never smoked in her life; ten months before that his father had died in a freak skiing accident, shattered against a ponderosa pine. Ashley had inherited the family business, the manufacture of knitting machines. Ashley, an associate professor of ancient history at Cabot Community College in Los Angeles, had detested the factory—with its machines that groaned like exhausted animals, foul smells, deafening noise—since his first visit as a child. He had always stayed away, despite his father's insistence, blandishments and finally browbeating. "Gutless," he had said with contempt to his only child, "that's what you are. It takes guts to run a business. You don't have it." "It has nothing to do with guts," Ashley had replied. "I'm not interested in business. It's that simple."

After his father's death Ashley felt he had no choice. Though he wondered whether perhaps it was something else, a need to prove his father wrong. Bitterly, Ashley took a leave of absence from Cabot and attempted to run Ashley Textile Machines, Inc., known in the industry as ATMI and founded by his grandfather, a man saddened that his one and only grandson had not followed in his footsteps and become an engineer. But as decisions on pricing concessions, new product development and labor union grievances were brought to him, and problems of cost overruns, late deliveries and customer quality complaints needed his attention, Ashley began to suffer from headaches, pain in the lower right quadrant of his stomach and a persistent ache in his upper back. He visited doctors, took medication, but the symptoms worsened. Worry about ATMI, his health, was no longer something he could set aside but had become an insistent roiling mass, maggot-like, in his skull. Then he grew certain that those around him held him in contempt, the way his father had, and were secretly trying to undermine him. He confided this to his wife who suggested he see a shrink. He did see a shrink who said he had transferred his hatred for his father to those around him, then gave him medication. Finally, despite his feelings of guilt, Ashley, who felt both himself and the company heading toward extinction, could stand it no longer and with the encouragement of his dying mother sold the business. He now suffered remorse: he had betrayed his grandfather and father, men of courage and perseverance who had founded ATMI and made it prosper.

Ashley lectured to his classes, grew more demanding of his students, intolerant of their errors, stricter in his grading, came to loathe their slouched bodies, skeptical faces. What had once enthused him he now found trivial. What did Babylonia and Assyria matter, or the Peloponnesian War, or the Roman Empire?

All struggles for power, the dominance of men over other men. He had rid himself of the yoke of the family business yet his symptoms did not improve. The dean of the history department, to whom Ashley had now taken a dislike, regarded him with an estimating eye and urged him to take a vacation, travel, get away. Now in summer recess, Ashley, who in reflective moments recognized that suspicion of everyone and everything had insinuated itself into his life like a fine dust, decided the dean was right. He considered London and Paris then remembered that his father, in his attempts to interest his son in the business, had once taken him to Prato, outside of Florence and the textile capitol of Italy, to visit customers. Ashley remembered the trip, his only journey outside the U.S., as a confusion of conference rooms, gibberish language, black coffee, and a constant struggle to stay awake. But he recalled Florence, the great cathedral in the center and the gentle flow of the Arno, as something exotic and grand, and so Ashley now found himself, newly arrived, in the Grand Hotel in the Piazza Ognissanti, staring across the Arno and contemplating the flight of a bird.

Ashley, though feeling jet lag as mush in his head and a heaviness in his legs, decided it was too early to go to bed. He left the hotel and trudged toward the center. Pedestrians crowded the sidewalks, groups of men lounged against the walls, chatting, smoking. Scooters buzzed by, their noise amplified by the narrow streets, causing him to wince and think of venomous wasps. The familiar headache was returning. What was he doing here, in this alien place? What was it after all but just another place in which to be lonely?

Ashley crossed the Piazza della Repubblica, the square a confusion of pedestrians, scooters and automobile traffic. Huge neon signs high above the square advertised liquors and Japanese hi-fi equipment. A car slowed beside him and a young woman, hair the color of aluminum around a heavily made-up face, massive silver hoops at her ears, called, *"Sei solo? Cerchi compagnia?"* Ashley peered down; she pulled open one side of her blouse. He stared at her naked breast, thought of sexually transmitted diseases, killer viruses tunneling into his body. *"Allora?"* the woman said to the unresponsive Ashley, then shrugged and drove off. Ashley watched her tail lights disappear, felt a throb of regret. A bus stopped beside him. People stared out with bored, patient eyes; he had the impression he was viewing time past, that the bus had been traveling with the same passengers for eons; then he was certain one man on the bus was him and wondered how he could be on the bus and on the street at the same time.

Ashley, sleep now a necessity, headed toward the hotel. He became aware of the heat. It radiated from the pavement and cement walls. He felt the night press upon him as though it had weight, a suffocating woolly substance. He was jostled by the crowds, had a slippery sensation, that somehow he had ceased to exist, the world hurrying by, he left behind, fluid and insubstantial. What was he doing here, at the end of the earth? He recalled the voice of his shrink, impersonal and grave, the voice of God: you can no more escape yourself than you can your shadow. His headache worsened.

The following morning Ashley awoke late, had a light breakfast at the Grand, checked the Fodor Guide to Florence that he had purchased before leaving the U.S. He thought he would visit the great central cathedral then decided to save that and opted instead for the Uffizi with its "unsurpassed collection of Renaissance art." Outside, glare pressed against his eyes and he hurried across the Piazza Ognissanti toward the shade of the narrow streets. He recalled his dream of the previous night: it still disturbed him. Burly men in black, armed with sledgehammers, were smashing the machinery of ATMI. He watched, filled with anguish, powerless to stop them. Glass tears fell from his eyes and shattered into a thousand fragments when they struck the cement of the factory floor.

Ashley waited in line amidst a throng of Japanese tourists and finally entered the Uffizi. He now stood before Botticelli's *Birth of Venus*. He contemplated Venus on her sea shell: she was all curves and contours, slightly pudgy as befitted a newborn. As Ashley stared at the face of Venus, which he found particularly beautiful, he became aware of a female presence to his right. He turned toward the woman and at the same moment she turned toward him. He looked at her, looked back at the painting, then again at the woman. "My God," Ashley exclaimed, "you're the spitting image of the Venus!" and he gestured toward the face in the painting.

"I've heard many lines," the woman said with a faint smile, "but that's the most original."

"But you are!" Ashley insisted. "You really are. You could have sat for the portrait."

"Don't overkill," the woman said.

"You're American, aren't you?" Ashley said.

"Yes," the woman answered, "and I gather you are as well." She turned toward the exit. "I think I've had enough museum for one day. Thanks for the compliment."

"Do you mind if I walk out with you?" Ashley said, though he had just arrived.

"Not at all," the woman answered. "It'll help keep the Italian wolves at bay, of which there's one every five yards."

They left the Uffizi and entered the Piazza della Signoria. Ashley squinted against the sun that burned down on the great square. "Where are you from?" he asked.

"Chicago," she said. "I'm a stewardess on American. I had a

two-day layover in Rome so I decided to visit Florence. I've never been here before and the place is important to me."

"By the way, my name is Ed Ashley."

"I'm Kimberly Clark."

A priest in black cassock, about Ashley's age, long aggressive nose, receding chin, leaned close to Kimberly. *"Benedetta è la mamma che t'ha fatta,"* he said and smiled wistfully. Ashley found him repellent, thought he resembled a serpent, and for an instant expected a forked tongue to flick out of the man's mouth.

"I wonder what that guy mumbled to you," Ashley said. "It didn't sound like a benediction."

"He said blessed is the mother that made you," Kimberly said.

Ashley turned toward her. "You speak Italian?"

"My parents are Italian," Kimberly said. "Immigrated to the U.S. from Naples. We speak Italian at home."

"But Kimberly Clark..."

"I was christened Carlotta Donadio, but I did modeling and my agent thought the Italian name too heavy. I changed it. I never much cared for it anyway."

"Any particular reason for choosing Kimberly Clark?"

"I read it on a Kleenex box," Kimberly said, "and liked it."

Ashley and Kimberly zigzagged past the groups of tourists in the piazza toward the raised loggia and the statues. Kimberly stopped before the bronze statue of Perseus holding aloft the head of Medusa, sword in his hand. Ashley, trying to avoid a professorial tone, recounted the legend that the head of Medusa had the power to turn all those who looked at it to stone. Perseus had burnished his shield and guiding himself by Medusa's reflection, lopped off her head. Kimberly did not respond or even acknowledge that she had heard, but continued to study the figures and Ashley did likewise. Gore oozed from the severed head and neck of the fallen Medusa; one of her arms drooped off the side of the pedestal. Perseus stood astride her body, below her upturned breasts, muscular right arm gripping his sword, blade horizontal, just beneath his genitals. The head that Perseus held above his own was calm, eyes closed. The face of Perseus was calm as well, the battle over, victor and vanquished clear. There was a murderous quiet to the statue.

"It's about rape and power," Kimberly said. "It has nothing to do with turning people to stone... In what way was Medusa evil? If you stayed away she didn't hurt you. Men dominating women is what that statue is about."

Ashley was about to comment that Freud had interpreted the whole story in terms of castration and staring faces in nightmares, but he saw as they moved away that Kimberly was upset and decided to say nothing. But one thing he had concluded: the airline stewardess with the face of Botticelli's Venus was no fool.

Pigeons scurried ahead of them as Ashley and Kimberly angled around the crowds. *"Che bella,"* said a young man in a body-hugging black T-shirt to Kimberly as they passed, leaning on the *b* sound. Kimberly paid no attention. Ashley had an impulse to kick the man in the groin. The sensation was new to him.

Ashley stopped to contemplate Michelangelo's *David.* "There was an artist with an eye for detail," he observed. "Notice that David's left testicle is lower than his right, which is anatomically correct."

"Hmmm," Kimberly said and moved on, apparently uninterested in David's testicles.

"Why is Florence important to you?" Ashley asked.

"Because my parents were married here. There was some squabble with in-laws so they wound up getting married in Florence instead of Naples. In the church of Santa Trinita. That's why I'm here, to visit the place. It's not far."

"Would you like to go there now?"

"It's closed until four."

"Well, in the meantime would you join me for lunch? I know *I'm* hungry."

They wandered along the Via Porta Santa Maria—sunlight lay like molten glass on the city—and found a trattoria on the Via delle Terme. Kimberly ordered for them both in Italian. Ashley thought he would try the capon breasts and Kimberly, who said she was suddenly starving, chose the *bistecca alla fiorentina.* He ordered a bottle of red Orvieto Classico. The chicken floated on a peppercorn sauce that bit Ashley's tongue and the entire dish reeked of garlic. He stared at his plate: the chicken stared back, somehow defiant. Kimberly's dish was an inch thick chunk of barely cooked beef that filled her plate and draped over the edge. She sliced the steak, gold and white bracelets gleaming against her sturdy wrist, blood oozing onto the table. Ashley thought her both magnificent and frightening as she attacked the meat. When she set down her silverware only a bare T-bone remained. They both finished the wine.

"Tell me about yourself," Ashley said.

Kimberly settled back, gave a wry shrugging smile, apparently loosened by the Orvieto. "I'm thirty-one years old and still trying to find what I'm good at. I married early, to the handsomest male in Hamilton High and a football hero to boot. After the sex business wore off I discovered he was about as intelligent as a potted plant. Then I modeled. The money was good but every guy around, from my agent to the photographers, was always trying to hit on me. I know I'm attractive, I'd be a fool not to know that. But life for an attractive woman is tougher than you might imagine. There's something destructive about beauty. I wrote a frankly autobiographical novel about the trials of an attractive woman and I have a literary agent trying to peddle it, but I can do a lot better than that book."

Ashley watched Kimberly as she spoke, felt tenderness flow through him and sensed he was falling in love. Perhaps all of his troubles had been but a preparation for this encounter. Life, after all, did not take the shortest distance between two points. He felt his life turning around.

"What about you?" Kimberly said. "What do you do? Why are you in Florence? I gather alone."

Ashley, trying to avoid any note of self-pity, described the loose ends of his life, his need to get away. But then, as if some invisible shackles that had long bound him had fallen away, he found that he could not stop. He spoke of his father who treated him with contempt yet Ashley had sobbed at his funeral, of the employees at the company who had tried to sabotage him, of his wife, her complaints steady like white noise, whom he had come to detest, of his students who had whined behind his back to the dean, and all those who had misunderstood him, doctors, colleagues, his own parents. Two vertical creases appeared between Kimberly's eyes, but he went on. He had the feeling that if he stopped talking he would cease to exist.

"Let's go find Santa Trinita," Kimberly interrupted and stood up. Her voice was that of a flight attendant.

"Yes, of course," Ashley said looking about him, momentarily confused and disoriented, the light in the room suddenly too bright.

"I'll ask the proprietor for directions," Kimberly said. "Shall we split the tab?"

Ashley wagged a finger. "Absolutely not. I want you to feel totally indebted to me." And he gave her what he hoped was a seraphic smile.

They turned onto a shady street. A shrunken prune of a

woman, sprawled on the ground against a wall, held a sleeping child; her hand, sere and dark, lay like a dead leaf on the child's head. As they passed, the hand shot out and grabbed Ashley's pants and the woman gibbered something, raising pleading eyes, mouth half open. For an instant Ashley stared down at her ravaged face, pink toothless gums, then he yanked his leg free, revolted. The child whimpered, the crone shouted after him. Kimberly said, "You should have given her a couple of lire. She said she's putting a curse on your head: no wish of yours will ever be granted. That's a heavy-duty Italian curse." They entered another piazza. The sun struck like a hot ingot, the city a sheeted glare, and as Ashley desperately searched for shade his stomach disgorged a mouthful of acid. Maybe his life wasn't turning around after all.

When they entered Santa Trinita, Kimberly genuflected then crossed herself. The place smelled of burning candles, dust and odors Ashley could not identify. He imagined it the breath of God. "I'd like to go to the altar alone," Kimberly said.

Ashley sat in the back, grateful for the coolness, and watched Kimberly's splendid legs as she walked down the long aisle toward the altar then sat on the front bench. His stomach, the lower right hand side, ached; it was the sauce on the chicken he decided, or maybe the wine, or maybe the heat, or maybe the curse of the old crone. What had possessed him to babble that way? She had stared at him like a tombstone but he had rattled on anyway. Ashley cursed himself for a fool. What now? Where to? He knew perfectly well what he yearned for. He looked down: his eye was caught by his hand: it lay perfectly still like some helpless and defenseless creature. Hastily, he looked away.

Kimberly returned, wiped her eyes. She crossed herself again when they left the church. It was the wrong moment, Ashley concluded, to ask for what he wanted. "I imagined my parents," she said, "young and innocent, my mother ten years younger than I am now, standing before that altar and taking their marriage vows. I tried to picture them, their life ahead, all anticipation and promise. I'm sure it hasn't turned out the way they imagined. I suppose it never does."

They did not speak for a while. Kimberly seemed lost in some private reverie. Ashley found they were once again in the Piazza della Signoria. He stopped, turned to Kimberly and said what was in his heart. "I must say, I feel very close to you... It would give me the greatest pleasure to sleep with you... I know you've heard that from lots of others but there it is. We have so little time."

"I've never heard it asked quite so sweetly," Kimberly said. "I don't want to disappoint you, Ed, but...how shall I put it? You're just not my type."

"What *is* your type?" Ashley asked, then, feeling he would do anything for her, went on, "I'm willing to become any type you want."

Kimberly gave him a smile, both beautiful and sad. "That's a fair question: what's my type? Well, I'm drawn to strong courageous men... That's about the best I can do."

"I'm perfectly willing to do something courageous," Ashley said, and did indeed feel full of courage. "What would you suggest?"

Kimberly gave Ashley an impish look, scanned the piazza. "Do you see that fountain, there near the middle? The one with the big white statue of Neptune in the center and the nymphs around the sides? How about climbing into it and walking across."

Ashley looked around, then wondered whether Kimberly was still under the influence of the Orvieto Classico. "There must be at least two-hundred people in the square," he said.

"Well, if there was no one in the square it wouldn't be an act of courage."

"I might be arrested."

Kimberly again gave her sad smile. "I told you, Ed, you're not my type."

Ashley turned and, brow drawn together, stared at the fountain, the great white statue, the square; he seemed a soldier readying for combat, assessing the terrain, assessing danger, then in long strides he headed for the statue.

"Hey, where are you going?" Kimberly said.

"To the fountain."

"I was only kidding," Kimberly called.

"No you weren't," Ashley called back.

Ashley dodged through the crowds, reached the fountain, climbed the one step, then hauled himself over the parapet, hanging onto a nymph's head for leverage. He lowered himself slowly: the water reached just above his knees. He was surprised at how cold the water was despite the heat of the day. He could hear the rising excitement of the crowd as he walked across the fountain. What Ashley had not reckoned was the slippery bottom of the basin. His foot skidded from under him, he grabbed for a nymph, missed, and wound up flat on his back in the water. Ashley hauled himself to his feet, spitting water, amidst great cries of laughter from the crowd. He reached the far side of the fountain, climbed over the parapet and into the arms of two carabinieri.

"Sei cretino, tu," one said. *"Cosa credi di fare?"* They both took an arm and started to haul him away.

Kimberly appeared before them. *"L'ha fatto per un eccesso d'amore,"* she said to the two young cops.

The policemen stared at Kimberly and perhaps decided that they too, in an excess of love, would have walked across the fountain for her. They handed Ashley over to Kimberly. *"Portalo a casa,"* one said, *"ha bisogno d'affetto."*

"Well, there it is," Ashley said with a triumphant smile.

Someone patted him on the back. *"Sei pazzo ma bravo,"* a

voice said. Ashley turned to Kimberly. "He said you're crazy but okay." And Ashley did indeed feel okay. He grinned and waved at the faces around him, all friends, all brothers and sisters. He had the feeling he had broken loose from invisible hoops that had bound him since childhood. His life was at last turning around.

"God, you reek of chlorine," Kimberly said.

Ashley, suddenly chilled in his dripping clothes and now sobering up, said, "I'd better get back to the hotel, shower and change... Will you come with me?" He was going to add "please" at the end of the question but refrained at the last instant.

Kimberly squinted at Ashley then said, "I have some gifts to buy. Tell you what, I'll meet you on the steps of the Duomo—that's the big church in the center—in about an hour." She gave him a smile both sweet and regretful, squeezed his arm and was gone.

Three taxis refused to take the soaked Ashley and so he hurried through the busy streets, turning the heads of passersby, feeling he was catching cold. A foul taste remained in his mouth, causing him to wonder what bacterial horrors the fountain water contained. Finally and mercifully he reached the Grand, no longer sure his life was turning around.

Ashley quickly showered then paused to study his body in the long bathroom mirror (the word melting came to mind), his reddish pubic hair, his pale organ, and felt a vague dissatisfaction. He dressed in a lemon-colored sport shirt and blue slacks, inspected himself in the mirror, decided he was unhappy with the colors, then headed for the door anyway. He took a cab to the Duomo and arrived less than an hour from the time he had left Kimberly.

Ashley stood on the steps of the great cathedral and scanned the crowd: no Kimberly. The steps were now in shadow but much of the square between the cathedral and the adjacent baptistery was still in the sun. Ashley checked his watch, carefully searched the crowd. Still nothing. Two nuns stood against the baptistery, backs bent, their habits forming identical black question marks in the sun. He thought their presence had an ominous significance. He walked across the square to the baptistery so he could view the steps in their entirety. Then he stared up at the immense facade of the cathedral, the structure that had so impressed him as a young man when he journeyed to Florence with his father and was the principal reason he had chosen to come to this city rather than another. He tried to make sense of the half acre of white, green and pink marble, the three great doors, the fluted columns and arabesque patterns, the figures of saints and apostles in the niches, the golden-hued mosaics above the doors. He peered at the great central window, its rosette a giant marble sunflower, wrinkled his brow, studied, but could not organize the complex edifice into a coherent whole. Lace, he finally decided, a gigantic embroidery in stone. Then he had the impression the facade was all glass, in delicate balance and tension, and a well-thrown rock would shatter it all. In fact, if no one were there he thought he might throw a rock; he imagined a wondrous explosion, a million shards of glass bursting outward. He looked up at the figures in the niches, humbly asked their help in convincing Kimberly to appear.

The entire square was now in shadow. The crowd had thinned, the vendors of cards and trinkets were gone, the Duomo was closed. He again stood on the steps, peering into the distance. Perhaps his memory had betrayed him, perhaps he was to meet her somewhere else. But he could hear Kimberly's voice distinctly, I'll meet you on the steps of the Duomo...in about an hour. But was her last smile and her touching of his arm a mute goodbye? His eyes now watered as though for hours he had been searching through mist for the tip of a sail or the dim outline of a landfall. He was certain that something vitally important was at stake: a place in his heart that only Kimberly could fill. Yes, he loved

Kimberly, for wasn't it true that if you long deeply for someone then you love that person?

There were only passersby now and he was alone on the steps. Pigeons came and went like blown leaves. An old man, gathered into himself, shuffled past, gloom emanating from him. Evening was settling in. Floodlamps came on illuminating the square and the facade of the cathedral with a chemical light. The scene appeared distorted, like a Van Gogh landscape. Ashley glanced at his watch: he had been waiting for three hours. He thought of time, of his own life flowing away, gray, featureless. He had an intimation of his own decline, a momentary queasy feeling as when he viewed an x-ray of a part of his body. He imagined his own demise: cancer like his mother, prostate cancer perhaps; the thought transformed itself into an inner substance and he felt a dull ache in his groin. He tried to recall his mother's face, the memory weathered by time—like those statues eroded by wind and rain—now a shadowy simulacrum of its former self.

Perhaps Kimberly had been an apparition, Botticelli's model come from the fifteenth century to test him in some way, a vision now returned from whence it had come. Or perhaps he was going insane, the entire encounter invented by a fevered brain. Those things happened. He was not well. His back ached and he leaned against the still-warm facade of the church. An odor emanated from the interior: it seemed dangerous and unreasonable. What an idiot he was not to have asked her where she was staying. His life had not changed and would never change. He thought of the old crone and the curse she had placed upon him. "What nonsense!" he said aloud, but some primitive part of his mind refused to accept the verdict. He remained leaning against the wall. A fog settled over him blotting out all thought, all notion of time. He would stay there forever, turned to stone, as if some god had touched him and he had become part of the wall, like the figures in the niches. Then in the July night, his mind now empty of all feeling, he looked at the baptistery and saw her hurrying toward him. She came through the wall, translucent, moving lightly, her dress long and white and flowing as though it were a wedding gown. He experienced a great flooding of relief as though in some way his life had been spared, a death sentence commuted. He wildly waved his arms and Kimberly Clark, born Carlotta Donadio, Botticelli's Venus, waved back in that funny way beautiful women wave.

The Visit

I am seventy-two years old and have decided to think seriously about death. I am not sick, my cholesterol, blood pressure, PSA and basic metabolic panel are all normal, though I do suffer from spring allergies and a certain cynical view of life. I am active, make it a point to walk briskly every day, and own a business. But in the last months, as I shave, I have come to scrutinize my face, the deep lines incised around my mouth, the liver spots on my temples, the skull beneath the skin, and see in all this my own mortality, and not that distant either. No point shrinking from it, I decide. The right thing to do is face it squarely.

My wife Julie, five years younger than I, an ex-professor of French literature, considers this a useless and maudlin exercise, and quotes La Rochefoucauld: "Neither the sun nor death can be looked at steadily." Well, I'm going to try. For insight, I search the words of the poets. "Death in itself is nothing, but we fear/ To be we know not what, we know not where," says John Dryden. This is true, well said, but not enlightening. What about the philosophers? All *their* profundity comes down to is that death gives value to life, makes it precious and important to live fully. Julie comments that this is obvious. Since it's impossible to know what's on the other side—though the way to bet, she feels, is that there is nothing on the other side—then all death can ever teach you is the preciousness of life.

But now a problem develops which is more important than my sorting out death. My company, a manufacturer of quality leather goods—attache cases, luggage pieces, toilet article kits—is suddenly in deep trouble. I have made the error, no doubt due to laziness, of allowing one customer to account for half of my business. That customer is now looking for a forty percent price reduction or he's going elsewhere. He claims he can buy comparable product in the Far East at half the price he's paying me. He's willing to pay slightly more for a Made in U.S.A. label, but that's it. There's no way I can reduce my price by forty percent and stay in business. I have a dinner appointment with their V.P. Materiél (the accent mark appears on his business card), a new man whom I have never met, to try to dissuade him from the price reduction, which may well be hopeless, or at least have him split his orders for a while as I hustle for replacement business.

I'm preparing to leave the house, mentally trying to strengthen the arguments I will use with him at dinner, when the doorbell rings. It's Glen Eustin. I'm surprised, puzzled and both pleased and displeased. The unwritten rule is that we phone to see each other. But we have had no contact in months, though I did call and leave a message and Julie did as well. Neither of these calls were returned. So in a way I'm pleased and relieved to see him. "I'm sorry to barge in on you this way," he says and smiles, his self-deprecating signature smile that I once found irresistible. "You're about to go out... I can come back another time."

I now notice that Glen does not look well. His face is thinner, complexion yellowish, cork-like, and the whites of his eyes yellow. "I have a few minutes," I say, and invite him in, out of the damp February night. Actually, all I have is about ten minutes, if that. His handshake is moist, uncertain.

"I really *am* sorry to barge in this way," Glen says. "I should have called."

"It's all right," I say. "Sit down. Sit down. How are you?"

He looks around as if checking whether anyone else is in the room, in the house. He has that haunted ill-at-ease look he had when he badly needed a drink. It occurs to me that he might want a drink, but Glen is an alcoholic, has been in AA for years, so that can't be right. He's hesitant, as if not prepared for my simple, How are you? "I miss Carolyn," he finally says. "Tonight more than ever. I was staring at her picture then I went and dug up our wedding album... I can't believe how young we were then. And how beautiful she was. You were best man, remember? Then on impulse I decided to come over, hoping you'd be in. I just didn't want to be alone... For some reason I couldn't bring myself to call."

I'm about to bring up my dinner engagement but instead, on impulse as well, say something that Julie and I had talked about months ago, casually, then dropped. It suddenly seems important and so without preamble I say, "Julie and I are going on a barge cruise this summer, in France, on their inland waterways. We'd like you to join us. As our guest. We've talked about it and I was going to call you. Three is good company, especially with an old friend. We'll float through the Loire valley, check out the cathedrals, eat good, chat, like old times–"

"I can't possibly, " Glen interrupts.

"Why? Have you already made plans for the summer?"

"By the summer I'll be long dead."

"What?"

"I have liver cancer," he says matter-of-factly then stares at me as if offering himself for inspection. I now become aware of the parchment texture of his skin and how yellow his skin and eyes really are.

"I am so *sorry*," I say, spacing the words, trying to come to grips with this horror while realizing how weak my words must sound. I reach out and put my hand on the arm of this poor stricken man that I have known for fifty years. "There must be something that can be done."

"Not really," Glen says. "The whole liver is infected so they can't operate and what's left is shot because of an old bout with cirrhosis. They don't even think chemotherapy will do any good."

"What about a transplant?"

"I've seen two specialists. Neither of them believe it would work at my age. Besides, there's a couple of year's wait for transplants." He gives me a sad resigned smile. "There's nothing that can be done."

There is a large clock in a brass case on the mantlepiece behind the couch where Glen is now sitting, an heirloom from my grandfather via my father. Grandfather was a clockmaker and constructed the timepiece—which is temperature compensated and which grandfather claimed was accurate enough to be used as a chronometer for navigation—with his own hands. It is indeed an extraordinary accurate clock. I glance at it now, at the lurching second hand. I should leave in the next five minutes. To keep the new V.P. Materiél waiting would be bad form indeed. But I can't tear myself away from Glen. Not yet at least—that would be more heartless than I can now manage.

"Would it be too much to ask you for a drink?" Glen says.

"Are you sure?"

"Yes, I'm sure."

I go to the liquor cabinet. "Cutty Sark okay?"

"Yes. Just straight. No ice."

Glen takes a gulp of his drink, seems to relax. "Where's Julie?" he asks.

"In San Diego, with our daughter."

He seems to relax further, pleased that we are alone. "When I learned about the cancer," he says reflectively, "I went through what I suppose are the usual reactions. This can't be true, there must be some mistake, why me, why now? Then thoughts like it's God's punishment for all the misery I've caused others while drinking, though I don't even believe in God. Then terror at the thought of dying, and soon." He stares straight at me. "You can never get used to dying, you know. There's not much point in even thinking about it... What I did was just curl up into myself. I didn't want to see anybody, didn't even answer the phone... I can *see* this thing. I stare into my body and see millions of murderous cells multiplying like maggots, feeding on my insides. Then I stare in the mirror, at the dye on my skin and in my eyes... It's death made visible. I'm ashamed of it, ashamed to be seen. I never go out in daylight. But tonight, Sam... Maybe it was the wedding pictures, but I just couldn't bear the thought of being alone."

I touch him again. "You're not alone," I say.

He smiles again, waves his hand in a dismissive gesture as if doing away with all he has just said, and speaks clinically, as if analyzing the life of another. "I'm past all those questions now. I'm working at something else, reviewing my life, trying to see what I did right and where I screwed up. Not that I can change any of it, but it has a certain importance."

"To effect closure?" I say involuntarily.

"Yes, that may be it. To effect closure. As though life is a book that needs a summary. An ending where you draw conclusions."

He has finished his drink and stares at his glass, it seems to me longingly. Reluctantly, I ask if he would like another drink. He nods yes. "The same," he says. As I pour the Cutty Sark it occurs to me that for Glen coming to grips with death simply means coming to grips with his own life, nothing more profound than that.

"Do you remember Keesler Field?" Glen asks as he takes a gulp of scotch. "Well, I've been trying to remember the songs we sang there while marching."

"There was *Wait Till the Sun Shines Nellie,*" I volunteer.

"The one I liked best," Glen says, "was *Bamboo Bungalow.* I taught the song to the kids when they were little and we'd all sing it together driving on vacation. Carolyn too... Those were happy times... When I die I'd like somebody to sing *Bamboo Bungalow* over my grave."

I let that weird thought go by and think back to basic training at Keesler Field, in Biloxi, Mississippi, where I met Glen. Since the army was into doing things alphabetically, and since Eustin is alphabetically close to Ewell, we were often assigned to the same details. We were both from New York, both unhappy, and drifted toward each other. But even at that early age I found something vulnerable about Glen Eustin. He was forever doing foolish things, like violating the fundamental rule of army life and volunteering, or staying out beyond curfew, or missing reveille. I always tried to protect him, protect him from himself and from the sharp edges of the world, and I came to love him.

"Singing," Glen says. "That's what I remember most about the Army. I asked my dad if they sang songs when *he* was in the Army. He brushed that off and said I was lucky that I got in the war late and never went overseas. He did fight but he never talked about it." I recall Glen's father, Paul Eustin, press agent, chain smoking, driven. Paul's clients included some of the top entertainment personalities of the time: Peggy Lee and Mario Lanza among others. But his most promising star was Frank Sinatra. It was Paul Eustin who came up with the idea of paying a couple of dozen bobby-soxers to scream and swoon while Sinatra was singing onstage at the Paramount theater in New York. Eustin hit it right for those initial screams were the catalyst for the mass hysteria that catapulted Sinatra to superstardom.

Paul Eustin died of a heart attack when his son was twenty-three, and Glen dropped out of school to take over the business. I remember visiting Glen. He was sitting in his father's office, behind the desk. I recall the wing-back executive chair he was in—it appeared immense and Glen seemed shriveled and minute within it. Now the press agent business requires imagination and hustle to keep your client's name before the public. It also takes diplomatic skill in dealing with those clients, typically egocentric types, not always stable, that require much stroking. To be charitable, I can say that Glen was just too young for the job. The business collapsed in three months.

Incredibly, Glen now starts to sing. "We'll build a bamboo bungalow for two, big enough for two my darling, big enough for two, under the bamboo, under the bamboo tree... Why don't you sing too, Sam? Like old times, when we were kids, let's sing together." He sings louder, with gusto, waves his arms. The whole silly business is irresistible and I find myself singing along. "If you'll be M-I-N-E mine I'll be T-H-I-N-E, I'll L-O-V-E love you all T-I-M-E time. You are the B-E-S-T best of all the R-E-S-T rest, I'll L-O-V-E love you all the T-I-M-E time, rack 'em up stack 'em up any old time, Match in the gas tank, BOOM! BOOM!" And Glen throws back his head and laughs and laughs. "The army wasn't all that bad, was it?" he says still chuckling. "In a way it was a chosen time... Funny how distance makes all things beautiful."

This high moment strikes me as an opportune time to take my leave. I'm about to stand when Glen says, quite soberly, "I thought of writing down the lessons of my life. Pass them on to the children. It's foolish, I know. How can you ever transfer experience?" He makes an uncertain gesture. "But it's funny, I've thought about it and to tell the truth I'm not sure what the lessons of my life are." Glen pauses, gives his self-deprecating smile. I can see exploring the lessons of Glen's life stretching far into the evening. I glance at my grandfather's timepiece, feel a desperate need to leave. And yet as I stare at Glen, at the face of a dying friend, a man I once loved—who has come to me, reaching out to the oldest living relationship in his life for comfort—I cannot find it in myself to say the words, "I have to leave."

"I keep thinking back to Carolyn," Glen says, his speech now overly deliberate. "I carry her picture around, like a good luck charm, to ward off evil spirits, danger... Do you want to see it?"

"Yes, sure," I say.

Glen carefully removes a photograph from his wallet and reverently hands me the picture of the young and extraordinarily beautiful Carolyn. A lump rises in my throat. Sooner or later everyone who knew Carolyn developed a crush on her. And that included me. I loved her and fantasized over her, saw her always through a cloud of desire. In those years I envied Glen his wife, his glamorous father, his life. I recall that we would all meet at Carolyn's mother's beauty parlor, Margo's, on 34th Street in New York, opposite Macy's. Carolyn worked in the shop under her mother and learned the trade. But Carolyn, energetic and smart, a born businesswoman, wanted to get out on her own. I suggested they come to Los Angeles, where I had found opportunity, and this they did. Carolyn opened a beauty parlor in Westwood, using money lent her by her mother. The shop prospered and Carolyn opened a second in Santa Monica then a third in Beverly Hills, all called Perm City. Glen, it developed, had a flair for hairdressing and because of his personal attractiveness and charm, drew many customers to the shops as he worked in one then another.

Glen returns the photograph to his wallet, stares at a wall as though it were a landscape; he seems to be listening to a distant sound. "I read my dreams," he finally says. At my puzzled look he goes on, "When I went through analysis, my psychiatrist thought dreams were windows to the soul. But since they're quickly forgotten, she asked me to write them down as soon as I woke up. I have a whole notebook filled with the dreams of twenty years ago. When I can't sleep, which is often, I read my old dreams. They're quaint, sort of innocent, and they tell me something about my life then. They also get me sleepy.

"I don't know why I bothered with law school," Glen goes on. "It must have been a mid-life crisis, but Carolyn went along with it, paid for it... Imagine getting a law degree at fifty. Ridiculous! What I really wanted to do was write a book on drinking, a brilliant, insightful counter-culture thing. I even started it but didn't get very far." I can see that Glen intends to helter-skelter review his life, free associating in his search for meaning. His gaze is focused well beyond me, toward distant space, remote time. I could be an adjacent passenger on an airplane, strangers on the same flight. I am simply an ear to listen, listen to things I already know. Yet, like the wedding guest before the ancient mariner, I cannot choose but hear. "I never did practice law," Glen says. "Who wants a fifty-year-old inexperienced lawyer anyway? I screwed around with real estate and odd jobs as an arbitrator. It took me away from Carolyn and the business and maybe that was the point of it all. To make it on my own. I always drank but that's when I became a *serious* drinker."

His speech is now a bit slurred but the words appear to come easily. "It was Carolyn who pushed me into psychoanalysis. Her theory was that if I could find the cause of my drinking I'd be able to overcome it. Well, in analysis I learned a lot about myself but kept right on drinking. I must have been hell to live with, especially when I turned up at the shop drunk. Carolyn finally gave me an ultimatum. Get into a detox program or get out of my life. That's when I went to Scripps then into AA.

"AA is a very practical outfit. They don't care *why* you're an alcoholic any more than a doctor cares why you have a strep throat. AA figures alcoholism is a disease and all they want to do is cure that disease. It worked for me." Glen raises his glass. "Here's to AA," he says and drains his drink then gives me a huge grin. "But AA is a big commitment. What with going to meetings three or four times a week, then I sponsored other men... That also took me away from Carolyn... But none of it matters now, does it?"

As Glen continues to return to Carolyn, I come to realize how much that loss has devastated his life, how missing her has become an eternal state. Carolyn died in an automobile accident two years ago, while rushing from one Perm City to another. And Glen—perhaps remembering the disaster that resulted when he took over his father's business—wanted nothing to do with Perm City and sold it almost immediately.

Glen rotates his empty glass but I avoid offering him another drink. "All the kids turned out badly," he says in a puzzled way and blinks slowly. He looks around confused, as if sightless. "You have to ask yourself why."

I recall Julie commenting on how spoiled and undisciplined the Eustin children were. In the end, his oldest, a boy, became a druggie, both using and selling, did time in prison, and is wanted for armed robbery. Glen helped him flee the country and he now lives in Venezuela, with a woman, and they have a child. Glen used to send him money every month and I suppose still does, taking the position that whether the boy is five or fifty, he remains Glen's son and his responsibility. His daughter Paulette, named after Glen's father, lives in a commune outside Albuquerque, and his youngest, Ellice, is gay, a sometime dental hygienist who relentlessly sleeps around. The last time I saw Ellice she had a multicolored butterfly sewn on the crotch of her jeans.

"I always get stuck on the same point," Glen says. "What went wrong? Everything I touched fell apart, from my dad's business to the children. If it hadn't been for Carolyn I'd have fallen apart too."

Grandfather's clock stares accusingly at me. At last I find the courage to stand up. Glen looks at me in surprise. "I want very much to sit here with you," I say. "I want to stay with you all night. But I can't." I explain my dilemma.

"Of course," Glen says. "I understand. Your business is important." He goes to the liquor cabinet, fills his glass with Cutty Sark and drinks it all as though it were water, then shudders. "Goodbye then. I doubt if we'll ever see each other again. You go to your life and I go... Well, you know where I go." But he does not go to the door. Instead, he just stands in the middle of the living room, swaying slightly. I take his arm. "Let's go, Glen." He jerks his arm free. "You see me as a failure, don't you, you the big businessman. You look down your nose at me. I'm a hairdresser, just a shit hairdresser, hanging around a lot of women, and a failed lawyer too." Then he squints into my face. "Smart man," he says, "tell me. Where did I screw up?"

I'm astonished. There's no irony in his voice as there was when he raised his glass to AA; he really wants to know. "It doesn't matter anymore, Glen. Just go home and get some rest... Do you want me to call a cab?"

"It matters," Glen says. "It matters. Pretty soon I'll get plenty of rest. Tell me." He sways before me, peers at me, actually searching for the key that would explain his life.

I must leave, but then I contemplate this bitter old friend. What is there to say that those years of psychoanalysis hadn't already said? It occurs to me that there is a fault line running through Glen Eustin, and all his misfortune is but the outer consequence of this inner defect and that defect had forever determined his fate.

"I really don't know where things went bad for you," I say gently. "You're smart and charming..." I search for a useful thought, words that might somehow transform what little remains of Glen's life, then decide that only truth now matters. "Maybe you just lacked discipline. Maybe you were done in by your virtues."

"My virtues?"

"Yes...charm...intelligence... Maybe you substituted those for hard work."

He continues to squint at me. "I don't get it."

"You depended on charm rather than hard work to get by. Then you made excuses for failure. Since you're smart, the excuses were very good." I'm suddenly aware how brutal this must sound, and worse, my own feeling of condescension as I say this. I have an urge to finish the job by blurting out, You were born in the wrong place at the wrong time. You would have been a great success in the court of Louis XIV. But this I cannot say.

Glen continues to sway before me. "And the kids? Don't tell me, let me guess. Since I couldn't impose discipline on myself, I couldn't impose it on the children either. How's that?" He seems pleased that he was able to put all that together.

I nod. "That's probably right."

Then his look changes to a sneer. "What bullshit!" he exclaims. "What simplistic arrogant bullshit."

"Do you want me to call a cab?"

"Fuck you and your cab," Glen says. "I don't need any of your routine sympathy. It must make you feel good to see how I screwed up my life. Makes your puny little life look like a great success." I gently steer him out the door. He's parked in front of the house, fumbles with his keys then stops and turns to me. "You know," he says, and seems suddenly primitive, feral, "one thing about dying—it's liberating. I can now say to you what I've wanted to say for years."

Now there is so much more to say, a great weight of things unsaid. I don't want him to leave, but there's simply no time. I turn toward the garage. "Sam," Glen calls after me. "You always wanted Carolyn, didn't you? I could tell by the way you looked at her that you would have given your eyeteeth to fuck Carolyn."

"Glen," I say, "everyone wanted to fuck Carolyn. That's the

downside of having a beautiful wife. But Carolyn never put out for anyone but you."

"How do you know that? How could you possibly know that?"

"Goodnight," I say. "God bless. I'll call."

"I was about to leave," the V.P. Materiél says, fixing me with a hard brown stare.

"Thank you for waiting," I say, humility being in order. "Sorry to be late," though I offer no explanation for my lateness.

The V.P. proceeds to give me a tutorial on his business. His speech takes on a mercantile fervor as he explains the workings of the new global economy. A patronizing note creeps into his voice. He's much younger than I, no doubt sees me as obsolete. But what he's saying is all bull. I stop listening. In his place I see the jaundiced face and eyes of the dying Glen Eustin. I should have stayed. All that anger... Was it because I deserted him, like so many others surely have? And as he may see Carolyn having done? He expected me to protect him—which is probably why he came to the house—protect him as I had half a century ago in Keesler Field. And this I should have done, because as I look at the arrogant face of the V.P. Materiél, his eyes stony as a snakes, I see that my cause is lost. I will lose his business, all of it—there will be no splitting of orders—lose it now, tonight. His meeting with me may be some need for a power display, or maybe the idiot *did* think I could meet the Asian price. One thing I do know for certain: I don't like the man and I'm pleased that I kept him waiting. He doesn't give a damn about my company. I lost his business the day he came on board, no doubt with a mandate to cut costs, and decided to seek proposals from China, Korea, or wherever it is he's going.

Glen had asked where he screwed up, but despite his insistence I now see he really didn't want to know. Instead, he wanted to be touched and comforted, not psychoanalyzed again. He had had enough of that.

"Excuse me," I say to the V.P. Materiél, "I have to make a call." I find myself singing *Bamboo Bungalow* as I head for the phone. I'll try, I tell myself, I'll try, but in the end no one can protect you from the sharp edges of the world. And no one, not even saints I suspect, can come to grips with dying. Glen had it right; Julie had it right: to examine death can only mean to examine life. After all, when you think about it, that's the only thing you can possibly know.

The Light of the East

Chandor, whose full name was Atal Harkishan Chandor, had an unhurried way of speaking. His accent was clicking Indian, but he never searched for words and had a vast vocabulary. He spoke softly and sometimes you had to strain to hear, but his speech had a mesmerizing effect, beyond the sense of the words, and you found yourself relaxing, as though the sound were softly running water.

We worked at Leru Laboratories in Culver City. The place was owned by Rolf Hansen, a big good-natured Swede, and there were just five employees. Hansen, an engineer, hustled around the aerospace companies in L.A., Ventura and San Diego counties looking for design and fabrication work for test equipment. These were one of a kind units that companies didn't want to bother making in-house. They gave Hansen the specs and he or I, the only two engineers at Leru, designed the unit, Chandor, the draftsman, drew it up and one of our two technicians built it. The work was varied, interesting and not terribly demanding. The only female employee was Ingrid, a girl in her early twenties, secretary and maid of all work, who was also Hansen's niece.

Leru Laboratories was located in a strip mall in what had previously been a luggage store and the place retained a vague smell of leather. Hansen had a clothes-closet size office and Chandor, Ingrid and I shared the only other office. Chandor was a meticulous draftsman. He did not work quickly, but steadily, evenly, without erasures, the way he spoke, and both his electrical and mechanical drawings were works of art. His printing was particularly beautiful, the kind you see in old patent applications, and it seemed to come to him naturally. He was able to work on his drawings and speak of something entirely different at the same time.

While we all dressed casually, Chandor always wore a suit, charcoal in color, a white shirt and a dark tie. Once a day, around mid-afternoon, Chandor would stop work but remain at his drafting board; his eyelids would drop like heavy shutters and he would sit without stirring for ten minutes. Nothing budged him, not the phone, not talk around him, not even the screech of a power saw. He just sat, unmoving as a monument, but there was a tautness about him and you did not have the impression that he was asleep.

Chandor was a strict vegetarian and usually brought his own lunch, packed in individual-serving Tupperware containers. He carried his lunch to work in an elegant black leather briefcase. He loved cauliflower, broccoli and fresh fruit, particularly apples and pears which he said were scarce in India. For a beverage, he drank soy milk. Sometimes we would eat out, the three of us who shared the office, at a diner down the street. Chandor was short and squat, dark skinned though his features were Caucasian. But it was his eyes that caught your attention: they were large and black and steady as you might imagine the eyes of a hypnotist to be. They seemed to have a particularly hypnotic effect on Ingrid—a tall, awkward, innocent-faced blond girl—whose mouth would slowly drop when Chandor concentrated the steady pressure of his gaze on her.

Chandor spoke of his bodily functions with the ease with which one speaks of the weather. He told us the color, volume and consistency of his bowel movements and nasal excretions. Though this may sound disgusting, the naturalness with which Chandor did this gave it an innocent, child-like quality, and though it was embarrassing it was not offensive.

In remembering Chandor and his nonchalance with regard to his bodily functions, I recall an incident that made me aware of how different from us he really was. It was late afternoon in winter, drizzling and already dark outside. In our little office, Ingrid, Chandor and I were at work. Each of our desks had its own light and there was a coziness and warmth to the room. Though no one spoke, about us was the intimacy of old friends. In that moment of quiet and closeness, Chandor farted. It was a beautiful fart, sustained, full-bodied, with a slight tremolo to it. Chandor was extremely courteous. "Excuse me," he said. Neither Ingrid nor I uttered a word and there was no odor. But the fart hung in the air like a profound statement, never to be forgotten.

Chandor was a Hindu and over lunch he would sometimes discourse on his religion. Not that he was trying to proselytize. "Christianity proselytizes by persuasion, Islam by force of arms, but it is all pointless," Chandor said. "There are many paths to spiritual liberation. Why impose your path on another?" After he said this two vertical creases appeared between his eyes and he added, "It must be monotheism that causes it." His hand, strong and blunt, made a dismissive gesture. "Having but one god, you are forced to conclude that there can be no other, and everyone but you is misguided." I must admit, he had a point.

"If there are many gods," Ingrid said, "how do you decide which one to pray to?"

"Each Hindu family has a favorite god," Chandor answered. "Ours was the goddess Kali. Perhaps because my mother was such a strong personality, she chose our family god to be a woman."

"Did you have much religious training?" I asked. Not that I particularly cared, but we were relaxing after lunch and I liked to hear Chandor talk.

"I went into an ashram at the age of twelve," Chandor said, "and studied for six years under the Maharishi Agit Singh, a most holy man, a believer in infinite compassion, infinite peace, infinite love..." Chandor took on a distant look at the memory of his beloved teacher. And Ingrid took on a distant look as well, as if vicariously sharing the memory of Chandor's holy mentor. "The Maharishi was an incarnation of Vishnu," Chandor continued. "His eighth reincarnation. Miraculously, he remembered fragments from all his previous lives."

"Atal, do you really believe that?" I asked, or rather the engineer in me asked.

"Of course," Chandor answered, but he was in no way indignant. "I believe this in the same way that you believe in evolution. In fact, the reincarnations of Vishnu follow the path of evolution. From the fish to the tortoise to the boar to the half beast half man, then to man the axe wielder, man the cultivator, and man the warrior king... His last incarnation, Kalki, has yet to appear." I glanced at Ingrid: she appeared to be drinking all this in, round-eyed, as if at the ultimate font of wisdom. In that moment, face innocent as a sunflower, she seemed terribly vulnerable and open to attack.

But in a way I could understand Ingrid. For when Chandor spoke of Hinduism you sensed in him a latent power. Of strength contained and held in reserve, of one meant for larger things than bending over a drafting table at Leru Laboratories.

One day, while Ingrid was out on an errand, Hansen came in, made phone calls, paid bills, then sat with Chandor and me in our office and complained of the time he was wasting on these administrative tasks. He had had Ingrid keep the books and pay the invoices, but she had screwed things up so badly that Hansen decided to do this himself. And since Ingrid was Hansen's niece, the good-natured Swede couldn't bring himself to fire her. Now Ingrid wasn't stupid, maybe naive, maybe impressionable, but not stupid. I think she just wasn't cut out for detail work like bookkeeping and her mind wandered while she was doing it. "I have taken a course in economics," Chandor said. "If I can be of assistance to you in this regard, Mr. Hansen, I would be pleased to help."

Hansen cast an eye on the meticulous drawings on Chandor's drafting table. "Well Atal," Hansen said, "I might just take you up on that." And that Hansen did. So in time Chandor kept the books and wrote out the checks for invoices and payroll for Hansen to sign.

When a piece of test equipment had to be built quickly, a tech would make a copy of Chandor's partially finished drawing to get an early start. Once, a tech inadvertently spilled coffee on Chandor's original. "You fool!" Chandor shouted. "You blundering idiot! Look what you have done." This outburst, from the soft-spoken Chandor, stunned us all. Nor did Chandor limit himself to these few words, but ranted on long after the tech had apologized. Days later, when the tech had almost completed the circuit board, a hot soldering iron was found lying on the board. Left overnight, the iron had burned a hole through the board and ruined it. The tech swore he had not left the iron on, and even if he had it would be resting in its holder and not on the circuit board. Chandor made no comment.

Chandor had to be the only guy in Los Angeles not to own a car. He had an apartment not far from the office and walked to work. Since public transportation in L. A. is practically non-existent, I asked him if he didn't miss an automobile just to get around. "Getting around does not interest me," Chandor replied. "Besides, physical things are impediments. One can become a slave to physical things. Americans, unfortunately, are obsessed with them. And since you can never have enough of things, you continue to accumulate them until you die, suffocated by things." Chandor gave me the penetrating look that always preceded his conclusion. "Material reality is an illusion," he said very seriously. "The ultimate truth lies beyond it."

Trying to keep the conversation focused on the practical and away from the metaphysical, I asked, "But tell me, Atal, when you want to go to church, for example, to pray, isn't that a hassle...with buses and all?"

"But we need no churches to pray," Chandor said. "There are no Hindu congregations, no Hindu priests. We have wise men but no priestly order. We have temples but no churches. In fact, strictly speaking, we are not a religion at all. We are a collection of thoughts and attitudes toward the divine." He gave me his serious look. "Truth is one. We need no special location to find it."

"I see," I said, though I didn't see at all.

Once, in the office, Ingrid, who no longer had much to do, asked Chandor, "Atal, you said that you spent six years studying under your holy man. What did he teach you in all that time?"

Chandor continued his drafting work as he answered. "There is the spiritual and there is the physical. In the physical, through concentration, visualization, meditation, he taught me to control the functions of my body. For example, I can stop the beating of my heart."

I looked up from my calculator. "You can stop the beating of your heart?"

"Yes."

"For how long?"

"Perhaps twenty seconds."

"But why would you want to do that?"

"When the world is too much with you then stopping all internal bodily motion restores your connection with the universal and you find inner peace."

"Can you demonstrate that, Atal, while I hold your pulse?" the skeptical engineer in me asked.

"Oh no," Chandor answered. "I would not do this for frivolous reasons, like a circus performer. I do this only when I feel the need."

"What else can you do?" Ingrid asked.

"I can drink a fluid and urinate it minutes later. I do this for purification purposes."

"I can do that with beer," I said.

Chandor treated this comment as beneath his notice. "Anything else?" Ingrid asked.

"I can hold an erection for hours," Chandor said.

Ingrid stared at him. "You can?"

"That I'd like to learn," I said.

"It takes many years to achieve this," Chandor said seriously. Chandor's sense of humor, I'm afraid, was not highly developed.

Ingrid continued to stare at Chandor. I wondered if she was thinking what I was thinking: that this could be put to a test.

In the following months I noticed an odd thing happening. At quitting time Ingrid and Chandor disappeared together. Chandor hopped into Ingrid's Saab and off they went. They made an odd couple: squat dark Chandor and tall blond Ingrid. Then I noticed over time a change in Ingrid's vocabulary. She snuck in words and phrases like "avatar" and "blinding light" and "seeing god with the third eye" and "self-transcendence" and "hearing celestial music" and "tasting divine nectar" and "sensing the vibrations of the universe." She took on a dazzled look when she said this, of one who was indeed seeing the light. I really had only one question for Ingrid but I couldn't bring myself to ask it.

Then one day neither Ingrid nor Chandor showed up for work. The following day Hansen stormed into the office. "That fucking Indian!" he cried. From friendly, good-natured Rolf Hansen, that was quite a statement.

"What happened?" I asked.

"He and Ingrid ran off. She left a note to her mother that Atal has shown her enlightenment and spiritual regeneration. He even got her to change her name. She signed the damn note Janatra. Can you beat that? That swami shithead turned her mind to oatmeal."

Two days later Hansen stormed in again. His feelings toward Chandor had escalated. "That goddamn fucking Indian!" he cried. "The son of a bitch cleaned me out." Chandor, in charge of the books and checks, had written checks to himself in the total amount of $10,000, meticulously forging Hansen's name. He skipped town with both the niece and all of Hansen's working capital. "I told the cops," Hansen said gloomily, "but I doubt if the amount of money is enough to get their attention."

Some months later I received a card from Ingrid. On one side was a picture of Chandor; it took me a moment to recognize him. He had let his hair grow to shoulder length so it framed his face. The photo had been retouched because his skin was lighter than I remembered and his eyes even larger. He bore a vague resemblance to Jesus. His name below the picture was changed to Maharishi Bhagwan Prebhuda. "We have founded an ashram," Ingrid wrote, "The Light of the East, dedicated to personal salvation. Life is preordained and I have now found the path meant for me. Truth is one though people may call it by many names. May you unite with the Supreme. Love, Janatra (Ingrid)." The card was postmarked Portland, Oregon. I decided not to mention this to Hansen who, having replenished his working capital, hired a new draftsman and not bothered to replace Ingrid, had returned to his previous good nature.

A second card arrived two months later, postmarked Mill City, Oregon, the same picture of Chandor on the front. "Many are coming to join us. They know that while the West may produce great men in politics and science, it is Asia that produces the giants of spirituality...Jesus, Moses, Mohammed and, of course, the Maharishi. We are learning submission to the Perfect Master. In his will is our peace. We are all his children. Love, Janatra."

Months later I received another card, also postmarked Mill City. This card carried a new picture of Chandor, hair longer yet, this time slightly wavy, eyes larger yet, head framed in light like the medieval portrait of a saint. Below him were the words The Light of the East. "I am healthy, holy, but not always happy," Janatra wrote. "I try to exhale all my doubts, inhale the energy of the Master, become a wave of bliss on the ocean of the universe, but it's not always easy. Do not try to contact me." There was no signature.

Another card, badly smudged, arrived months after the last one. "The mantras are giving me terrible headaches. I have lost my cosmic consciousness. Wearing a sari has become a pain in the ass. So has meditation. The Maharishi now demands total loyalty. No one can question his word. DO NOT TRY TO CONTACT ME !!! Ingrid."

Eighteen months after Ingrid disappeared with Chandor, Hansen showed up at the office with a tall woman. "Look who's back," he said triumphantly. It took me a minute to recognize Ingrid. She was pitifully thin, cheeks drawn, hair limp. She looked at least ten years older. "She finally dumped that fucking Indian," Hansen said. He looked his niece over. "Take her out to lunch," he said to me. "Buy her a good meal. It's on me. She could use some fattening up."

"Is the diner still around?" Ingrid asked. "Let's just go there."

"So what happened?" I asked the haggard Ingrid after we took a booth looking out on the boulevard.

"The Maharishi got himself badly confused with God," Ingrid

said. "At first, after he got a group together, we'd just study Hinduism and the paths to salvation. But he advertised and we kept getting new members. You'd be amazed at how many suckers there are looking for salvation. Then he began to make demands on us. We had to be strict vegetarians, wear Indian clothes, chant on schedule, work and pray on schedule. I mean you didn't have a minute to yourself. We were all children of God he told us but we needed enlightenment. That was his favorite word, enlightenment." Ingrid looked around the diner, peered outside. She had a hunted look, as if afraid she was being stalked.

We ordered lunch. Ingrid decided on a rib eye steak. "But enlightenment was expensive," Ingrid said, "and people had to pay for the privilege of being enlightened. He already controlled our lives, but then he tightened the screws. He not only dictated how we dressed and when and what we ate and the work we did around the ashram, but when we could go to the bathroom and when we could speak to each other. Every day he had us go through hours of chanting and praying. He gave each of us our own personal mantra. But it wasn't free. You had to pay for your mantra. Actually, it really didn't matter what your mantra was. If you repeat anything often enough it loses all meaning. Anyway, giving money was a kind of loyalty test.

"He leased a thousand-acre farm that had been abandoned as unproductive and had us do farming. Here, look at my hands." Ingrid held out her hands. They were heavily calloused. "That comes from farming as a form of enlightenment." She studied her own hands but with a special piercing sadness, of one who had once believed in something greater than herself only to find it false and mean. "When I suggested that we just go into town and buy groceries at the supermarket, I got punished with five days of silence, when no one could speak to me, and I had to spend all my time alone chanting and meditating...

"All the women had to wear saris when we weren't working. Then he gave everyone new names, spiritual names he called them, all Bengali, his native language."

Our food arrived. Ingrid made a clasping motion with her hands, then stopped. "That's another thing. The Maharishi blessed what we ate. But before eating we had to fold our hands in prayer, nod toward the Maharishi and thank him for our food." She illustrated this with a kind of parody. "Thanking the Maharishi got to be a habit." She gave me a bitter smile then attacked her rib eye.

"When did you decide the guy was a flake?"

"I was in denial for a long time. When you believe, *want* to believe, it's tough to accept that your belief is false. The Maharishi discouraged sex, even between the married couples. He said it distracted you from the spiritual. But he demanded massages for himself from the women and took turns sleeping with all of them. That's when doubt started.

"Then he insisted that earthly goods didn't matter. You shouldn't own more than you can fit in the trunk of a car is what he said. In fact, he had me sell my car to pay for my mantra and enlightenment. But while *we* couldn't own worldly goods, the Maharishi bought himself a big Mercedes. The guys in the ashram would fight for the privilege of driving him around. That's when something in me clicked over and real doubt set in. Then he had his house redone in some Indian style. Oh, I forgot to mention that. He had his own house while we slept in a dorm, a converted barn. I might also mention that the Maharishi thought Americans are obsessive about hygiene so he discouraged bathing. The dorm smelled like a locker room."

"Why did you write do not try to contact me?"

"At first the Maharishi allowed us to get mail, make phone calls, even receive visitors. Then he decided that contacts with the outside world were bad for our unity consciousness. Then he went hard over. Outsiders were sinful, unworthy, ignorant. They were unfit and there just was no place for them in the great enlightenment. He would have violent fits of anger when he heard of an unauthorized contact with an outsider. And you were punished by being forced to assume a humiliating position—for example, squatting on all fours like a dog—for hours. He also deprived you of food. He ripped out all the phones except for the one in his house and forbid all visits and all mail. When an outsider appeared, say a meter reader, like someone with a contagious disease you wanted to warn him: stay away from me or I'll be punished." Ingrid nodded, mouth compressed—an innocent who had experienced the rise then the total destruction of belief. "The last cards you got were snuck out."

"But there must have been some good moments..."

"Yes, in the early days, when I trusted. And those who joined the ashram were all good people. Everyone was searching for something—love, understanding, to make sense of it all—and each saw an answer in the Maharishi." Ingrid shrugged. "He was ambiguous enough so you could interpret what he said to mean whatever it was you wanted it to mean... I really did like the people, enjoyed working and talking with them, even enjoyed chanting together... They were all desperate though. They wanted to succeed, to find whatever it was that was missing in their lives." Ingrid now gave me a thin sad smile, gestured with her calloused hand. "But in the end 'succeed' only meant pleasing the Maharishi. And that was impossible because he was insatiable. But they tried. You can fall in love with your chains, you know. Some did. They hung his portrait over their beds like that of saint."

"What made you finally quit?"

"I'd already concluded that the Maharishi, in spite of all the spiritual talk, was just another guy drunk on power. Then the place had become suffocating. Life was just a perpetual chain of work and chanting and prayer and meals and attending to the needs of the Maharishi, every second programmed. Worse than the strictest monastery. Then one day—and this you won't believe—the Maharishi told us that in a dream he learned that he was Kalki, the final incarnation of the god Vishnu. He insisted that we call him Your Divine Grace and worship him. That's when I decided I'd had enough bullshit to last my whole life and had to get out."

"Did you just up and leave?"

"Oh no! I thought about it for weeks. I had no money and the farm was miles from anywhere. But I knew where the Maharishi kept his strongbox of cash and where he hid the key. One evening I said that I was sick and absolutely had to lie down. It took some courage, but while everybody was at evening prayers I took all the money from the strongbox. It really wasn't that much. Just the Maharishi's petty cash, about $3,000. The real stash was in the bank, in a money market account earning interest. I snuck out when everyone had gone to bed and walked all night to Mill City. All the while I kept looking behind me, scared to death they would find I was missing and catch up with me and I'd be punished. I hid whenever a car came down the road. From Mill City I took a bus to Portland and a plane home." Recounting her escape must once again have triggered apprehension in Ingrid because she anxiously scanned the diner as if expecting to see an enraged and vengeful Maharishi materialize in a corner.

"Do you think the Maharishi will try to retaliate?"

"No, but I have nightmares about that. But then the Maharishi is too busy recruiting new converts to worry about defectors. And the three-thousand dollars, like I said, was only petty cash."

"Were there other defectors?"

"Some. The family of one young guy sued the Maharishi for unlawful imprisonment. The Maharishi had a good lawyer and won the case. His point was that anyone who joined The Light of the East did so of his own free will. It was no different than joining a Catholic convent or the army."

Ingrid had polished her plate of steak, french fries and green beans. She looked up, bluish crescents beneath her eyes, a face disfigured by the bitter wind of betrayal, a far older Ingrid than had left Leru Laboratories only a year and a half earlier.

"Let me ask you a question," I said. "When we were yakking in the office, Chandor said he could hold an erection for hours... Was that true?"

"Did he say that?" Ingrid gave a scornful laugh. "It's all bullshit. He couldn't hold an erection any longer than anybody else."

Mutiny on the Bounty

"I'd like you to lend me $10,000," Simon says. We're at a table in the bar of the Bob Burns restaurant in Santa Monica. Simon watches my reaction to his request the way the accused watches the jury file into the courtroom.

I have known Simon for some thirty years. In all that time his income has rarely strayed over the poverty line but at no point has he ever asked to borrow money.

"Jesus, Norman," I say, "that's a lot of cash. What's happening?"

"It's to produce a musical, a musical adaption of *Mutiny on the Bounty*. Joel is doing the book and Ulpio the music." I take a hit of my Bloody Mary. Joel is Joel Wax who works in Hollywood as a third-string scriptwriter and Ulpio is Ulpio Pineschi, a journeyman composer who works for Disney on film background music. Neither of these guys is in danger of being nominated for an academy award. Simon is a lyricist who these days stays off welfare by writing jingles, freelancing for ad agencies.

"I thought musicals cost hundreds of thousands of dollars to produce," I say.

"They do," Simon says, "but to get backing we need earnest money. Cash that we put up as evidence of good faith." He takes a swallow of his Compari and water. "This musical is good stuff, Sam. I've never felt this confident before. It's going to be bigger than *Phantom of the Opera*." He nods as he says this, in agreement with himself.

I met Simon when we were both freshmen in Engineering at UCLA. In his sophomore year Simon switched majors, improbably to English. I though he'd flake out on that too but to my surprise he plugged along all the way to a Ph.D. He wrote his doctoral dissertation on The Sexual Element in the Novels of Henry James. I considered this an extraordinary feat of imagination. Having dipped into Henry James myself, I think the man's books are about as sexy as street maps. After his Ph.D. Simon taught at Cal State Fullerton for a while then was tossed out for seducing two of his students. What Simon really wanted was to be a prodigious novelist like his beloved James. He did manage to write about half a novel which he kept revising for years then finally abandoned. I think he just knew too much, expected too much of himself as a writer and so was never satisfied. He worked for ASCAP then drifted into songwriting. He had some modest early successes and one near-hit in a song called *Harmony,* and both Dean Martin and Sammy Davis Jr. recorded a Norman Simon song, but neither recording sold much. Simon desperately wanted the boss of the rat pack, Frank Sinatra, to record one of his songs but that never happened. Simon, being stubborn, kept on plugging. After a while, it was all he could do. But one of the great divides in this world is BR and AR, Before Rock and After Rock, and Simon never made it across that divide.

"Norman," I say, "I hate to be a killjoy, but suppose this thing flops—and most musicals do flop—how will I ever get my money back?"

"Greta says she'll repay you."

Greta is Simon's fourth wife. She's a pop singer, does everything—country western, rhythm and blues, Latin, you name it—and works in a club in West Hollywood. She's twenty years younger than Simon, thrillingly slender, and has a terrific butt.

"Let me tell you about this thing," Simon says. "It'll boost your confidence." He then goes into how they're adapting the plot of *Mutiny on the Bounty* to a musical. He stares at me with the insistence of a hypnotist as he explains.

I finish my Bloody Mary, order a second. I should tell you straight out that Simon is the most egocentric individual I have ever known. It doesn't matter on what subject you start, from literature to the origin of the cosmos, you always wind up talking about Simon. Simon spent years in psychoanalysis. I don't know if it did him any good, but I figure what psychoanalysis really did for him was allow Simon to talk endlessly about himself. So for three or four hours a week he rattled on about Simon and his mother, Simon and his father, Simon and his wives, Simon living with Simon. No doubt heady stuff to a guy whose single focus in life is himself.

To tell the truth, I don't like Simon. He's a trifle obnoxious and he's always telling me how he's about to make it big. Once, losing all patience, I said to him, "Make it big, Norman, then tell me about it. I'm not interested in forecasts." He's also a man without a sense of humor. You might ask why I bother seeing Simon at all. Good question. I never call him; he always calls me to get together and I rarely say no. I think I see him to gain a relative measure of where each of us, though we came out of the starting gate together, now stands in life. I own a successful business while he's always wallowed around on the ragged edge of poverty, living off his various wives, even having them pay for his psychoanalysis. Maybe that's a stupid reason to see someone, because he makes you feel superior, but I think that's why I see him.

But I do envy Simon one thing: his success with women. He has a bright poetic intensity about him, the way you imagine the great English romantics— Shelley, Byron, Keats—did, that appeals to women. So he slept with many and married some, but none of his marriages ever lasted. After a while I suspect the women tired of listening to Simon discourse on Simon. Maybe they also tired of supporting him. But Simon was always happily married, it's his wives that weren't. Since there was never any money to divide up and he willingly left the children with their mothers, his divorces were always friendly.

I must admit I also envy Simon the ease and friendliness of his divorces. I recently went through a bitter divorce that set me back financially and was murderous emotionally.

Simon, incredibly, is now singing to me, sotto voce, one of his *Mutiny on the Bounty* songs. I've finished my second Bloody Mary and order a third. As Simon is crooning away, I'm thinking about Simon's current wife, the lovely Greta, when an idea enters my mind, hovers there like some enchanting bird, becomes more bewitching by the second. I take a long swig of my third drink to work up the courage to broach it.

"Norman," I say, startling him out of his singing, "I've got a proposition for you." His face lights up. "This is the deal. I'll lend you the money if you let me sleep with Greta." You might say I should have been more artful in making my proposal, but then you can't beat clarity.

He squints at me as though his buddy of thirty years has metamorphosed into a Martian. "What?" he says.

Now that it's on the table, I warm to my proposition, the vodka in three Bloody Marys getting an assist. "I'll lend you ten grand if I can sleep with Greta over one weekend, say from Friday night to Monday morning." Simon is staring at me, evidently not sure whether this is some sick joke or a serious proposal.

"I'll even sweeten the deal for you," I go on. "You can pay me back over two years, five grand at the end of each year and no interest. Sleeping with Greta takes care of the interest."

"Is this some perverted humor you're trying on me?"

"I'm serious," I say, and I *am* serious, *feel* serious, as I add for emphasis, "never been more serious in my life."

"That is a disgusting unnatural idea," Simon says, his mouth turning down as if he'd found a worm wiggling in his Compari. But he makes no move to leave.

"But it's all win-win," I say. "Everybody gets what they want. You get your ten grand and I get to spend a weekend with Greta."

"And Greta?"

"Greta makes an investment to give you, and therefore her, the chance to beat *Phantom of the Opera* and become a millionaire. That's not a bad tradeoff. Besides, we're both men of the world. Greta is your fourth wife and you're her second husband."

"It's prostitution."

"Don't label things with polarizing words, Norman. It's a simple transaction that benefits everybody."

"You shithead," Simon says. "You slimeball. You really *are* serious."

"Don't resort to name calling, Norman. We are what we are. Life is filled with tradeoffs. This one hurts no one and benefits everyone."

"I have to talk to Greta," Simon says, then peers at me as if he's reading my DNA, no longer sure who I am. "I suppose we should never complain when people reveal themselves," he finally says. "For now we see them as they truly are." He then gets up and leaves without saying another word or even looking at me. I must say, he carried that off nicely. Of course, that left me with the tab.

I wait in the lobby of the Beverly Hilton, the hotel where my tryst with Greta is to take place. I've reserved a suite with a Jacuzzi in the bathroom large enough to hold a regiment. Damn the expense. Our rendezvous is for seven. At seven-thirty Greta hasn't shown up so I figure maybe she, or Simon, got cold feet. I wait on, scanning the entrance, hope dimming, when to my joy Greta appears. She's wearing no makeup, old baggy slacks, and a nondescript sport jacket. “Jesus, Greta,” I say, “you look like some homeless type.”

“Norman’s idea,” she says. “He doesn’t want me to look appealing.”

“Listen,” I say, “I haven’t had any dinner and I’m starved. Do you want to eat something? We can eat right here in the hotel.”

The maître d’ leads us to a darkened corner table, probably to avoid Greta’s outfit being too prominently displayed. I order a steak rare, a bottle of red wine, girding for the main event. Greta orders swordfish then, after the waiter leaves, says, “Where’s the money?”

I reach into my jacket pocket, hand her an envelope. “Ten grand. A cashier’s check made out to Norman, like we agreed.”

Greta peeks at the check then stuffs the envelope in her purse.

I pull out a second envelope. “Here’s a promissory note for you and Norman to sign. It’s no big deal. Take it with you. I’ll trust you to sign it.”

The formalities over, I search for some icebreaker subject to thaw the arctic atmosphere. I ask about her singing career. She answers laconically. Then she says, “Norman had a sandwich named after him.”

I’m startled by this off-the-wall revelation. “He did?” I say, trying to fake being impressed. I mean, you have to admit, having a sandwich named after you isn’t exactly up there with a Nobel Prize.

“Yeah. Mort’s Deli on La Cienega. Named a sandwich The Norman Simon. Mort’s an admirer of Norman’s songs. Norman says having a sandwich named after him means more to him than that Ph.D. of his.”

“What’s in the sandwich?” I ask.

“How the fuck would I know what’s in the sandwich?” Greta says with disgust.

I once again search for a subject to talk about then conclude there's only one subject that we have in common. "How come a smart guy like Norman," I ask, "with all his education, wound up spending his life writing songs?"

Greta stares at me, probably trying to assess whether this is a serious question. I've now adjusted to the dim light. Even without makeup Greta has a lovely face, terrific bone structure. I drink the wine and despite Greta's distant attitude feel myself falling in love with her. I'm pleased to see she's drinking the wine too. "Norman believes in the power of popular song," Greta says. "Not that Baby, Baby rock crap, but the older stuff, like Rogers and Hart. *Blue Moon, My Funny Valentine, A Small Hotel,* that kind of thing. Stuff that stays with you, that becomes part of you. That's why he writes songs and that's why I sing them. To give people something to hold onto."

I gaze at Greta's lovely face, see her in a new light. "You're right," I say and I'm not faking it: she *is* right. "I have trouble remembering the PIN number at my ATM machine, but I have no problem with stuff like"—and I sing—"'the very thought of you,' or 'diamond bracelets Woolworth doesn't sell, baby,' or 'I get no kick from champagne.'"

"You're way off key," Greta says, and cracks the shadow of a smile. I love her more by the minute.

"But all those were songs of another time," I say. "They're prehistoric. They don't work anymore."

"That's our problem," Greta says and again the suggestion of a smile touches her face. She could be a da Vinci Madonna. "But you stand a chance in musical comedy. A lot of that has stayed traditional."

I eat my steak, drink the wine. "Norman and I yak a lot about popular song," I say. "I pointed out to him that they're all about sex, but sex where consummation never happens. People are always singing about yearning, unrequited love, betrayal, self-pity. How or why they wind up in that mess you never find out. He said it doesn't matter."

"He's right," Greta says as she finishes her swordfish. "In popular song only the unexamined life is worth living."

I stare at Greta and have no reply. The new light in which I see her is glowing brighter, multicolored.

We finish our meal. Neither of us wants dessert. "I'm stuffed," I say. "Would you like to take a walk? Get some fresh air?" No point rushing things. We have the whole weekend. Besides, I feel heavy after all that food, the wine.

We walk along Wilshire Boulevard into the cool southern California night then turn south onto Bedford and away from the traffic. It's quiet, a breeze blowing, pleasant after the crowded restaurant. I take Greta's arm. She lets me do this. We walk awhile without speaking. Then a voice behind me, a calm solid male voice, authoritative, says, "Stand right where you are. Don't move. Don't turn around." An object, cold and hard, is thrust against the nape of my neck.

"Hand over your wallet," the voice says. "Now!"

My mouth is suddenly dry, hands cold. "How do I know that's a gun you've got on me?" I say. This dumb question is probably a regression to my scientific education, an engineer seeking data.

He shoves hard, my head snaps back and I stumble forward. "Do you want to bet on it?" the voice says.

I hand back my wallet. "Now your watch." I comply.

"Your pocketbook, lady."

Greta swings her pocketbook twice from side to side. Then, I suppose not wanting to take the gun bet either, she hands back her purse. "Both of you just stand there like good kids and keep facing forward for five minutes," the voice says.

I hear running footsteps retreating behind me and turn. The

figure is disappearing into the night then vanishes around a corner.

"He has the check," Greta says and suddenly smiles at me, a mournful but splendid supermodel smile.

"And he has my wallet with all my credit cards." Then for some unaccountable reason I start to laugh and Greta laughs and we're both laughing. Maybe it's because we're both overjoyed that we're alive and unharmed, but we're both laughing like idiots.

"Don't worry about the check," I say, now desperately in love with Greta. "It's made out to Norman. Unless he can prove he's Norman Simon, Theodore the Thief won't be able to cash it. I'll write you another check."

"That's nice of you, Sam," Greta says.

We walk back toward the Beverly Hilton. Greta takes my arm. "This may sound like a confrontational question," I say, "but I don't mean it to be... Tell me, how come a smart girl like you married an egotistical schmuck like Norman Simon?"

Greta stops, lets go of my arm, raises an eyebrow. "Hey, I thought you were his friend?"

"I am, sort of," I say, "but that doesn't change what he is."

"I think you have Norman sized up wrong," Greta answers soberly. We resume walking and she again takes my arm. "He's a very caring individual but terribly insecure. He's working at things now, like making amends to his old wives, getting to know his children... One day, when he was very unhappy, he said that he thought he took a wrong turn somewhere, somewhere in the beginning. I suggested he go back to basics, try writing again. He took me up on it and he's working seriously on a novel. I've read some of it and I think it's pretty good. He's also learning to listen."

Greta slows her step, eyes scrunched, she seems to be trying to formulate an important thought. Then she stops altogether and turns to me. "He now listens to me carefully, as if he's making up for all the times he didn't listen at all. I think that through me Norman has discovered the fallacy of his life." She pauses a moment. "It's simple, really," she finishes. "He never cared about anybody other than himself."

The light in which I see Greta is now brilliant, kaleidoscopic. "Why did he go along with my proposition?" I ask.

"He didn't want to. I talked him into it."

"Why?"

"The *Mutiny on the Bounty* adaption is important to him. He sees it as his last chance."

"Will this *Mutiny* thing work out?"

"Tough to say. Some of it is pretty good."

We continue walking, then I ask, "Are you interested in sex with me, Greta?"

She gives me a rueful smile, squeezes my arm. "Sorry to disappoint you, Sam, but no, I'm not." Then she says in a businesslike way, "But if you insist, I'll do it. A deal is a deal."

"I'll walk you to your car."

"What about the money?"

"You'll have it in the morning."

We peck each other's cheek. "Give Norman my best," I say as Greta gets into her Toyota Celica. I watch her drive off. I really do love her. I think that's why I didn't insist on the deal.

Rainstorm

Mist covers the windshield. Kreider leans forward to peer through it, then switches on the defroster again. Two clear elliptical patches appear on the lower section of the glass then spread to the rest of the windshield. The rain picks up and Kreider turns the wipers on high; they make frantic banging sounds as they struggle unsuccessfully to clear the water. Traffic now slows to a walk. "We'll have to get off 101 if we expect to get to Point Mugu by eleven," Kreider says.

"We can take 405 and 10 to Santa Monica then the coast route north," I volunteer.

Kreider shakes his head. "Four-o-five won't be any better than 134," he says. He glances toward me, suddenly apprehensive. "You got all your charts, demo equipment?"

"Yeah, sure," I reply. "Everything is in the two cases in the trunk. It's all there. Don't worry."

"I get paid to worry," Kreider says then surveys the traffic, which has now mysteriously speeded up. "You know what?" he finally says. "Let's take 101 to the Valley, then we'll cut down to the coast by one of the canyon roads. There's a map in the glove compartment. Check it out, George, can you?"

I study the map. "We can take Topanga or Malibu Canyons, or Decker Canyon further on," I say. "Decker is the closest to Point Mugu."

"They'll all be jammed," Kreider says. "What's the smallest, the least traveled?"

"Well, there's N9, something called Ramirez Canyon. That's the skinniest line on the map that gets to the coast."

"We'll take that," Kreider says.

I check my watch. "We've still got two hours before the appointment with Reynolds," I say by way of encouragement.

"Yeah," Kreider says, but does not appear encouraged. "If John is there and we're not, we're dead. And the company is too." He's over-dramatizing but not by much.

I glance at Kreider. He's a mesomorph of a man, big oblong head and the body of a linebacker, but he looks tired. And well he should. He's been working fourteen-hour days for months, executing John Cole's commands with the relentlessness of a bulldozer. It seems as if everybody in the company is working on the same project. Cole has mobilized all the resources of Aerosystems to convince the Navy that he has the answer to the fleet's biggest problem. They're terrorized by the possibility of attack by a hoard of surface-hugging cruise missiles, like the French Exocet, lost to their radars because of sea clutter, impossible to spot until it's too late. But Cole, the president of Aerosystems and probably the most brilliant engineer on the planet, has conceived a super accurate anti-missile system that'll locate and blow away the Exocets as well as revolutionize fleet air defense. Cole's solution has been analyzed every which way, simulated, mocked up, and considered from every angle short of building the damn thing. We all think it'll work. Even the skeptics among us concede that maybe it'll work. But the Navy is struggling with the problem on its own and has not asked for a proposal from anyone. Cole's problem, *our* problem, is getting the Navy's attention.

"Do you think Cole will be able to stall things if we're late?" I ask.

Kreider gives me a sneer, makes a disparaging noise. "Admirals don't wait," he says. "Reynolds is a busy man. He said he'll be at the Naval Air Station until noon, then he's gone. We've got from eleven till noon. That's it." Kreider is the project engineer on the program. A man never in doubt.

The traffic accelerates as we pass through Glendale then slows to a crawl again when we hit North Hollywood. A squall of rain strikes in a white sheet and despite the struggling wipers the windshield becomes practically opaque. Traffic stops. Kreider strikes the steering wheel with his fist. "Shit!" he exclaims.

I'm not banging on anything but I feel the same way. The company is barely staying alive, Pentagon spending down to a trickle, and Cole is going for broke on the Navy's anti-missile defense. I'm sure that every mind in Aerosystems right now is totally in sync: the future of Aerosystems, Cole's future, *everybody's* future, depends on Cole's ability to persuade Reynolds that we've got the answer to the Navy's problem. And here are the guys with all the data and demo equipment Cole needs to do the job stuck in a rainstorm. The words "we should have left earlier" are on the tip of my tongue but they are, after all, useless, so why bother. The weather forecast had predicted showers but not this. When we left Pasadena the rain was just a drizzle.

Kreider asks me to crack a window as he switches on the defroster again. It seems like we've been crawling along for days. I check my watch. We've got an hour left to get to the Naval Air Station at Point Mugu and our rendezvous with John Cole and the all-important Admiral Reynolds.

Kreider may look tired but I no doubt look a hell of a lot more tired. I'm in charge of system analysis and I've probably put in as many hours as Kreider. But I don't have his muscle mass, his energy reserves. I'm slated to give the system feasibility pitch to the Admiral though my head is filled with mush. I'm the kind of person who needs sleep and lots of it, but last night was a no-sleep night. I pray that my nervous system will rise to the occasion and I will do a credible job in front of the Admiral and John Cole, assuming we ever get there.

Last night was an emergency room night. Our four-year-old son Matthew had an episode, probably triggered by the wet weather. My wife, attuned to his every sound, must have heard him wheezing through the walls because she ran off to his room. She's become expert at assessing the boy's condition: by the color of his face, the way he speaks, the droop of his eyes. She scrutinizes the retraction of the skin at the base of his neck, counts respirations, listens to the wheeze. Matthew's asthma has become the focal point of her life. She's compulsive about keeping the house clean, dusts and vacuums every day, and protects him as though he were the boy in the bubble—afraid to let him near a child with a cough for fear he'll catch cold, afraid to let him near an animal for fear it'll trigger his wheezing, and is terrified by cigarette smoke, as though it were Sarin or Zyklon B. The boy is loaded with drugs—prednisone, theophylline, cromolyn; sometimes they work and sometimes they don't. The doctor says he'll grow out of it. The doctor, who looks like Albert Schweitzer, which is itself encouraging, says confidently to my wife: as the boy grows his windpipe will enlarge and relieve the problem. My wife hangs on to this, repeats it, belief growing with each repetition. Last night at two in the morning she carried Matthew into our bedroom and switched on the light. The poor kid's wheezing sounded like the high note on an accordion. "George, look how contracted his neck is," she said in a panic, then insisted we take him to the emergency room and I couldn't talk her out of it.

We waited, sitting on metal chairs under fluorescent lights in a green-walled room while the doctors took care of stab wounds, broken bones, heart attacks, bleeding ulcers, etc. etc. My wife kept bugging the nurses. Then, brusque and impersonal, they gave Matthew an adrenalin shot. He was better in seconds. But then he complained that his head hurt. His hands were shaking; it breaks your heart, your kid's little hands shaking. No, I didn't sleep much last night.

We finally go over the rise of 101 and into the San Fernando Valley. The freeway is as wide as a football field, five lanes in both directions, all jammed. Los Angeles doesn't handle rain too well. It's ten-thirty-five when we finally reach N9, the Ramirez Canyon turnoff. The rain has let up some and Kreider guns his Thunderbird through the switchbacks, heading south toward the coast. He was right: there is no traffic.

I think back to last night. As we waited in the emergency room my wife complained her usual complaint. She wants a house, one with a decent size yard, and not an apartment, so Matthew can play outdoors and get fresh air. She wants hardwood floors everywhere because they don't trap dust the way carpets do. I think she's grasping at straws, searching for a miracle, but I promise we'll buy a house as soon as we can. No point emphasizing the sorry state of Aerosystems.

As we speed along we close on the tail of a car in front of us. Kreider edges close to the car, flashes his headlights. No way to pass on this narrow curvy road unless the other car pulls over. Then the car in front of us fishtails, skids and slides into a ditch, turning over when it hits the ditch. In disbelief, I watch it all happen, an improbable slow-motion movie, right there before our eyes.

Kreider brakes, pulls over and we both run to the overturned vehicle. The rain has slowed to a drizzle. The car is an ancient Ford Pinto, on its back, windows smashed. The tires in the air are completely bald. Inside, the man behind the wheel is hanging upside down. The steering wheel has jammed back and pinned him to the seat. He's unmoving, blood dripping from his face and into his hair, a huge shard of glass rammed into his cheek. A woman in the adjacent seat is hanging by her seat belt, body strangely contorted, and moaning, "My leg, my leg."

We stand there an instant. "Do you have a cell phone?" Kreider asks. "No," I say.

"Let's get back to the car," Kreider says. "We'll have the guard at Point Mugu call 911, or maybe somebody else will come along."

"Do you just want to leave these people here like that?" I say. "They may be dying."

"Get back in the car," Kreider commands. His face could be carved of granite.

"Well goddamn it, Pete," I say, "if you didn't want to help, why did you stop?"

"I wasn't thinking straight," Kreider says. "Let's not waste any more time. Get in the fucking car."

When I try to recollect my thoughts as they were at that moment, I'm not sure I had any thoughts. Or maybe I was thinking of a house with hardwood floors and a big backyard. I just don't remember.

Kreider concentrates on driving and does not speak for the rest of the trip. Maybe he's thinking of the future of Aerosystems and everybody's job. Or maybe he's only thinking of his own job. Or maybe he's not thinking of anything at all. By the time we reach the coast route and head north toward Point Mugu, the picture of the two upside down heads—one dripping blood and the other moaning—has become surreal, as though it were something dreamed that had not happened at all. When I think about it now, I ask myself what could we have done anyway?

We reach the Point Mugu Navy guard station at four minutes after eleven. Kreider's objective is surely the same as mine but no doubt more intense: find Cole and the Admiral. *Now.* Kreider does not mention the accident to the guard. Nor for that matter do I.

Still Life With Green Chair

I try logic. "Look," I say, "it's simple. I earn seventy-five dollars a week. We can't live on my paycheck alone. At least not now. Then you're only twenty and I'm only twenty-three. We have all the time in the world to have babies. *Now* just doesn't work."

She sits in the green chair and watches me pace the room. She has long brown eyes in an oval face; when I remember her now I think of a Raphael Madonna. When she is unhappy her eyes harden and her mouth tightens. "I don't want to have an abortion," she says, voice precise, each word one small stone piled on the other.

I stare out the window of our basement apartment—living room, kitchenette, one bedroom—to the legs of the pedestrians walking by, good burghers of Flatbush, in the bowels of Brooklyn. "What's the alternative?" I ask, turning to her.

"We'll make do," Ruth says. "Poorer people than us have children."

But I persist. I hustle around, visit family planning clinics, get thrown out of a couple, and finally am given a lead by a sympathetic young woman with four rings in one ear. "He's a refugee doctor," she says by way of explanation. But Ruth does not want to visit the man. "No," she says. It's not a "Gee, I don't think so," kind of no, but a hard implacable no. We've been married for a year and a half and have known each other since we were children. But this impenetrable steel wall, the word *no* etched into it, I have never before seen in her. But I continue to badger, become more insistent, frantic, time itself hostile, something irrational taking over. Finally, she says, "I'll see your doctor but only if you promise to leave me alone afterward. That you agree the final decision is mine and you won't hassle me. This isn't a simple difference of opinion we're talking about."

I agree to this. Wouldn't you? The important thing, the only thing, is to get her to the doctor. Besides, morning sickness is setting in, making her miserable. Maybe she'll come around.

The doctor's office is on the ground floor of an apartment building on Queens Boulevard; there's no receptionist, no sign on the door, no shingle outside. I wonder whether he's licensed to practice medicine in the U.S. The doctor speaks carefully and with a pronounced German accent, but it is not unpleasant, rather the way I imagine Freud would speak. In fact, he resembles Freud: long pale face, deep crevices falling away from the wings of his nose, a neatly trimmed gray beard that adds gravity to his words, dark sorrowful eyes—the eyes of one who has seen much misery yet is not hardened to it—, the face of a gentle man. His office is small, overpowered by a huge desk in dark wood, chipped in places, papers strewn over it. Behind him, on a credenza, is a statuette of an oriental sage, hands clasped and eyes closed in contemplation. A dusty plant sits in a corner, illuminated by a shaft of sunlight from a streaked window. He does not wear a lab coat and though the room is warm he has on a heavy charcoal-gray suit, lapels too wide, like something out of nineteen-thirties mitteleuropa. A door leads back to what must be his examining room.

The doctor is practically deaf and we have to shout for him to understand. To my surprise, he tries to talk us (me) out of it. He says that women are most elastic at Ruth's age, childbirth easiest. Then there are certain risks to the procedure...

"What risks?" I yell.

"Possible hemorrhage. Possible scar tissue formation so she cannot have children in the future..."

"How likely are these things?" I cry.

"Not likely," the doctor answers, "but they are not impossible." He nods at both of us in a wise grandfather way, seems to approve of something. "Have the child," he finally says, "it will make you both happy." I wonder whether this advice is his way of making peace with the Hippocratic oath.

"We don't want the child," I yell further.

Ruth does not budge but stares straight ahead, sullen, expressionless.

The doctor sighs, rises from his chair, smiles an understanding smile at Ruth. "Shall we go to the other room so I can examine you?" I nod encouragingly at Ruth. She contemplates me for a long moment, looks at me in a way I have never seen before, as if something unsayable and irreversible has been settled between us. She turns away, hesitates, then disappears into the back room with the doctor. When they return there are tears in Ruth's eyes. "She is very healthy," the doctor says, "and would have a beautiful baby."

"How much?" I ask at a slightly lower decibel level.

He looks at me carefully, seems to understand something beyond the question. "Three hundred dollars," he answers then goes on, apparently with reluctance, "in cash please, and in advance."

When we leave she says, "You know very well, Michael, that I don't want to do this. I will think about it further, but remember—it's my decision. And remember also: don't hassle me about it."

"Yes, sure," I say, "but it's for the best." In retrospect my voice is oily, that of a salesman peddling an inferior product. I take her arm and add in a confident you-and-me tone, as though it were a mathematical truth, "We'll have kids another time."

She does not answer, then after a time says, "Where in the

world would we find three-hundred dollars?"

"We'd borrow it from Peter," I say.

We don't speak for a while and I think the subject closed when she says, "I've always detested Peter."

I sigh. "How you feel about Peter is not the point. He's my friend and he'd lend us the money."

We are in the living room, she in the green chair. The chair is wing-backed, stuffed, a nubby green and white fabric, but in memory the white is gone and the chair is pale green. We bought the chair second hand and cleaned it ourselves. We also have a couch, second hand as well, slightly spavined, with a gray-green geometric pattern. A modernistic coffee table sits in front of the couch: a wood base with holes in it like a Henry Moore sculpture and a glass top. A single floor lamp on a long curved stem, like a freakish bird, is the only illumination in the room. But what I remember most vividly is the green chair and a somber Ruth hunkered in it. All of our furniture, including the kitchen table and four chairs and bedroom set, were purchased with our wedding gifts. I study her as if she's a problem to be solved, then feel a compulsive need to again go through my arguments, to sell, to persuade, and cannot keep myself from doing this. I gesture decisively, point a finger as if it were a pistol, then have the odd feeling that I'm arguing with myself.

"I thought you promised to leave me alone?" Ruth says. "Why are you bombarding me with all those words? I'll make up my mind. Just stop talking." Tears roll slowly down her cheeks. I come to her, try to hold her, but she pushes me away. "Just leave me alone," she says.

She asks her friends for advice. One says yes, another says no and the rest tell her to do what's in her heart. There's no question of approaching her parents, traditionalists that they are. From time to time, as she sits in her chair, she looks around the room with apprehension, as if expecting to find some dangerous animal crouched in a corner.

We grew up in the same impoverished Brooklyn neighborhood, went to P.S. 149 and Thomas Jefferson High School together, and I helped her with algebra and she helped me with history. Out of the crowds and confusion of high school we gravitated toward each other, confided in each other and were accepted as a couple before we ourselves knew that's what we were. It seemed so natural that we fall in love, marry. We went with friends to Jones Beach on hot summer days, slept overnight under the boardwalk, made love in the sand. It was on the beach that Ruth found the chestnut. It lay in the sand, though how it got there neither of us could explain. It was hard, lustrous, dark brown with lighter striations. Ruth considered it beautiful and the improbable place where we found it, as if dropped in our way by the hand of God, made it a talisman that she thought would protect us against misfortune. She kept it in the nightstand beside our bed.

I cannot stop talking and do not try, promise be damned. Erosion, I decide, will get the job done. She finally says, "All right, Michael, you can shut up now. It takes two to raise a child and make a family. If you're so set against it then it will never work." She comes out of the green chair and to her feet, suddenly a mature woman. "I will do this, but I can't say how our life together will be afterward. But there's one thing I do know—it will never be the same." Then her voice takes on an acid tone I have never heard her use. "It takes courage to have a kid. You don't have it. All that bull about money and we've got plenty of time. That's all gutless babble." Raw contempt stares at me.

When we come in for the operation (for that's how I think of it), the doctor is all business, face an impersonal mask. I hand him the money, folded and held with a rubber band, which he drops in a draw without counting. He then removes his jacket and dons a white lab coat, but before leading Ruth into the other room he says, "I want you both to leave here walking normally. The young lady will experience some pain but she will be able to walk as usual... Is this understood?" I nod. I wait in his office for it to be done, stare out the streaked window. People hurry by, innocently going about the business of their lives. On the sidewalk, in the shade of a tree, a dog licks his organ without conviction.

It is July and when we leave the doctor's office, "walking normally," the sun appears enormous, cloaked in a fiery haze, the air dense, hard to breathe. Ruth is pale, her face grim, granite-like. She refuses to take my arm. The boulevard, streets and houses appear unfamiliar, somehow sinister, and our own little apartment when we enter it is itself unfamiliar, small and shabby and sad.

After the operation there is some bleeding but no hemorrhage and in a week Ruth returns to her job. But apparently more than the foetus has been excised. She keeps to herself, speaks to me only when necessary, no longer shares her experiences from work, her conversations with friends. We could be two bureaucrats sharing the same office: polite, remote. Our easy intimacy, of those who came together at an early age, is gone. She grows testy over trivia, seems to go out of her way to pick a quarrel. Where sex had been the most pleasurable activity in our lives, the one that sealed our love for each other, she is no longer interested, and if she accedes is cold and unresponsive. Then she decides that she can no longer share our bed and sleeps on the couch. I conclude that the abortion was far more traumatic than I had anticipated and that a sacerdotal patience, relying on the healing that time brings, is in order. When I try to console her, to draw her into intimacy, she brushes me away, in her eyes a glimmer of the contempt that surfaced when she spoke of courage. Around the apartment we bump into each other: she now seems to take up more space than she physically occupies. A new reality lays thick and heavy on everything about us. We now rarely eat together and when we do we sit at the table, heads down, like monks, between us a great weight of unspoken things. The tablecloth is now spotted and grease-stained but neither of us bother to wash it; the pattern seems to carry a message of dissolution and ruin.

So I wait for scar tissue to form around her memory of the old German doctor and his operating room and what was lost there. But things do not improve. She sometimes ridicules what I say, the opinions I have, and does this even in the presence of others. Losing patience, I ask her what is happening: does she really hold a contrary opinion or is making me look foolish what she's after. She stares at me as if what I said was more ridiculous yet. "I am my own person," she says, eyes hard and mouth set, "and I'm entitled to my own views." She has become a stranger. She now sees her friends rarely; in an unguarded moment she reveals that all people, men and women alike, now arouse in her a faint revulsion. I wonder whether she now views herself as a kind of leper, one who agitates her little bell and says, "Do not come near me. I have destroyed a life."

All this happened fifty-one years ago. We separated exactly nine months after the abortion, on a sunny sweet-smelling April morning. I commented to Ruth, a hunk of lead in my heart, that it was a shame to leave each other on such a lovely day. She answered, not unkindly, head tilted, "Goodbye Michael." When packing she came across the chestnut and tossed it in the trash.

The divorce was final three years later, when she remarried. She never communicated with me after the divorce. I don't know whether she ever had children, though I hope she did.

I moved to Los Angeles, remarried twice, worked as an engineer for North American Aviation then Hughes Aircraft. Finally, I started (and still own) my own business, the fabrication of precision parts for the aerospace industry. My third wife died a year ago and I write this sitting alone in our house in Malibu. The house, all ten-thousand square feet of it, sits on an acre of mesa in the Malibu hills overlooking the Pacific. The desk in my study faces a wall of glass that gives out onto the ocean. Sometimes, evenings, I watch the sun, a glowing red coin, sink slowly into the sea, then the sky flares dull red shading to yellow then purple, the ocean dark gray and finally black, all light drained from the world. Then I am touched by apprehension: I have always mistrusted darkness, thought of it as hiding evil.

I have no children. My seconds wife, it developed, could not have children, which is just as well because our marriage was an error for both of us. I don't know what her natural hair color was because she kept changing it. She was a master of makeup (at which she spent hours) and when she was done her face seemed fabricated of plastic; she had an insatiable need for new clothes, and yearned for an acting career. I learned that she slept with anyone whom she thought might further that career. When I think of her now I imagine a line of studs jumping on her as if she were a carousel in an amusement park. It turned out that all we had in common was sex and when that wore off there was nothing. In the end we do not explain our marriages.

My third wife, whom I married when I was in my fifties and she in her late forties, had grown children of her own, and we were both emotionally beyond starting a family. We were friends: an intelligent woman whose counsel on any subject I valued. Was there love? Affection yes. Love? Hard to say, but if it's hard to say then I suspect it was not there. Love and marriage need not go together.

I stare out the glass wall at the sky and the water; this morning they resemble each other, both shades of gray, like the open shell of a giant mollusk. When I turn my head the bones in my neck make small clicking sounds. I should be visiting customers: business has slowed and I just laid off a dozen men. The aerospace market has shrunk, concentrating itself north and east, away from southern California: Boeing in Seattle, Lockheed Martin in Maryland. I should be hustling civilian business. But as I think of this a deep fatigue overwhelms me and I realize that I have stopped caring. My business was my life. Now I can't say that anything is my life. The other day my shop foreman showed me a photograph of his first grandchild, a boy he claimed looked like him. He was very proud and I congratulated him and agreed that the infant did indeed resemble him. I have friends but many of my old friends, men I knew for years, are now dead. At my age, friends, one by one, disappear, and of course I see in their death the beginning of my own. The losses are irreplaceable. One does not make new friends in one's seventies.

I should sell the business while there's still something to sell. But what then? The money is meaningless. I would spend the rest of my days staring at the sky and the sea, waiting to sicken and die. I could travel I suppose, though I have no desire to do this. Time zone changes bother me. Then sightseeing never held any interest for me. Only work did. Sometimes I experience a throb of longing and have thought of finding Ruth and by some miracle returning to the easy intimacy that existed at the beginning. But I would not know where to start looking; besides, she may well be dead, or an old crone, or a happy grandmother surrounded by a hoard of pink-cheeked children, each lovely enough to be in a Raphael painting. No, the idea is absurd. I have thought of going back to Brooklyn and finding the basement where we once lived and where the green chair sat, and looking in there once again. I see it as a still life: the chair, the freakish bird lamp, the couch, the Henry Moore coffee table. But the building was no doubt torn down long ago and the neighborhood has surely decayed. Then what would be the point?

It is indeed strange that I fathered a child at the age of twenty-three, then never again. In some odd way, though I am the least suspicious of men, I sometimes have the feeling that Ruth placed a curse on me. She had offered me a chance for family and when I spurned that, by some occult magic she saw to it that the chance would never again occur. But setting that nonsense aside, had I really believed the "too little money and plenty of time" logic I hammered her with? Or was I indeed "gutless" as she said? Though it's difficult to reconstruct one's state of mind as it was half a century earlier, I know now that we indeed could have made do. I could have worked harder, worked longer. I was just plain scared, though of what exactly I cannot tell you. Perhaps of a drastic change in my life and my relationship with Ruth. But then not having the child changed my life far more. Ruth warned me of this. I just wasn't willing to listen, to understand.

When I look back across seventy-four years of life, I realize that the best time of that life were those eighteen months in my early twenties in a basement in Flatbush. I sometimes imagine how my life would have been different had I allowed Ruth to have her way. My son or daughter would be a man or woman of fifty and Ruth and I would be proud of him or her and no doubt the others. And perhaps they would be part of the business and make of it one of the great enterprises of America. Or perhaps they would be failures: those things happened too. But either way, like my shop foreman, I would probably be a grandfather.

I stare out through the glass wall, past the memory of the basement apartment, to the great ocean beyond and now, toward the end of my life, in fantasy uselessly change what is unchangeable. There is now a frightened place in my head that nothing can fill, not work, not friends, not anything.

An Afternoon at the Movies

in homage to Delmore Schwartz

The scenes are grainy, stark black and white, like those old silent films. The movie is sparsely attended. On the screen is my mother, in her early twenties, plain-featured, straight black hair framing her face, large uncertain eyes. My Aunt Beckie, shorter, stouter, five years older, is packing. Beckie is using a portion of her precious savings to take my mother, emigrated a year earlier from Poland, to the Catskills for a three-day vacation. Don't do it! I want to yell to my mother. Don't go! It will lead to poverty and misery for your entire life. But the two young women happily put their belongings together in a dilapidated cloth suitcase and laughing and carefree set off on holiday.

The scene shifts to woods and mountains. The sun is high overhead when a chime sounds; young men and women hurry toward a narrow rectangular building marked The Eatery. Tables are in long straight lines, benches on either side, like an army mess hall. Food is served on large platters that are placed at intervals along the tables and the guests help themselves. My mother's eye is caught by a young man facing her one table over from where she is sitting. His face is drawn, ascetic; he wears metal-rimmed glasses that give him a scholarly appearance. The man is my father. My mother notices that he does not greedily grab food the way the others do but politely waits. He looks in my mother's direction and their eyes meet. She gives him the suggestion of a smile.

It is now evening; the chime sounds again. My mother and aunt enter The Eatery. My mother looks around, finds my father, and steers her sister toward his table and they take places opposite him. When the food arrives he waits for them to help themselves, but my mother says, Here, pass me your plate and I will serve you. Thank you so much, he says, eyes opening wide, how kind you are. My mother introduces herself and her sister. My name is Samuel my father says, but a bit sadly, as if he is the last in a long line of Samuels. They all come partially to their feet, impeded by the benches, and shake hands with old world formality, my father bowing slightly with the handshake.

My aunt regards my father with an estimating eye and apparently does not like what she sees. Perhaps the man is too ethereal for her, does not have the down-to-earth look of a breadwinner. They leave The Eatery together and my father invites the two sisters for a walk; my aunt demurs but my mother accepts. What do you do? she asks. I own a small metal parts company, he says. I'm appalled by this incredible untruth. That's a lie! I shout in the darkened theater. Heads turn. Hey, what's with you? someone says. Pipe down! calls another.

My aunt introduces my mother to another young man but as his gaze wanders over her body she backs away. She tells my aunt that his eyes are too close together and his forehead too low. I agree with her assessment.

As if some gravitational force is at work, my mother and father continually drift toward each other. He is taller than she but narrow, frail-looking compared with her robust body. They walk together. Sunlight filters through the trees in soft gleams, dappling the ground. My mother comments on the innocent beauty of the day. Both seem caught up in a gentle vibration. My father shyly takes my mother's hand and she lets him do this. Then my father sneezes, apologizes as he blows his nose. Do you have a cold? my mother asks. Allergies, he answers. Pollen, dust, animals, all these make me sneeze. I am done in by innocent things. He gives my mother a sweet child-like smile and her mouth turns down in sympathy. And allergies will plague my life as well, and that of my brother and sister. Spring grasses, flowering trees, bananas, peanuts, in a long list will cause us to suffer, genetically cursed, we too done in by innocent things. My mother gaily points to birds and asks their names. My father tells her the names, usually wrong. On her last day my mother asks for his address and in a ceremonial way they exchange addresses, on bits of paper that my mother finds in her purse.

When my mother returns to the city, she eagerly runs each evening after work to the mailbox. She tells my aunt that she thinks often of the young man, that she found him handsome in a poetic way. My aunt dryly points out that poets generally die at an early age, usually of consumption and in a garret since they never have any money.

We see my mother taking piano lessons on an ancient upright in an elderly woman's apartment. It is evening and my aunt looks on approvingly as my mother peers at the notes and tentatively tries to translate them into music. When they leave it is Beckie who pays the woman for the lesson. In another scene my mother is in night school. By their accents it is clear that all the students are immigrants. The class, predominantly women, has been assigned *Tom Sawyer* to read. They take *Tom Sawyer* seriously as if it were history and not a novel. In another class the teacher lectures on the constitution and the three branches of government and my mother listens with rapt eyes. Should the constitution be changeable? the teacher asks. Absolutely not! The class is adamant. That is the law: it cannot be altered any more than the Bible can be altered. But the teacher patiently points out that times change and the constitution must change with it. He cites the abolition of slavery as an example. But he hastens to observe that while the constitution can be modified, it is difficult to do this, guaranteeing that it will not be changed for frivolous or transient reasons. The class nods approval.

My mother at the kitchen table studies late into the night then arises with her sister at six. They eat bread and jam while dressing, gulp a glass of tea while packing their lunch, then hurry to the subway. In stark black and white we see the shop where they work. Row on row of women, crammed together, are bent over sewing machines; the din of motors, gears, belts, pulleys fills the theater. Carts piled with material are pushed down the narrow aisles, often striking a chair. You idiot! You too should be on piece work! a woman with wild eyes shouts to the boy pushing the cart. She seems frazzled for an instant then she hurriedly aligns cloth, picks up her pace at the machine. You can almost smell the cotton dust that thickens the air. The camera skims across the women and comes to rest on my mother, her expression hard, focused. Then the camera zooms in on her hands—their movements smooth, rapid, precise—then to the feeder foot of her machine, the cloth zipping through, finally the blurred image of the high-speed needle head fills the screen. The clatter is deafening.

The sound track is suddenly quiet. We are again at the kitchen table. The two sisters are sipping tea from a glass. In this peaceful moment my aunt gazes tenderly at my mother, takes her hand, eyes shining. I know it is hard now, Beckie says, but this will change. You will have a good life. You will marry an educated man. You are not like the others. She speaks these words carefully as if they are fragile objects. I want, desperately want, my aunt to be right, for the movie to change the future. But I know that these events, unlike the constitution, can never be changed.

We see my mother, late in the evening, sitting at the kitchen table writing a letter. The screen is filled by her hand moving across the paper. Dear Samuel, she writes. Despite myself, I jump to my feet, shout, Stop! Don't do it! Tear up the letter! What's going on here? calls one of the patrons. An usher appears. Sir, he says to me, if you create another disturbance I will have to ask you to leave. My mother is at a mailbox. The letter slides into the slot and is gone. The mail slot stays fixed on the screen, somehow sinister, suggesting a meaning beyond itself.

My mother is sewing a dress, dark gray. She tries it on: it is ankle length, does not hug her body yet one can divine her narrow waist, ample bosom. We learn that the dress is for an important occasion. My father will introduce my mother to his family. She asks Beckie how the dress looks. My aunt grunts approval. My father comes to fetch my mother, comments on how attractive she looks. She takes his arm as they walk to the subway. His father, my grandfather, is a forbidding figure. He is dressed in dark clothing, has a full beard, sits unmoving as a boulder as he interrogates my mother. He will be dead of prostate cancer in twelve years. He asks my mother if she keeps a kosher home and she answers yes. She twists a handkerchief and does not meet the old man's eyes as she answers. He then asks if she can read and write. She answers yes she can in Yiddish and Polish but has difficulty in English. He does not seem pleased by any of this. My father's mother, my grandmother, watches from the shadows. She is a thin diminutive woman, black hair pulled tight around her head and looped in a bun, deep-socketed eyes. She will live to be ninety-six, spend ten years in my mother's home, criticizing her at every turn until my mother in despair finally prevails and has the woman, a querulous old prune, shipped off to a nursing home. My father's two brothers, one a carpenter and the other a tailor, are also at the table. But it is the old man who conducts the interview. The camera pans across the onlookers: their faces, expressionless, have the hard lines of those who have endured much at the hands of a hostile world.

My mother comments that they must be proud of their son

Samuel who manages his own company. They stare at her in puzzlement and my father makes a joking remark. She turns quizzically to my father: it is her first glimmer that my father will recount his life as he wishes it to be rather than as it is. Twice in his life he will retreat completely into a fantasy world and will require electric shock treatments to pull him out of it.

My grandfather asks my mother about her family. Her parents, she says, have remained in Poland and have no desire to come to America. Only her sister, her courageous sister Beckie, with the help of a friend, has come and saved the money for my mother's passage. Her two other sisters and a brother have remained, in a small enclave outside of Warsaw. Fifteen years later, every last one of them, my maternal grandparents, uncle, aunts and cousins will be wiped out in the Holocaust.

In the next scene my mother answers her sister's questions about the interview. My aunt carefully watches my mother. You don't like these people, do you? Beckie finally asks. They are plain people like us, my mother answers charitably. They have no doubt suffered like the rest of us. They have every right to judge the woman their youngest son wishes to marry. You marry the man's family as well as the man, my aunt observes.

At Beckie's insistence, my mother invites my father to their apartment for tea. It is Sunday afternoon, my mother has spent most of the day cleaning, baking almond biscuits. They sit at the kitchen table—there is no living room—my father opposite my aunt. He is dressed in a suit and tie, white shirt with a high collar on his long thin neck. His hair is already thinning. He sips tea, nibbles on one of my mother's biscuits, stares earnestly at my aunt but seems forlorn. She asks about his life. He came to America from Odessa, he tells her, when he was seven, together with his parents and two brothers. They came to America to escape the pogroms then sweeping Russia. He is the youngest of six children, three of whom died in a cholera epidemic. He went through the sixth grade but then had to leave school to earn a living. What do you do to earn a living? Beckie asks, fixing my father with an x-ray stare. He no longer speaks of his own company but says he is a salesman selling plumbing supplies. Where and for whom? my aunt persists. He cites names, places, then seems to warm to the subject, speaks of trips to Hartford, Boston, elsewhere in New England. In disgust, I mumble to myself, What baloney! Tell her the truth, for God's sake! He sells potatoes off a pushcart in an outdoor market in Brooklyn. That's what he does. Just tell them and be done with it. But no, he embroiders his travels, his lies darting about like mercury under my aunt's interrogation. Do you have a business card? my shrewd aunt asks. My father's gaze shifts, he makes a show of checking his wallet, shrugs, looks sad, and says he will send her one. She asks about his ambitions. He says something about night school and studying law. But my aunt's expression is now one of profound skepticism. My mother serves more tea, offers my father another biscuit. The light in the room is suddenly very white.

It is a mistake to marry him, my aunt says. He is a dreamer, a wishful thinker and no doubt a liar. But he is kind and good and needy, my mother says. All men are needy, my aunt answers, but that has little to do with their ability to provide for their family. He has the soul of a poet, my mother says. My aunt ignores this and goes on: At the least make it a long engagement so there will be time for him to reveal himself to you.

It is a summer evening and my parents are strolling in a park. She holds his arm. They kiss and kiss again. They sit on a bench, embrace further. I cannot say whether it is he or she who pulls the other to the grass behind a bush. Mama, Mama, I say under my breath, what are you doing? Don't go there. Don't do this! A lump rises in my throat. But their future will proceed inexorably, unchangeable. In breathless haste they make love. They do this in scene after scene, neither can get enough of the other.

My Aunt Beckie is crying. Why did you let this happen? she sobs. My mother tries to comfort her. All will be well, she says. We love each other. All that I wanted for you is gone, Beckie says bitterly. Then in a hoarse voice she shouts, I curse the man who did this to you. I curse him for the selfish pig that he is. It was my doing as well as his, my mother answers quietly. Do not speak badly of him. But my Aunt Beckie will speak badly of him for the rest of her life. She will forever treat my father with contempt, for his illnesses, in which she does not believe, for his inability to make a living, for the poverty in which he will plunge her sister and their children. In times of particular dislike, throughout her life, she will curse the day she decided to take her sister to the Catskills and wish that lightning had struck her as she left the house. To this my mother will never reply. The child my parents have conceived behind the bushes in the park is me. No longer can it be a question of a long engagement.

The wedding is held in my grandparents' house. There are few people but the small room appears crowded. On one side stand my grandparents, uncles and cousins, and on the other my a Aunt Beckie and some women friends from the shop where Beckie and my mother work. My mother's dress is light in color, just touches the floor, a dress she designed herself and sewed on a borrowed machine. My father is solemn in a dark suit. During the ceremony, the camera fixes on my Aunt Beckie's face, her expression—that of one attending a funeral not a wedding—changes several times as if some drama, the death of hope perhaps, is playing itself out in her head, then she starts to cry. My father stamps on the ceremonial glass and everyone yells Mazel Tov! Here the movie ends and my mother's long life of poverty and struggle begins. She will raise her family, tend to a forever-ailing husband,

and take in work as a seamstress, our primary source of income, laboring far into the night on a treadle sewing machine for the rest of her life. Yet never once in all those years will we, my brother and sister and I, ever hear her complain about her lot or her marriage.

We file out of the theater. The lump is again in my throat and tears in my eyes. Of course, none of it was changeable. They are all dead now, my parents, my Aunt Beckie, my uncles. My mother died at the age of seventy-seven of a massive stroke. We all thought that our dependent father would not last a year after his wife's death. But he lived on alone for nine more years, surrounded by photographs of my mother, in the closet her dresses and shoes, bits of time he could not part with. He became a member of a Golden Age Club and wrote poetry that he read to senescent world-beaten faces, mostly women, gathered in a semi-circle around him. In this my mother was right: in his old age my father gave vent to the poetic soul my mother had glimpsed within him. He died quietly in his sleep. We do not know of what.

Fountain of Youth

I am seventy-three years old and a widower. I putter about, take an occasional course (literature, French language, computers), have lunch with old men like myself, wander around the mall and wish I had done some things differently. I have four children and nine grandchildren sprinkled around the U.S. of A. They call me occasionally in discharge of their filial duties, sometimes visit with me when business takes them to L.A., then disappear into their busy lives.

I see women, enjoy their company, but, though tempted, avoid entanglements. Through an ad for an "escort service" I met a certain Cecile, a brisk middle-aged no-nonsense woman, who arranges "escorts." In Cecile's case at least, escort is a euphemism for prostitute. To cut to the bottom line, I lost my sexual powers some years ago. I get pleasure by performing oral sex on the woman. I have tried to understand why I enjoy this. I suspect that at an advanced age one develops a certain fascination with the vagina. Picasso's late nudes are filled with views of the vagina. A desire to return to the womb, perhaps, to be reborn?

Though I am Caucasian, I ask Cecile for the services of non-Caucasian women. They strike me as more exotic, or perhaps one attributes a different order of sexuality to races other than one's own. And so I met Kwan Li.

Kwan Li is Chinese, a river rat from Shanghai who smuggled into the U.S. with her brother three years ago. It's difficult to tell her age—she herself isn't sure—but I would say mid to late twenties. Her brother was killed in a gang war with Hispanics, a bloodbath that claimed five lives and was described in vivid detail in the

Los Angeles Times and on local TV. Kwan Li is wide-faced, wide-hipped, with excellent legs, a splendid bottom, skin that appears translucent and black shrewd eyes. She asks me with some apprehension whether I find her breasts too small; she understands that American men favor large breasts. Her apprehension is endearing. I assure her that her breasts are in perfect harmony with the rest of her body and her other attributes more than make up for any deficiencies in that area.

Back to the bottom line and the miracle it is my purpose to recount. In my first rendezvous with Kwan Li, I go through my usual routine and while in the act discover, to my astonishment, that I have an excellent erection. I switch to the traditional method and complete the act quite successfully. But there is much more. That night and the following day I'm buoyant, optimistic, vigorous. I stare at myself in the mirror: my eyes are surprisingly clear and the wrinkles in my face appear less deep. I prowl the house, restless, alive with energy. In the newspaper, I focus on businesses for sale, find myself reviewing them seriously. This is madness, I tell myself. I sold my business, a shop that manufactured special purpose attachments for textile machines, five years ago, a year before my wife died. I have a sizeable nest egg so there is no reason for me to even think about this. Is it euphoria over having achieved penetration when I no longer thought it possible, or something else? In three days the energy dissipates and I am once again my seventy-three-year-old self.

I make another appointment with Kwan Li, we go through the same act as previously, and the result is the same. The following day I am once again restless, hungry with ambition. I seriously investigate the purchase of a business, a manufacturer of high power switches. The owner, a man younger than I but not by much, eyes me skeptically. In several days the Kwan Li fix (for that is how I think of it) wears off and I let the idea of the purchase slide away, a kind of mental aberration.

Now Kwan Li is not my first Asian. I have had others but never with the same effect. I decide to experiment and ask Cecile to procure another Asian for me, specifying that she must be Chinese and around the same age as Kwan Li. Cecile has no doubt seen much kinkiness among her clients and treats their odd tastes as the most natural thing in the world. The girl is indeed about Kwan Li's age or younger and if anything more attractive. I go through my routine. Nothing. It's the way things have been for years. I feel no spurt of energy and the following morning look even older than I did the day before. Back I go to Kwan Li. By God, there it is: the same effect.

I think about all this and decide that there is something in the vaginal secretions of Kwan Li that produces the magic. I ask Cecile if I can have the services of Kwan Li every third day for the next several months. Cecile hesitates: she doesn't like her girls becoming too dependent on a single client. I offer to pay a premium and Cecile finally agrees. To my astonishment, as the weeks go by I find the lines in my face smoothing, my energy level skyrocketing. I work out in a gym, my muscles bulk, I lift weights with the kids. Throwing aside all caution, I buy the switch business and plunge into the operation, visit customers, distributors, discover the weaknesses of the product line, set about fixing them.

It is clear to me that the key to my future lies with Kwan Li and the current arrangement is too tentative. For one reason or another she may be snatched from me, and so I ask Kwan Li to quit working for Cecile and come live with me. (I must tell you that through all this I have taken care not to confide in Kwan Li why she is special. "Is this how you do with all ladies?" she asked me once. Absolutely, I said. She shrugged: she too, like Cecile, no longer questions the kinky behavior of her clients.) I offer Kwan Li a steady salary, better than she is earning now, but Kwan Li eyes me warily. When I insist she tells me she is concerned about being thrown out when I tire of her, or of becoming a prisoner, even a slave. Such things, she says, are common in Shanghai. I finally offer her a large up-front bonus, all cash, and she accepts. She brings with her a small jade Buddha, chipped, that she places beside the bed. "Bring good luck," she says.

I wonder whether the effect Kwan Li has on me is universal. I'm tempted to ask a friend of my age to go through the same drill with her to test this but I wouldn't know how to ask. Then I'm fearful. If the man did comply he might become addicted to her as well, with consequences that I can't foresee. Still, I believe there is some chemical unique to Kwan Li that could in fact be isolated and synthesized, and would provide the elixir of youth in a bottle.

Kwan Li, it turns out, has no interest in housekeeping and even less interest in cooking. Day by day she grows more restless, mopes around the house, grumbles at small things. She begins to understand the hold she has on me. I try to get her to work in my business—stockroom, bookkeeping, computer data entry, anything. I want to keep an eye on her, keep her engaged. But none of this interests her. Then one day she disappears. In desperation I call Cecile who, now abrupt with me, says she has no idea where Kwan Li is. Besides, Kwan Li is not the most reliable person in the world.

By the fifth day after her disappearance I find that I'm shuffling my feet as I walk, and at the office my secretary glances at me apprehensively and asks if I am well. I beg Cecile for another Chinese, hoping (no, desperately wishing) to find another Kwan Li. Cecile, a business woman after all, complies but ups her rate. Though I try half a dozen, none have the Kwan Li effect.

After three weeks I give up on Kwan Li and am wondering how to rearrange my life when Kwan Li surfaces. She looks tired, bedraggled, and has lost weight. She refuses to tell me where she's been. She peers at me. "You look much older," she says. "That's because I've been worrying about you," I say. "You worry about my pussy, not me," she says. Kwan Li is no fool.

Things return to normal, but now I know that somehow, some way, I've got to isolate the magic elixir in Kwan Li. And do this quickly before Kwan Li disappears again, this time possibly forever. But now Kwan Li makes another demand. She is not happy living with me, it makes her feel like a concubine. She wants an apartment of her own. At first I say no, look fierce when I say it. Then I repeat for emphasis: no, a definite and total NO. But Kwan Li has dealt with far fiercer characters than I. Stubbornly, she insists. "You want pussy, I want apartment." Kwan Li is a believer in basics. So what would you do? What would anybody do? I find her an apartment. She furnishes it in what I would describe as Asian whorehouse traditional. The dominant colors—of the chairs, drapes, rugs—are shades of yellow. "Yellow bring good luck," she tells me. Her chipped little Buddha, more good luck, is beside her bed. Furnishing the place keeps her happily busy for a month. But my resolve to extract the magic elixir is now stronger than ever.

The metallurgist at the company is really a chemist and he tells me that he studied under some high type organic chemist at UCLA, a certain Guy Besso. The man may be retired because that was ten years ago and he was old at the time. But on inquiry I find that Besso is still around, so I make an appointment to see him based on some trumped up story. To enter Besso's office you pass through a laboratory of zinc counters and sinks where men and women in white coats are bent over bubbling glass tubing, Bunsen burners, flasks, beakers; an odd odor like marsh gas hangs in the air. I find all this promising.

Besso's office is that of a man who never throws anything out. Books, papers, journals, folders are everywhere in the cramped space and litter an ancient desk. An oddball clock with zodiac signs and a swinging pendulum is in a corner. A computer, an anachronistic object in the room, like finding an automobile in a medieval engraving, sits on a credenza behind his desk. Besso looks about my age, great bald dome of a head, liver-spotted hands. He regards me doubtfully: I am a non-student and probably trouble.

I decide to start dramatically. "How old would you say I am?" I ask.

Besso looks puzzled. "You said you wanted to see me about consulting work for your company. Is my guessing your age relevant to this?"

"Yes it is," I say.

Besso sighs, studies me a moment. "I'd say you are in your late forties. Fifty at the outside."

"I'm seventy-three," I say.

"You're well preserved for your age," Besso says without batting an eye, clearly a man not easily astonished.

"There's a reason for that," I say, "a strange and remarkable reason. Now promise to hear me out on this because it's why I'm here." Besso takes a surreptitious glance at the zodiac clock, sighs again—his students have no doubt heard many such sighs—and nods for me to go on.

I explain, as delicately but as clearly as I can, my experience with Kwan Li and its effect. Besso scrutinizes me as if I'm an object, then his eyes slowly narrow as my recitation goes on. "I'm a busy man..." he says.

"So am I," I say and, because I can see the idea enlarging in his mind, I add, "Believe me, I am not crazy. I am not a crank, not a nut. I own a company and I'm a practical and realistic man. What I'm presenting to you is evidence I've obtained with my own senses."

"What do you want of me?"

"I would somehow obtain for you a sample of this woman's vaginal secretions and ask you to determine in what way they are unique. I would of course pay for this."

"I don't have any idea what the chemical composition of normal secretions are. How can I determine in what way this woman's are unique?"

I can see that Besso is a natural passive-aggressive. No creativity in evidence here. My turn to sigh but I adopt a positive approach. "UCLA has a huge medical school and hospital. How about enlisting the services of the ob-gyn department to get samples?"

Besso leans back, glances toward the swinging pendulum of his clock, then takes on a benign grandfatherly expression. I sense philosophy in the air. "Men have sought the fountain of youth for millennia. Regardless of your experience, it does not exist. I believe that you believe. But I can assure you that you are wasting your time." The unstated conclusion to the sentence is "and mine."

I continue doggedly. "Let us put this to the test," I say. "You are an experimental scientist, a believer in results. If I obtain a sample for you, would you be willing to test its effect on laboratory animals? I don't know if it'll work on non-humans, but it's worth a try in order to convince you."

Besso hesitates. "You said that you would pay for this?"

"Absolutely," I say. "I'll pay and pay up front if you like."

I propose to Kwan Li that we celebrate her new apartment by going out to dinner. Kwan Li is flattered: not many men take Kwan Li out to dinner. Wearing a clingy pale yellow shift, black hair flowing down her naked back, a scent of jasmine about her, she really is a knockout. I take her to Carruthers, one of the best restaurants in L.A. She is doubly flattered. I offer her one cocktail then another. In the euphoria of being on display publicly, she accepts and becomes dizzily drunk. Actually, she's not bad company, sort of droll. When we return to her apartment, no doubt filled with gratitude, she says, "I give you plenty pussy tonight."

I tell her that I always want some of her, whether she is there or not. Then I make my proposition: I'd like to bottle some of her fluid, always have it close, and in that way always have some of her with me.

She laughs and laughs, says I'm a crazy old man but crazy in a nice way. So she agrees and we go through our number and with some awkwardness I manage to get a sample of Kwan Li's magic elixir in a vial which, at home, I carefully stopper and place in the refrigerator.

The following morning I hustle over to Besso with my precious vial. He says it'll take some time to set up the experiment. I point out that the stuff may be perishable and he'd best hop on it right away. Two days later Besso calls me. He's beside himself with astonishment. He injected the elixir into some old mice. Almost immediately they became frisky, behaved like young bucks, and were jumping on all the female mice around, in fact were jumping on the males too. Besso has become a believer.

Besso sets about trying to isolate the magic elixir. He cajoles the gyn department at the hospital for smears of normal fluid, then deploys the full armory of modern chemistry to determine its composition—mass spectroscopy, nuclear magnetic resonance, x-ray diffraction, infra-red signature analysis—then does the same for a precious droplet of Kwan Li's secretion. Subtle little differences appear but this could well be noise. Besso conjectures that whatever the substance may be, it probably doesn't last too long. He needs fresh samples.

Kwan Li has become testy, is no doubt bored, and decides

what she really wants is a car, a Jaguar. I patiently point out that she has no driver's license, doesn't even know how to drive. Besides, she's in the U.S. illegally so she couldn't get a license even if she learned how to drive. She waves all this away. Many Chinese girls drive, she says, even without a license, and she wants to drive and she wants a Jaguar and that's it. Kwan Li reduces things to their simplest terms: no Jaguar, no pussy. So I give her driving lessons in an empty high school parking lot late afternoons and weekend mornings. I'm severe with her, try to stretch things out. She's actually quite well coordinated and surprisingly confident behind the wheel. But I'm tough on her, set up cardboard boxes for her to parallel park and yell when the car touches a box, ask her to make u-turns without touching the curb, back up in a straight line and so on. All the while I'm milking fluid out of Kwan Li as if she were a cow, take my own dose and pass the rest on to Besso.

Besso repeats the mouse experiment with identical results. He's enthused. Out of scientific curiosity, he tries the elixir on female mice: no effect. He hastens his chemical analysis, notes minute differences, a slight change in a complex protein molecule. He shakes his head, doubts if that small difference accounts for the magical effect. Worse, he doubts if a molecule that complex can be synthesized.

My fighting for time with Kwan Li is a losing battle. To tell the truth, she now drives better than I do. Her reflexes are quicker and she's confident. "Time to buy car," she says. Her manner is definite, the implication of not buying an automobile is clear. We visit a Jaguar dealer. She would like a yellow car; besides bringing good luck, she tells me that in Chinese tradition yellow is the imperial color. I point out that yellow is too bright; it draws the attention of the police if she happens to be speeding. I suggest a non-committal asphalt color. We finally agree on sky blue. She insists the car be in her name. No dummy Kwan Li. So we buy her car. She drives it off, happy as a kid with a new toy. Much fluid forthcoming in gratitude. I must confess I'm becoming quite fond of Kwan Li.

Besso has found other small differences. He doesn't know if these are meaningful, just experimental noise, or possibly contamination in the various fluids. He does not look hopeful. I try to cheer him up, point out that Edison needed over a thousand failures before he hit on the proper material for the filament of the light bulb. Finally, though with some trepidation, I suggest that Besso try a smidgen of Kwan Li's elixir on himself. That might give him the creative charge he needs. He looks at me dubiously. "Not directly from the source," I tell him, "but from the samples." He seems relieved.

While Kwan Li is tooling around in her sky blue Jag, Besso appears rejuvenated. Damn if the elixir didn't work on him as well. He redoubles his efforts, discusses the problem (hopefully in an academic way) with his colleagues, assigns some slave labor graduate students as helpers. I'm getting antsy. There is no telling what Kwan Li's next demand will be. There are changes in her—in dress, makeup, the way she walks, holds her head—a growth in sophistication. She could be in a TV commercial as she emerges from her Jag, wearing Porsche sun glasses, Giorgio Armani clothes. All this is costing me a fortune.

I travel on business, meet with my children. They stare at me in astonishment: I don't look much older than they. What is happening? Why am I back running a business? They say they're happy for me but they look wary. They might sense something unnatural occurring. Of course I'm not about to tell them about Kwan Li and the elixir.

Besso does statistical analysis and finds that most small differences disappear from sample to sample and concludes that these are caused by noise or contaminants. But there are two differences that are constant from sample to sample and it is on these two that he concentrates. He tells me that the two differences are aspects of the same thing: they form a ring molecule, difficult but not impossible to synthesize. And so Besso struggles around the clock, charged himself by a touch of Kwan Li, to synthesize the elixir. He is almost there, he claims, but cannot succeed in closing the ring. What he does manage to synthesize he tries on the mice. Nothing. As he and his assistants battle on, Kwan Li decides that she must have jewelry.

Kwan Li likes jade, she tells me, Chinese royalty having decked themselves in jade for millennia. I complain that she will ruin me, try to slow her down, but Kwan Li cannot be slowed down. She visits jewelry stores and finds that the sparkle of diamonds causes jade to pale in comparison. I tell her no and that's it. Kwan Li pouts and keeps her legs tightly crossed. My life has become a race between Besso synthesizing the elixir and Kwan Li driving me into bankruptcy. I wonder whether it makes sense to tell Kwan Li of the unique treasure she possesses, cut her in on the deal, make her part of it. That way she might prove cooperative. But I decide against this: as Cecile said, Kwan Li isn't the most reliable person in the world. There is no telling how she would react.

I check in on Besso. He looks as if he hasn't slept in days and his gaze is focused somewhere on the other side of the galaxy. He talks of tetravalence and carbon-hydrogen double bonds and cyclo molecules and strikes me as crazier than his lab rats. I despair but then a bubbling Besso, hippety-hopping around with excitement, says he thinks he's discovered the secret of how to close the ring. He draws one of those weird diagrams hooking together carbon and hydrogen atoms and adds a touch of potassium and nitrogen. The shape looks curiously like a vagina. He points to the potassium link. "That's the pearl in the oyster," he says. I have no idea what he's talking about.

After days of labor Besso manages to synthesize several precious droplets. He tries it on the mice. Eureka! Old mice leap about and copulate madly. Throwing caution to the winds, Besso touches a smidgen to the underside of his tongue. "It must be absorbed by the mucous membranes of the mouth or nose," he tells me. "Swallowing it wouldn't work: the hydrochloric acid in your stomach would disintegrate the molecule." The effect is almost immediate. Besso jumps around like the mice. I wonder whether it's the elixir or a placebo effect. I bring this to Besso's attention.

"You try it," Besso challenges me. He tells me to open my mouth, raise my tongue, and he touches the tip of a pipette containing the elixir to the underside. The jolt is almost immediate: euphoria, a feeling of immortality, one can climb Everest, screw a thousand women, run the world. "It's undiluted," Besso says. "That's what gives it its kick." He stares at me in awe. "It's the thing itself."

"What now?" I ask.

"We have to test its long-term effects," Besso says. "I'll keep giving it to the mice and see if any negatives develop. In the meantime I'll work on improving the means of synthesizing."

"Congratulations!" I say and give the staid Besso, who's now like a kid, a big hug. Then Besso backs away, takes on his solemn look, and says, "We must arrive at a business arrangement, the two of us. This may be very valuable." Even though I contributed all the money, I decide not to haggle. "Let's just make it fifty-fifty," I say. "I think it's fair and it's the simplest." Besso readily agrees and I have my attorney draw up a contract.

I get tough with Kwan Li. "No diamonds," I tell her. "You can have some jade but that's it."

Kwan Li must sense that something has changed. She looks at me shrewdly, doesn't insist. Days go by. "You no eat pussy anymore," she says, puzzled. "You fuck normal." I shrug, tell her I'm reformed. I'm getting a fix every couple of days from Besso's elixir.

Then one day I go to find Kwan Li and she's gone. Not only is she gone but so is her Jaguar and all the furniture in the apartment as well. Either she moved somewhere else or sold it. She's too practical to have given it away. I feel a real sense of loss. If she planned to return she would not have taken the furniture. In the bedroom, by a window, sunlight glistens off a small green object. It is Kwan Li's jade Buddha. She must have inadvertently dropped it in her haste while packing. I feel tender toward the object, put it in my pocket.

Besso calls with bad news. The elixir has a very short shelf life. In only a couple of days the molecule comes apart and the drug loses all potency. The old batches, that he slaved so long to make, are now worthless. He has tried refrigeration and freezing. This adds a day or two but no more. He has to continuously make new batches with all the labor this entails for him and for his assistants.

"What does it take to stabilize the drug?" I ask.

"I don't know," Besso says and sounds despondent. "Penicillin had the same problem. It took twelve years and a program second in size only to the atomic bomb project to make penicillin stable."

"We've learned a lot since the penicillin days," I try hopefully.

"I believe the expedient course of action," Besso says, "is to go to the drug companies and see if they're interested in doing it. We would license them. They've got the people, the equipment, the know-how..."

"They're a wily bunch," I say.

"Maybe so. But what we have is commercially useless."

"Let's think about it," I say.

I miss Kwan Li. I know that's strange, but I wonder what's become of her and whether she might be in trouble. And what is she doing for money; she spends it like water pouring over a falls. I call Cecile: she doesn't have a clue as to Kwan Li's whereabouts.

On the streets I find myself scanning the cars, searching for Kwan Li's sky blue Jag. Once, I go to Chinatown and wander the streets, on the lookout for her car.

I continue to pray that Besso will succeed in extending the shelf life of the elixir. In this Besso is not successful. He spends time fabricating the precious droplets for he has grown as dependent on the stuff as I have. We agree to approach the pharmaceutical companies. He expects me as a businessman to do it but I suggest that we go together. Alone, I might get thrown out as a nut. I need Besso with me for credibility.

While I'm trying to arrange an appointment with someone high enough to matter, at Merck or Pfizer or Glaxo, I get a call from an agitated Besso. He wants me to come over immediately. Three of the lab rats to whom he has been feeding the elixir have died. He opened them: two had massive cancers of the pancreas and the third cancer of the liver. Besso, it is clear, is a worried man. "We're not rats." I point out.

"Ninety-eight percent of our DNA is identical to a rat's," Besso says. "That's why we use them as experimental animals." Then slowly and solemnly he adds, "I've decided to stop taking the stuff. I'm as addicted to it as you are. It's changed my life. But if I want to keep living, I must stop. I suggest you do the same. Otherwise you will finish the same as those rats."

"Suppose I decide to take my chances," I say.

"I can't help you," Besso says. "It takes three days to make a batch. I can't use my laboratory to make this for you. Use your friend as the source."

I ignore that last remark. "I'm willing to pay to do it," I say. "Hire a couple more assistants if you have to."

Besso shakes his head no, is still solemn. "This is a poison," he says. "You might not think so at first, but that's what it is. Judging by those rats, as soon as you start taking it you're on the road to dying. If those rats are any indication, dying will happen quickly. The stuff makes you flare like a Roman candle then you're gone."

"Is any of it still around?" I ask.

"Maybe one dose."

"I'll take it."

Then I have a moment of doubt. Would Besso intentionally kill the rats then claim the elixir killed them in order to have the elixir to himself? But I study the solemn Besso and decide that Machiavellian behavior is beyond him. Then, of course, there is our contract.

I continue my search for Kwan Li. Finally, I call Cecile and offer her money if she will question her other Chinese girls to see if they know of Kwan Li's whereabouts. A week later Cecile calls. Kwan Li has gone to Taiwan as the consort (Cecile's word) of a wealthy industrialist.

I'm fading, my energy level dropping. I come to work late, the staff peers at me with apprehension. My life—youthful vigor, women, my ability to forcefully drive the business—depends on the elixir. I plead with Besso: I'm willing to accept the risk. I'd rather go out as a Roman candle than just fizzle and disappear. He shrugs, agrees to help me, but absolutely refuses to make the stuff in his department. We find a small laboratory that he then instructs. The price is ridiculous but I accept. A droplet every two days. I think Besso agreed to this to establish whether the long-term effects on humans is the same as on rats. Then I learn from a chance remark by a lab technician that Besso is freeloading on my output and taking a fix himself. When I confront Besso with this he sheepishly confesses. He is performing creative research at a level he has not attained since young manhood. What he is doing is exciting, the cutting edge, etc. He can't stop—it's just too important. So much for all that solemn speech making.

Life goes on. All of Besso's rats are dead, mostly from cancer.

Then I glimpse the real Besso: in a frightened voice he tells me that he is not well. He is losing weight, has pain in his upper abdomen and back. He looks haunted, tells me he is afraid to see a doctor, afraid of what the doctor will find. Even a man as rational as Besso can be irrational. Finally Besso agrees to tests, x-rays. Like his rats, Besso has pancreatic cancer. He now looks like hell, ancient and shrunken. "So much for the fountain of youth," he says bitterly. "Meeting you was the worst thing that ever happened to me. This is what came of it." He gestures at himself.

I stop the laboratory work, stop the elixir. The view of the dying Besso has pushed aside all philosophy about Roman candles. I put my business on the market. I just don't care about it anymore.

I have returned to what I was, but with a difference. I lie awake nights listening to my body, feel phantom pains, in fear of the cancer that killed the rats and is destroying poor Besso. Sometimes I think of Kwan Li, her yellow-toned apartment, her sky blue Jaguar, how classy she looked when we went out to dinner. She now seems, like the elixir itself, unreal, a supernova that flared then disappeared. Like her, I have placed the small jade Buddha on the nightstand beside my bed; maybe it will bring me good luck as well; it sits there like a memory. Sometimes the Buddha and I contemplate each other and I recall Kwan Li and those remarkable months. She was worth every penny I spent on her. How ironic that the fountain of youth resided in the vagina of a Chinese prostitute. Of course, Besso would tell you that it wasn't a fountain of youth at all but something far more sinister. Yet I cannot say that I'm unhappy. Unbelievably and magically, I was given my youth a second time. It lasted only a year but it was a time of miracles, when I was granted once again, however briefly, the gift of being young.

Stalking Jenny

I died two weeks ago at the rather unfair age of sixty-seven. The irony of this is that only three days earlier, at my annual checkup, my cliché-plagued internist declared me healthy as a horse, in the pink, and fit as a fiddle, in that order. Yet forty-eight hours later I was slumped beside my John Deere JX75 mower, the lawn only half cut, dead as a doornail, as he would no doubt phrase it.

Since *how* one dies always seems to interest people, I'll briefly describe this unhappy event, not that there's anything particularly unique or heroic about it. Someone up there clamped a steel vise to my chest and was ferociously tightening so that it was crushing my insides, the pain shooting out to my shoulder, neck, even my jaw. I thought I was falling and held onto the mower. Breathing became impossible and I did fall, though I don't remember hitting the ground; then the pain dissolved and I experienced a floating sensation coupled with a deep sense of tranquility. The landscape closed around me, pearly and strange, my peripheral vision gone, and I was in a tunnel moving ever faster toward a distant point of light. The world shot by like images in a slot machine as I whizzed down the tunnel but I don't recall ever reaching the light. The next thing I knew I was dead. There was no fanfare, no flights of angels singing me to my rest. Just dead.

I must say, I was at least mildly surprised. Though I knew I would have to die like everyone else, deep inside I did not believe it would happen, at least not anytime soon. I never smoked, exercised religiously, my HDL and LDL were in the right ratio and I was not overweight. But I lived under a genetic cloud: my grandfather died of a heart attack at age fifty-six and my sister suffers from chest pains. Still, I thought that somehow I was immune and could go on and on. Alas, wrong. Through an advanced health care directive and in keeping with the California Uniform Anatomical Gifts Act, I had donated my organs to whomever might benefit from their use, but after cooking under the Los Angeles sun for a couple of hours before my wife came home—she had been off to her allergist for her thrice weekly allergy desensitization shots—and found me, those organs were useless to anyone and they ultimately went up in smoke along with the rest of me.

It turns out, however, that before shipping you off to somewhere in that great beyond, Higher Authority allows you a certain period to wander the earth, moving freely forward in time to a maximum of ten years. Presumably, the purpose of this exercise is for you to see how you screwed up the lives of those around you while you were alive, though this was never explained to me. So I search out my wife Jenny, now of course the Widow Jenny, five years younger than I, to see how she's coping. Quite touchingly, my ashes are in a shiny brass urn on the nightstand on my side of the bed, my picture beside it, and my voice is still on the answering machine.

Jenny has joined a widow's support group in Brentwood, where we lived. I'm surprised to find that when she speaks of me I've been elevated to sainthood. "He was a fine man, considerate, responsible…a good father…" and she breaks down and sobs into her hands while the other widows pat her, hold her and say they understand. Gone are the quarrels, the suspicions, the subtle but continual battle of wills that defined our life together, all apparently obliterated in that great fire in the Ashes to Ashes Crematorium in West L.A.

I decide that mourning is dull and fast forward two years.

Jenny has sold the house and moved into a condo in Westwood. The brass urn, now tarnished to a dusky gold, is an art object on the mantelpiece in the living room, my picture has disappeared from the bedroom—and in fact is nowhere in evidence in the house—and the voice on the answering machine is her own. She has tinted her gray hair chestnut brown, once her natural color, drives a red BMW 330i convertible and works out every day at the Westwood Bally Total Fitness Club. Every muscle in her body has been tightened and toned and she looks younger than when I died. She also met her current boyfriend at Bally's. (I say "current" because she may have had others in the intervening two years, but I haven't bothered to check.) He looks about Jenny's age, a retired marketing honcho for a furniture chain. He works out like a demon—on the treadmill, Nordic Track, stationary bike, all the weight machines—seems desperate about it, but despite all that effort his muscle definition isn't what it ought to be. His hair transplant isn't a total success either. They leave the gym arm in arm, his body exuding the sweet chemical smell of deodorant, and repair to her condo. He surreptitiously pops a Viagra and they lovingly shower together. Well what the hell, I'd do the same.

I fast forward another couple of years. Jenny is still in the same condo and I'm still on the mantelpiece. But she no longer works out and the furniture exec has disappeared. We have three children and eight grandchildren, one daughter in San Diego and a son and daughter in L.A. Jenny is now into grandmothering, spends much time babysitting the grandkids, offering our children advice which is both unsolicited and unheeded. She has also gone spiritual, tried Zen Buddhism, dipped into Hinduism, then finally settled on Siddha Yoga and the teachings of a certain Swami Ruktananda. A photograph of the Swami—prominent cheekbones, red dot between penetrating eyes and Lincolnesque beard—hangs on the wall in the bedroom like the portrait of a saint.

One Labor Day Jenny treks from L.A. to Meredith, New Hampshire, on Lake Winnepesaukee to visit the Shree Ruktananda ashram, seeking, as she tells our skeptical San Diego daughter, spiritual renewal. After she gets there she calls the daughter and in a reverent voice tells her that the place has a special vibrancy: the grounds, the buildings, the paths through the woods, all exude a loving and tranquil energy. She enthusiastically goes through the ashram routine of meditation, chanting, study, earnest talks, etc. etc. Her guru, a man who speaks much of divine consciousness and has the complexion of pressed turkey, piously mentions the need for *dakshina* to spread the Swami's message. I'm sorry for her, there with all those flakes, a piece of fine crystal mixed in with gravel, but there's nothing I can do.

She calls our son, a busy man, and excitedly tells him she is experiencing unity with God, a mystical awakening, and is entering an inner spiritual realm she never knew existed. His advice: keep your checkbook firmly closed. Then it turns out that Jenny has a horrific ragweed allergy: sneezing, runny nose, itchy eyes, scratchy throat, trouble breathing, and against which no antihistamine seems to help. She calls her allergist, whom she blames for this attack. He patiently points out that her shots are against southern California pollens and these do not include ragweed. All this is screwing up Jenny's meditation, not to mention her unity with God, so reluctantly she leaves. But not before ignoring her son's advice and contributing a good chunk of my hard-earned cash as *dakshina* to the Siddha Yoga cause.

I fast forward a year and a half or so and all has changed. Apparently disillusioned with spirituality, Jenny now spends much of her time sitting alone and contemplating the walls of her condo. The children invite her over but she often declines, complaining that her arthritis is acting up and her knees and back hurt when she walks. She does indeed walk with a defeated stoop, shrunk into herself. Sometimes she will babysit the grandchildren but is impatient with the stupid things that kids often do and scolds them excessively. Soon, she's no longer asked to babysit. Often she cries alone. She doesn't bother to tint her hair: it's again gray and hangs limp. Her red BMW is gone and she now drives a Ford Taurus, of a charcoal color. My heart goes out to her, sealed off from the world that way, a woman who in the old days could be as commanding as Cleopatra. She should bestir herself, take a course, travel, join a club...do something, anything, but get out of the house. Instead, she sits alone, the room airless, curtained, dark; you can almost see the buzzards circling overhead.

I fast forward another year, expecting her to be gone, but to my surprise find her at dinner with a man who looks surprisingly like me and is about her age. From their conversation I gather he is a retired insurance company actuary, sometime poet, amateur violinist and a widower. They shyly hold hands, speak of each other's children and appear altogether in love. I backtrack in time, searching for the moment of their first meeting, and find it in a Ralph's supermarket. They are both in the produce department, at the oranges, and they both reach for the same orange. "It's yours," he says gallantly. "They're not very different one from the other," Jenny says. "You take it." They continue this Alphonse-Gaston number until finally he takes the orange. "How do you know the best ones?" he asks. This is not a Little-Red-Riding-Hood-amidst-the-oranges question—there is no irony in evidence here—the man seems genuinely interested in Jenny's criteria for the choice of oranges. Jenny eyes him carefully—there seems to be a Proustian moment of recognition—then she proceeds to give the man a Cliff Notes version of Oranges 101. "First, I look for a smooth skin," she explains. "A pebbled skin means the peel is too thick and the orange was picked past its prime. You're also paying for a lot of skin rather than pulp. Then the color should be a rich orange. A light color means the orange isn't ripe and it won't be sweet." He listens to this with rapt attention as if she's explaining the riddle of existence, then smiles a sweet smile. "You know your oranges," he says. His voice is rusty as if rarely used. "Thank you," Jenny modestly replies. "I'll bet you know your apples too," he says.

It's clear to me, touched by the simplicity—nay, the sheer goofiness—of their exchange, that these two don't want to leave each other. The man must have an extremely discerning eye or be desperate because to me at least Jenny looks like hell. She's wearing a disheveled house dress, rundown Easy Spirit walking shoes, hair a mess and no makeup. "Do you live nearby?" he asks rather hesitantly. I think their conversation has hit a flat spot but Jenny, apparently hearing the knock of opportunity, comes out of her shell, answers seriously, and with feline patience guides him along the aisles as they shop together. When they are in the checkout line, he says, "My name is Joseph," but diffidently, as if not quite sure whether she really wants to know, about him a submissive anticipation. When they say goodbye in the parking lot, after exchanging phone numbers, he bows with old world politeness.

I follow them through the succeeding weeks. He invites her to a rehearsal of the amateur string quartet of which he is a member. The group slogs through Schubert's *Death and the Maiden.* "When is the performance?" Jenny asks. "But this *is* the performance," a bearded fellow answers. "But I thought this was a rehearsal," Jenny says. "There are only rehearsals," Joseph sadly replies. He seems to be commenting on his own life.

He invites Jenny to dinner. She has perked up. She leaves her hair gray but it's chicly combed, she walks more erect, the condo is clean, her clothes neat. She helps Joseph straighten his house, they embrace in the bedroom, she guides him to the bed and carefully and gratefully they make love, though for a while Joe seems to be having technical difficulties.

Joseph tells Jenny he has written a sonnet to her. They sit side by side on the worn fabric couch in his living room; the moment is serious as if they are about to embark on some solemn journey. She snuggles close as he recites his poem.

> It pours over us a cold inky fog
> And grips the wanting heart with weariness
> Whispers in the ear a sickly monologue
> And wrinkles the flesh long made motherless.
>
> To know the world through the living touch
> And walk the fields where life abounds
> My lonely love do we ask so much
> Must we only listen to life's sweet sounds?
>
> Come close to me and the fog dissolves
> Like black night before onrushing sun
> And the whirling world ceases to revolve
> In trembling touching pleasure we are one.
>
> The inky night drapes round us with a clammy touch
> Where oh where is the simple love we need so much?

Frankly, it sounds sophomoric to me but there are tears in Jenny's eyes when he looks up at the end. They hold each other for the longest time and I tactfully leave them to themselves.

Joseph and Jenny see each other more and more often. He takes her to dinner at Valentino's then to a concert at the Music Center, Beethoven's Violin Concerto. "The greatest piece of music ever written for the violin," he says, eyes shining with a soft light, and Jenny, who in my recollection is tone deaf, nods sagely in agreement. They meet each other's children. Joe has a son and a daughter and four grandchildren. The boy is a computer programmer and has the sweet retiring manner of his father. His daughter strikes me as a bossy take-charge type, which is probably what Joe's late wife was. The daughter is a buyer of young women's wear at Macy's. She inspects Jenny and her outfit with a critical eye, but Jenny does not wilt and stares right back at her. Apparently Jenny and Joe pass muster with each other's children because after much serious discussion between them Jenny sells her condo and moves into Joe's house. I'm pleased to see that in all of her changes of household Jenny carries the urn, like the statue of a saint, with her.

I watch Jenny slowly take control of Joe's life. She buys his clothes, donates his nondescript furniture, the pieces near the window faded by sunlight, to Saint Vincent de Paul and redoes the house in Henredon traditional. It occurs to me that maybe the problem between Jenny and me was that we were both first borns, that neither could stand being subject to the will of another, and we could never resolve the tension this created. Though we did have some wonderful times together and occasionally, shining from far back, the light of those times comes to me with renewed brilliance.

They decide to travel. Jenny, who is of Irish descent (née Jenny Rowena Kilkenny) and whose grandparents emigrated from Limerick, wishes to visit Ireland while Joe, who is Jewish, would like to go to Israel. They decide to do both. Joe is enthusiastic about Dublin, home of Joyce's *Ulysses* and *Sweet Molly Malone*, and wants to see the lake isle of Innisfree, assuming the place exists, the site of Yeats's lyric poem, verses that Joe loved as a young man. Jenny, in turn, makes enthusiastic noises about the Holy Land.

I peek out to the end of the ten-year time horizon allowed me. Jenny and Joe are still together, in domestic tranquility, and I conclude that unless one of them sickens theirs will be a life of cloudless skies as they live out their days together. They visit their children, bring gifts for the grandkids at Christmas and birthdays, go to concerts. Joe has a poem accepted by *Poetics* and this is a cause for great celebration. Their friends are mostly Joe's fellow musicians and women Jenny meets doing volunteer work at Saint John's hospital in Santa Monica. They both drive a Honda electric car, hers light green and his dark blue, to do their part in reducing pollution. Joe, a man bothered by any irregularity in the machinery of life, is shielded by Jenny from bill-paying, shopping, repairing, and all the little nuisances that shadow our days.

I return to the seven year point. They garden, visit the local nursery and choose roses in shades of orange in honor of where they met. When they speak of that meeting it's always transposed to a higher key and takes on the mystical significance of an Old Testament encounter. The sunny side of their garden is now vibrant with Pat Austins and Joseph's Coats and Orange Celebrations. One morning, when Joe is out, Jenny takes the brass urn, now tarnished to a dull black, and sets it down in the rose garden. She goes to the garage and returns wearing green gardening gloves and carrying a spade. She then carefully sprinkles my ashes around the orange-headed roses. She turns over the ground, mixing the ashes into the soil. She stands there for a long moment and contemplates the ground and the roses, then returns the gloves and spade to the garage and enters her house with the empty urn.